#6

D0103591

WHAT READERS ARE SAYING ABOUT
BRIDES OF THE WEST

"Once again, Copeland ... omplex
characters to fully involve her ... another

outstanding

entry into the Brides of the West series."

· THE ROMANCE READER'S CONNECTION ·

"*Hope* is another fun, inspirational outing from seasoned writer
Lori Copeland. . . . It's easy to see why romance readers are circling
their wagons around the Brides of the West series!"

· LIZ CURTIS HIGGS ·

BEST-SELLING AUTHOR

"I just loved *[Hope]*! Only Lori Copeland could weave a knee-slapping tale with
such a beautifully redemptive message. Her characters are delightfully

funny and unpredictable,

and her plot is full of refreshing twists and turns. I can't wait for her next book!"

· TERRI BLACKSTOCK ·

BEST-SELLING AUTHOR

"*Faith* is one romance that will sit on my limited shelf space
and be read over and over." L.C.

"I love stories that are both uplifting and realistic, and *Faith* and *June* really
fit the bill. God bless you and may you continue to brighten people's lives
with your God-given talent!" K.L.M.

"Absolutely magnificent! The stories are

fresh and exciting

and inspire me to greater faith and service for God. God has anointed
you for a mighty work through your wonderful novels." K.M.

HEART
QUEST.

Romance the way it's meant to be

HeartQuest brings you romantic fiction
with a foundation of biblical truth.
Adventure, mystery, intrigue, and suspense
mingle in these heartwarming stories of
men and women of faith striving to build
a love that will last a lifetime.

May HeartQuest books sweep you
into the arms of God, who longs for you
and pursues you always.

Patience

LORI
COPELAND

Brides of the West 1872

HEART
QUEST

Romance fiction from
Tyndale House Publishers, Inc., Wheaton, Illinois

www.heartquest.com

Visit Tyndale's exciting Web site at www.tyndale.com

Check out the latest about HeartQuest Books at www.heartquest.com

Copyright © 2004 by Lori Copeland. All rights reserved.

Cover illustration copyright © 2003 by C. Michael Dudash. All rights reserved.

Author's photo copyright © 2002 by Elizabeth Maxely. All rights reserved.

HeartQuest is a registered trademark of Tyndale House Publishers, Inc.

Edited by Kathryn S. Olson

Designed by Zandrah Maguigad

Library of Congress Cataloging-in-Publication Data

Copeland, Lori.
　Patience / Lori Copeland.
　　p. cm. — (HeartQuest) (Brides of the West ; 6.)
　　ISBN 0-8423-1938-7
　　1. Mail order brides—Fiction. 2. Women pioneers—Fiction. I. Title.
II. Series.

PS3553.O6336 P38 2004
813′.54—dc22
                                                                                  2003016944

Printed in the United States of America

10　09　08　07　06　05　04
9　8　7　6　5　4　3　2　1

To Barbara Warren.
Every author needs a helping hand,
and Barbara supplies me with knowledge,
encouragement,
and much-needed spiritual uplifting.
Thank you, friend.

Chapter One

Patience Smith might have been surprised to know that her life had just changed dramatically. Sheriff Jay Longer didn't realize his had changed at the same instant.

Swinging a long leg over the saddle, the sheriff of Denver City, Colorado, climbed aboard his mare. His eye caught Dylan McCall hugging his wife on Main Street, right in broad daylight. And in front of the sheriff's office, too. He frowned. Was that any way to uphold the dignity of law enforcement?

A moment later Jay rode up to the waiting couple, sliding out of the saddle before the mare came to a stop.

Ruth McCall whirled to face him, her pretty face a mix of warring emotions. "We were in the shop. Mary was pinning the hem on Lenore Hawthorn's wedding dress— the bride's parents forbid her to try it on, so Patience was modeling it. A man burst into Mary's millinery and grabbed Patience. They went off in that direction!" She pointed west. "Go!"

"Honey, slow down," her husband warned. "I don't want you upset."

Tears brimmed Ruth's eyelids. "You have to *do* something, Sheriff!"

Jay frowned. Deliver him from newlyweds and estrogen-produced hysterics. All that sweet talk between the marshall and his bride should take place in the privacy of their home, not in the presence of people who might find it scratchy to watch. Of course, time was, when he still had Nelly, he might have been as love-struck as Dylan, but he'd have had enough sense of propriety to keep it to himself.

Sure, he would.

If he had Nelly back, he'd get down on his knees right out there in the middle of the street and tell her all the things he wished he'd said when he had the chance.

Jay casually straightened the brim on his Stetson. "She was wearing Lenore Hawthorn's wedding dress when she was abducted?"

Ruth nodded, tears rolling down her cheeks. "She was standing in for Lenore for the final gown fitting."

Jay glanced at Dylan, then back to Ruth. "Well, there's our answer. There's been bad blood between the Hawthorns and the McLanes for years. Ben and Lenore's wedding has set them off again—my guess is that the culprit has a connection with the groom's family."

With the Hawthorn/McLane wedding scheduled to take place tomorrow night, Jay figured that had to be the circumstance. Old man McLane was a crusty old reprobate, and he'd sworn to stop the nuptials between his oldest son and Hawthorn's youngest daughter. Apparently he'd found a way to interfere.

Ruth lifted a shaky hand to her forehead. "Sakes alive. The kidnapper mistook Patience for Lenore?"

Jay nodded. "That'd be my guess. What about you, Marshall?"

Dylan agreed. "That's the way I have it figured."

Denver City bustled in the background. An hour from now it would be dark, and a posse would find it impossible to track the young woman. Jay would have to set out alone and follow the trail until it got cold—or until he found Patience Smith.

"But *why?*" Ruth argued. "Why would anyone snatch a bride? What do they want with Lenore—Patience?"

The sheriff and the marshall exchanged sobering looks before Jay finally admitted, "Well now, that's hard to say." Could be a million explanations, but only one thing mattered. What would the kidnapper do with the girl once he discovered his mistake?

"Let's not panic," Dylan said. "When Patience tells the man that he's got the wrong woman, he'll probably turn her loose."

Whirling, Ruth bolted back into Mary's millinery shop in tears, and Dylan approached the sheriff.

"We've got a problem," the marshall said.

"Could be—then again, he might have realized his mistake instantly and let her go at the edge of town."

"Maybe—but if he didn't?"

Jay took off his Stetson and wiped his forehead. "Then you're right—we have a real problem."

Dylan stood by while Jay slid a Winchester Model 1873 into the hand-tooled rifle scabbard tied to his saddle. A cold wind buffeted the men's sturdy frames. Tomorrow night 1873 would be ushered out with parties and noisy celebrations, but Jay wouldn't be part of the festivities.

Dylan ran a hand across his face. "I still think I should be the one to go after her. Those girls and Ruth—they're like family to each other."

Longer busied himself checking cinches and stirrups. He knew Dylan had brought the girls all the way from Missouri to be mail-order brides, an arrangement that hadn't worked out. The orphaned young women were as close as sisters, so Dylan's bride's tears were understandable. "You're newly married, and you're the marshall. I'm single, the sheriff, and the crime was committed in my county."

Not that Jay wanted to go after this particular orphan. He'd had more than one disagreeable run-in with Patience Smith, the last occurring a couple days ago. She'd burst into his office carrying a bird with a broken wing and asked if he knew anything about setting bones. He'd calmly pointed out he was town sheriff, not town vet. He'd eyed the critter that scattered droppings on the office floor.

She'd eyed him back sternly, then asked if he was coldhearted.

He had to admit that he was—had been for a long time. And he wasn't in the bird-fixing business.

She'd left with the bird in hand, and the last he'd seen of her she was crossing the street, head held high, determination evident in her squared shoulders and stiff back.

Dylan's voice broke into Jay's musings. "The kidnapping took place in my town."

Jay sighed, knowing how stubborn McCall could be. "Look, let's not argue. I'm going after her, and I'm going to bring her home. That's my job; it's what I get paid for."

Conceding, Dylan stepped back. "I'll look after the town while you're gone. That much I can do."

Nodding, Jay gathered the reins between his gloves and mounted. "Finding her—finding anyone—in these mountains isn't going to be a cakewalk." The sheriff settled his hat more firmly on his head. He'd be lucky if he survived the search this time of year. January wasn't for the fainthearted. But he had another reason for going, one he wasn't going to mention. The wire he'd received today crackled in his shirt pocket. He knew what it said by heart. His gambling debts had caught up with him. The people he owed were coming to collect, and he didn't have the money to pay. If he wasn't here, there wouldn't be much they could do, and if he could buy enough time, maybe he would recoup his losses. And then again, maybe he wouldn't.

Turning the horse, he rode out of town due west. Somewhere out there a young woman was in danger, and as sheriff, it was his responsibility to rescue her.

He could only hope that Patience Smith was as tenacious with her kidnapper as she'd proven to be with him.

Patience decided that getting rid of trouble was like sacking fog. You grasped, fumbled, and blocked, but it kept coming. She shivered. The late-afternoon air was cold as granite, and she was wearing little more than lace and tulle.

She wanted off this horse, and even more, she needed to make sense of what had just happened. She glanced sideways at the man who held her on his horse and wondered about his intelligence. How could anyone mistake her for Lenore Hawthorn? Lenore had blonde hair, angular features, and blue eyes. Patience had brunette hair, a round face, and dark brown eyes.

The swarthy man's hold tightened. "Stop squirming, Lenore!"

"I'm not Lenore!"

"Yeah, yeah. That's what they all say." He set his spurs deeper into the mare.

"But I'm not Lenore!" Patience yelled.

"Shaddup!"

She swallowed back her mounting hysteria. The outlaw gripped her tighter around the middle and galloped around a curve. This mistake had something to do with the ongoing feud between the Hawthorns and the McLanes, she was sure. Hatred between the two families ran as deep as still water, and she feared there was no telling what fate awaited her if this man thought she was Amos Hawthorn's daughter. The families' insane feud had been going on for decades.

She frowned when she thought of Mary, Lily, Harper, and Ruth. The girls had all looked thunderstruck when this man had burst into the sewing shop and seized her. If the situation wasn't so grave, she'd laugh; but right now all she could do was cling to the horse and pray she'd survive the frantic ride.

The scoundrel was dirty and his rancid breath repulsed her. Where was he taking her? How soon would he accept the fact that she wasn't the intended bride? And then what? Would he dispose of her before she could convince him that he'd made a terrible mistake?

Relief suddenly flooded her. *Dylan.* Ruth's husband— or maybe the town sheriff, Jay Longer—would come after her. The bigheaded sheriff and she mixed like oil and water, but right now she wasn't particular about her rescuer. Considering their simmering animosity toward one another, she wondered if he'd even bother to come after her—but Dylan would make him. His job would make him. With his piercing blue eyes and hair as red as a Colorado sunset, Sheriff Longer was a hard man to understand. But whether he liked her or not, the tough-minded sheriff would not let this brigand get away with kidnapping a woman from his territory.

She clung to that belief as the horse's shod hoofs pounded the frozen ground. Wind stung her face and cold seeped through her bones. She had no protection from the wintry elements—no coat, only the lace sleeves of Lenore's wedding dress to protect her from the icy wind.

Suddenly, as if the hand of God swooped down and smote the enemy, the horse stumbled and pitched forward, throwing Patience and her captor over the animal's head. Patience went airborne. Seconds later she slammed into the frozen ground.

Lying motionless, she struggled to catch her breath, and then, dazed, she sat up in a feeble attempt to regain her bearings. She was alive! The horse lay prostrate on top of the kidnapper. She wished she felt compassion, an urge to offer assistance to the poor, unfortunate villain, but relief flooded her. She was free! The man must surely be dead, or very close to death; she didn't have the strength to even budge the horse to look.

Rolling slowly to her feet, Patience groaned. She tentatively tested her weight on one foot and then the other, and discovered that she could walk. Which she did, as fast as her injury would allow, grasping the hem of the fragile gown, trying to protect the sheer material from the rough trail.

Limping over the frozen ground, she sucked in deep drafts, the cold air stinging her lungs. Where was she? She had no idea; she wasn't familiar with the region. From the time Dylan had brought the five mail-order brides to Denver City, she hadn't ventured far from the outskirts of town. Her eyes searched the barren, snow-swept land, and she shuffled faster. She'd heard talk of prospectors in the area, how fiercely the men vied with each other for gold. Hysteria now threatened to overtake her as she realized she would freeze to death if she didn't find shelter soon. Her teeth chattered and her breath came in ragged gulps. *Walk, Patience. Walk like your life depends on it.*

Heartsick, Patience realized that in these circumstances, it actually did.

A blast of winter wind buffeted the sheriff, and he huddled deeper into the sheepskin-lined coat. The girl had only a thin, silk wedding gown to protect her from the cold. If he didn't find her soon . . .

Jay rode slowly, leaning from the saddle to search for tracks, but the frozen ground made tracking difficult. He didn't stand the chance of a snowball in a skillet of finding her, but he set his jaw in determination.

And then he spotted the dead horse. Dismounting and hanging on to the reins, he approached the carcass. His mare was skittish, and he had no desire to be stranded out here on foot. This was unfriendly country. If a man didn't freeze to death, he stood a good chance of running into a belligerent miner defending his claim.

Jay examined the animal, noticing a boot half hidden beneath the horse's body. When he had satisfied himself that Patience wasn't there, he mounted again. He had no shovel; he couldn't bury the miscreant. Animals would take care of what he couldn't. He nudged his horse and rode off slowly. Supposing the woman was still a captive, for it was possible the dead horse and victim had nothing to do with Patience Smith.

Then again, there was nothing to suggest that he *wasn't* the kidnapper, and when the horse stumbled she'd gotten away. If that were the case, where would she have gone? Running the questions through his mind, Jay came up with the same answer to both: most likely to one of the mining camps dotting these mountains or an isolated shaft, which would make finding her even more difficult.

He had been in these parts long enough to know that he couldn't go riding into camp dressed like a lawman. That would tip off the kidnappers that he was on their trail if she was still being held somewhere. He studied the rugged landscape, weighing his options. As far as he could see, there was only one choice open to him. Miners were a rugged lot, suspicious of strangers, so he'd ride into the closest town and get himself a shovel and a gold pan. Going undercover wasn't his style, but he was going to hit those camps disguised as a miner.

Chapter Two

Bitter cold air burned Patience's lungs. She had lost dexterity in her fingers a long time ago. She clung weakly to the hope that someone was looking for her— if she could only hold on, *someone* would find her any moment. She had wandered for hours. When darkness fell, she had curled inside a fallen log and wrapped herself in pine branches and dead leaves. She had survived the elements—but barely.

When she opened her eyes this morning, she realized that she had so many things she wanted to do—climb a tall mountain, eat a store-bought cake, make an edible blackberry cobbler. And if the good Lord was willing, find some way to make life easier for Mary, Harper, and Lily. Being single and alone out here in a man's world wasn't easy. She needed to find work, something that would pay better than clerking in a store or teaching school. If she lived.

Ahead, nothing moved. She was surrounded by icy nothingness. She walked on, the hem of Lenore's Irish lace gown dragging the uneven ground. Her hands felt like two blocks of wood. She crossed her arms over her chest in a feeble attempt to warm her fingers; her breath made heavy vaporous gasps. It seemed days since she had put on Lenore's lovely dress, standing motionless while Mary pinned the silken fabric. No other garment was as pretty as a wedding dress, but if she didn't find real shelter soon, this one could very well become her shroud.

The sun, a huge globe of pale, polar yellow, broke through a ragged veil of clouds, washing the landscape with a cold, clear light. Patience plunged ahead, aimlessly walking. Moving. She had to keep moving.

"Oh, God, help me. I need you!" she called out.

The words hung in the frozen air. She stumbled over unseen roots, having lost the road long ago. Brittle branches of winter-bound shrubs lashed her face. The wind brought tears to her eyes, which froze on her eyelashes. Shelter. She had to find shelter.

"God? Where are you? Can't you hear me?" He had always been near; Patience had always felt his presence, but not today. Not now. She felt completely, utterly on her own. She longed to lie down under a rocky overhang, out of the wind, just for a moment, but she pushed the thought away. To stop meant death.

When she did find signs of habitation, she almost missed them—a battered bucket, a small pile of mine tailings. She jerked to a halt, staring at a hole in the side of the mountain. A big hole covered with boards, but with a wooden door set in the entrance. A mine?

She paused before a shabby sign, the weatherworn letters almost too faded to read. Dropping to her hands and knees, she tried to make out the lettering burned into the old board staked to the ground. "Mul . . . Mle . . . Mule

Head." Her breath pushed between frozen lips, and she repeated the crude markings. "Mule Head?"

She sat back on her knees, staring at the deserted site. "Mule Head," she repeated. "What's a mule head?"

Bitter cold seeped into her bones, and her joints felt like raw meat. Shadows played across the weather-beaten boards nailed above the entrance to the big hole, highlighting the sturdy door.

Getting to her feet, Patience dusted off her hands. "Well, it isn't exactly what I'd hoped for, God, but the name of the shelter isn't important. Thank you."

Her head pounded and her stomach knotted with hunger. She desperately needed warmth and sustenance.

Wind shrieked through the mountain pass. She rattled, then banged on the heavy door. What if no one was here? Was this a deserted mine shaft? She pushed hard on the door and stepped back when it slowly swung open on creaking hinges.

Sunlight stretched higher in the New Year's Eve sky. Her eyes anxiously searched beyond the dim light, into a seemingly endless black void. "Hello!" she called, forcing the greeting from frozen vocal cords. Her eyes roamed the shadows.

There were bears out here—big ones—and she'd spotted herds of gigantic elk with big horns earlier this morning. She recalled that Ruth had almost died in a snowstorm. She'd shot an elk and gutted it, then crawled inside, pulling Dylan McCall in behind her. Had she failed to take those drastic steps, the newly married couple wouldn't be alive today.

Drawing a deep breath, Patience resolved to be as strong as Ruth. But she wasn't as strong as Ruth. She was a coward. She didn't have a gun—no way to protect herself from wild animals.

Teeth chattering, she studied the odd-looking construction. Some hundred feet from the main shaft someone had tunneled into a steep hill face, fashioning a dark earth chamber about eight by ten feet. A six-by-four, crudely built wooden door secured the hole.

Her breath caught and she refused to accept the absurdity of the situation. Kidnapped, and now at the weather's mercy. No. God was here; he was always with her. The thought assuaged any immediate concerns.

Stepping up on a flat, granite boulder that served as a step, she tried to see into the dimly lit dugout, but the effort proved useless. Her vision cleared, and she could barely make out the interior. In one corner someone had piled pine and juniper boughs. Two or three chunks of old tree bole were scattered about for tables. Close to the entrance, a crudely built fireplace with a small bed of coals dominated the west wall. Fire. Warmth.

She shook her head, refusing to believe her eyes. Did she risk entering and perhaps encountering something worse than kidnappers? What choice did she have? A few more moments in the cold and that would be a moot point.

Her gaze centered on the primitive lodging; she took a deep breath and stepped inside. *Wood. Please God, let there be firewood.*

She inched forward, shuffling, one step, then another. She stumbled and fell; her hands touched cloth. An arm!

Scrambling to her feet, she fought back a scream, but a shriek escaped anyway. She had fallen over a body—*a lifeless body*. There could be no mistaking the rigidity of those limbs. She backed up, moving deeper into the darkness.

A rustling sound from behind her sent her scrabbling for something to use for protection. Her hand closed around a short stick she recognized as a chunk of firewood. Not much use against a bear or a mountain lion. She gripped the club in both hands, straining to see in the fading light of the dying coals.

Something moved in the shadows, and Patience swallowed, caught between what was hiding in that corner and the dead man's body. She fought back a hysterical giggle. Between the frying pan and the fire.

Did that make sense?

Her eyes adjusted to the light, and now she could see that the figure trying to struggle upright was human, a small human.

A child.

She dropped the stick of wood, staring at the ragged boy who slowly rose on unsteady feet. "Who are you?" Patience asked.

The answer came in a thin voice. "Wilson. I'm Wilson."

Jay rode into Fiddle Creek with his badge in his pocket. As far as the residents were concerned, he was just another miner. He'd had a time finding clothes to match his new identity. For most of his life, when he could afford it, he'd dressed well, but today he wore pants with a hole in the knee, a shirt with a couple of buttons missing, and a hat he wouldn't have put on a scarecrow. It wasn't much consolation to see that he looked like most of the people he met.

A tinhorn gambler, resplendent in gray broadcloth with a beaver hat, strode down the boardwalk, looking for a game. For a minute, Jay was tempted. See if his luck had changed . . .

But duty came first. He had to find the Smith woman.

And a thankless task it would probably be. *She talks to birds! I ask you, what normal woman with any common sense would talk to a bird?*

Headstrong, too. He'd seen that. Stubborn as a cross-eyed mule. Well, it wasn't any skin off his nose. He wasn't looking for another woman, except in the line of duty. He'd had Nelly. All other women paled in comparison. No. Face it; he was a one-woman man. His woman had died.

He entered the mercantile, closing the door behind him. "Morning."

"Morning," the man behind the counter replied. "Help you?"

"Looking for a shovel and a gold pan. Some ornery critter stole mine."

"There's a lot of it going on," the clerk agreed, placing the items on the counter. "Anything else?"

"Got any licorice candy?" He had a sweet tooth.

"Yep." The clerk added the candy to the pile. "Don't I know you?"

"Don't think so."

"Seems to me like you used to do some prospecting over around Cutter's Gulch way. Jay something, ain't it?"

"Jay Longer. You've got a good memory. That's been a spell."

"Well, some have it, some don't. I never forget a face."

Jay paid for his purchases and left. Rum luck, hitting someone who knew him right off the bat. It had been a long time since he had prospected in this area. Never found any windfall. When it came to mining he was a jinx.

He stopped at Tillie's Café for breakfast. The hot coffee tasted good going down his throat. He was cold and tired, and he wanted a hot bath and a soft bed. He'd spent a long

morning working his way through small mining camps
scattered through the mountains. This afternoon he'd check
out Fiddle Creek. If Patience wasn't here . . . he shook the
thought away. She could be dead for all he knew—some
grizzly could have gotten her or another hungry predator.
He ran a hand over thick face stubble and hoped he didn't
run into too many other people he used to know. They'd
wonder about Nelly, and he didn't want to talk about her.
It still hurt to say her name.

Patience eased closer to the small boy. "Are you all right?"

"No, I don't think I am." The child spoke with an English
accent, like a drummer who had come to the store where she
worked one day, peddling notions. "I'm feeling puny."

She stepped closer, reaching out to feel his forehead. Her
hands tingled with warmth. "You're running a fever. Is
there a lantern—a candle I can light?" She had forgotten
how cold and hungry she was in the terror of the moment,
but now it came flooding back. She was alone in an abandoned dugout with a dead body and a sick child.

The boy's voice came back to her. "Yes, but I don't
know where."

*Lord, forgive me for thinking this, but we sure have different
notions of what might be considered help.*

She fumbled, locating a basket of pine knots, and held one
to the coals until it caught fire. Now she could see more
clearly. A crude cot had been built along the wall where the
boy was. He slumped down, pulling a ragged quilt around
his thin shoulders. A shelf held tin plates and cups and a few
containers of what she guessed to be sugar, flour, and cornmeal. She hoped there was coffee.

The boy stared at her with fever-dimmed eyes. "Are you real? I haven't imagined you?"

"I'm real enough. But we can go into that later. Right now, I'm going to build up this fire and fix something to eat. You lie down and cover up. I don't want you to get chilled." Speaking of chilled, her hands and feet were thawing, sending a hundred tiny prickles through her wind-frozen flesh.

She knelt before the fireplace, making a pile of wood shavings and twigs, covering it with small pieces of dead branches, blowing on the tiny flame until it caught. As soon as the fire was strong enough, she added larger pieces of wood, fanning until the sticks caught and the flames roared up the chimney. Warmth beat against her face, her hands, and body, wrapping her in a blanket of hot air. She knelt there until her joints loosened and her teeth stopped chattering. Aware that she had to do something about the dead person in the room, she rose and discreetly covered the body with a blanket.

Next, she rummaged through the meager store of supplies, finding a chunk of salt pork. Soon the smell of meat sizzling in an iron skillet filled the small space. While the meat cooked, she mixed cornmeal, baking powder, salt, and water, which she poured into a second skillet and pushed close to the fire. That done, she hunted for and found a can of coffee, filled the pot with water and grounds, and soon the fragrance of freshly brewed coffee filled the shelter.

Now to get the boy close to the fire, where he could get warm. She helped him to his feet, letting him lean against her until she had him settled in an old rocking chair.

"There. You'll be all right now." She tucked the faded

quilt around him, wishing she had some willow-bark tea to break the fever.

He bent closer to the flames, teeth rattling. "I still . . . think . . . I'm dreaming. Do you have a name?"

"I don't believe anyone ever called me a dream before. My name's Patience."

"Patience." He tried it out. "It's a strange name."

Well, *Wilson* wasn't all that great either, but she was too polite to say so. "My friends think it's a strange name for me. Patience isn't necessarily one of my virtues."

Stubborn, maybe. Patient? Never. She glanced anxiously toward the body on the floor. "Who's that?"

A spasm of emotion she took to be grief twisted the child's face. "He's the old prospector. He took me in when I had no place to go, and when he got sick I tried to help him, but he died."

The boy's forlorn face touched her heart. She wanted to take him in her arms and comfort him, but they were strangers. He would reject her efforts. Moving closer to the fire, she forked slices of meat onto the plates and sifted flour into the grease in the skillet, letting it brown. When it met her satisfaction, she stirred in water from the bucket sitting next to the door. Not as good as milk gravy, but it would be hot and, with the corn bread, filling.

When the gravy thickened, she filled the plates with food and poured the coffee into tin cups. Wilson reached for his plate, but she stopped him. "First we thank God for this food."

"Why? He didn't fix it."

"Don't you believe it. When I was stumbling around on the mountain, thinking I was going to freeze to death, God was leading me straight to this place where there was shelter, fire, and food. He sent me here to help both of us, and we're going to thank him."

Wilson stared at her with a skeptic's eye. "Perhaps so, but the prospector bought that food. He paid for it with gold he found panning in that creek out there. It didn't come from God."

Gold? Creek? The words caught her attention. A creek meant water. Water to drink, a necessity. And gold? Maybe she could manage to find enough gold to pay her way back home, if she ever found out exactly where she was.

"Wilson, you listen to me." She leaned closer, clasping his hands, noticing they were rough and chapped. "Everything in this world belongs to God. He allows us to use it. He gave that prospector the strength to pan for that gold. He led me here to be with you, and he's going to take care of us. Never doubt it. Now bow your head because we're going to thank him for all he's done for us."

The boy started eating the moment she finished saying amen. He ate with the desperation born of hunger. How long had he been here alone with a dead man? She placed another slice of meat on his plate. He needed it more than she did.

"How old are you, Wilson?"

He thought for a moment. "Eight—I think."

"Where are your parents?"

"They're dead. The cholera killed them. The prospector found us, and he helped me bury them. He took care of me until he got sick."

The picture was all too clear. Wilson had no one now. Eight years old and alone. Sometimes the world was a sad place. Patience knew what it meant to be alone. She was an orphan too. Before she had come to Denver City with the other mail-order brides, she had lived in an orphanage.

"Is there a town nearby?" She had to let the others know she was safe; Mary would be worried sick about her.

"Fiddle Creek. About a forty-five-minute walk from here."

She made a bed for Wilson in front of the fireplace, thinking he would be warmer there. Once she'd made him comfortable, she added another log to the fire, carefully banking it with ashes. If she was lucky they should have coals in the morning.

Rolled in her own blanket, she sat on the hearth, staring at the smoldering coals, grateful for shelter, for food and warmth. God had brought her here and she praised him for it, but with the blessing had come a new responsibility.

Wilson lay curled close to the fire, looking younger than his years. She studied the sleeping child's feverish face. Any plans she made would have to include him. The two of them were bound together, fighting for their lives in this formidable wilderness.

For all of her brave words, she felt alone.

Resting her head on her knees, she silently called for help. Tears wet the bedraggled cloth of Lenore's wedding gown. She wanted to go home.

Stretching out on the hard ground, Jay rolled tighter into his blanket. Stars hung low in the sky, and a crescent moon barely illuminated the landscape. He'd forgotten how peaceful it was out here. Maybe if he spent more time out of doors, enjoying creation, he would spend less time at the gaming tables. He'd been a fool to keep playing when he was losing, but he had kept telling himself the next hand would be the winner. Well, the winning hand never came.

His thoughts turned to Patience. Where was she tonight? She wasn't in Fiddle Creek. He'd searched a couple more nearby camps, asking discreet questions, but no one had seen her. It was like she had vanished into thin air. But he'd keep looking. He'd stumble over information sooner or later. He couldn't help wondering what she was going through if she was still alive. She was a little thing, just the right size to fit in the curve of a man's arm. The way Nelly used to.

He pushed the thought away. Nelly was gone, and he wasn't interested in Patience Smith. She was a job. Find her and take her home. That's all he had to do. Nevertheless, he found himself thinking of her out there in a flimsy wedding gown. She would have found shelter by now or she wouldn't be alive. This country was rough on women. He shifted to a more comfortable position and closed his eyes.

Yet sleep wouldn't come. Images of a young woman dressed in a wedding gown kept him awake. Tempted as he was to quit, he couldn't. She was out there somewhere, and it was his responsibility to find her—dead or alive.

Chapter Three

Patience bent nearer the fire and tried to soak up its paltry warmth. The flames had burned low, letting the frigid air seep back in.

"I'm *so* c-cold." Wilson huddled beneath a blanket, teeth chattering. His fever had broken sometime during the night, and he looked more alert.

"I know you are." She bit her lower lip, wondering how long they could survive the elements. One lone log remained, and she had hoarded it the past hour. After much internal debate, she'd taken off Lenore's gown and put on a pair of wool pants and a shirt that were hanging on a peg. The old prospector's clothing swallowed her frame, but the warmth overrode any fashion concerns.

She knew by now the moon had slid behind the tallest mountain and darkness blanketed the mine. She stirred up the fire, seeking the coals' meager warmth. Come morning she had to find more firewood. They must have heat to survive. She didn't know what time it was. The prospector didn't appear to have had a clock, and she didn't feel up to stepping outside to check the sky. How would they know when it was light outside if they were buried in the depths of the earth?

Her joints were stiff and sore from her wild ride, the fall from the horse, and the stumbling around in an attempt to find this place. Sleeping on a stone hearth trying to stay warm hadn't helped matters. She had an ungrateful thought, quickly squelched, that it would have been nice if God had led her to a house with a comfortable bed. She immediately felt ashamed. God had promised to take care of her needs, not her wants. She had needed shelter, food, and warmth. He had supplied all three. Wilson had needs too. If God had sent her to care for him, who was she to complain?

"Where did you come from, P?"

She looked up. "What did you call me?"

"P. I like it better than Patience."

She suppressed a grin. "And what's wrong with Patience?"

His eyes twinkled with mischief. "Possibly nothing, but it seems a bit pretentious."

She laughed. "Perhaps you're right. Regarding where I came from, I was kidnapped."

His eyes grew wide. "Really?"

She nodded. "Really. There was an accident, and the kidnapper and his horse were killed. I wandered around in the cold until I found this place."

Wilson's features sobered. "Why were you wearing a wedding dress? Did you get married?"

"Oh, no." She smiled, wishing she had, but she hadn't met her intended yet. She explained the circumstances, and the boy nodded.

"What are you going to do now?"

"I don't know. Try to find my way back to Denver City, I guess. Whatever I do, I'll take you with me. I wouldn't leave you behind."

Wilson picked up the poker and stirred the fire, making

the flames come to life. The dancing light threw the planes of his face into sharp relief. Patience picked out the clean-cut features, the shock of carrot orange hair, which was almost as bright as the flames. Put him into better clothing, put a little meat on his bones, and he'd be a good-looking boy, she realized. He had nice manners too. Someone had done a fine job of raising him. And educated. All those big words, like *pretentious*.

Now he looked at her, his expression grave. "You can stay here and run the mine."

"Mine?" She had forgotten about the mine. How could she forget something like that? "What kind of mine? Productive or played out?"

"Oh, there's gold all right. The old prospector worked it a little every day, even though the mine's haunted. Some days he got a fair amount of gold."

Patience gasped. *"Gold?* There's really *gold* here?" Her face fell. "We can't work the mine; it isn't ours."

"We can claim it. Nobody knows the old prospector's dead. It's ours for the taking."

"Ours?" She eyed him doubtfully. "And what do you mean, the mine's haunted?" She didn't believe in ghosts.

"Gamey O'Keefe. His spirit lives in the Mule Head, but the old prospector paid him no heed. He worked the mine anyway."

"Did the old prospector ever see the ghost?" She'd put this to rest right now.

"I don't know, but it's haunted all right. I've never seen anything either, but I've heard things."

"Well, when we see the ghost, we'll worry about it. Until then, I prefer to believe he's just a superstition." Patience pursed her lips thoughtfully. "And we could . . . honestly claim the mine?"

"Sure—it's ours for the taking. I can't claim it for myself because I'm only a child. No one would take me seriously. But you could claim it in both of our names. You'll have to do it quick because there's a lot of unscrupulous people around who'd love to get their hands on this piece of property."

She could tell from Wilson's earnest expression that he wasn't sure if she would include him in the venture, and she hastened to assure him, "I wouldn't leave you out."

But still, the idea of running a mine was overwhelming. There was so much she didn't know. Excitement flickered through her, in much the same way as the slow flames flickered around the heavy firewood.

Gold! Think of all she could do with the money from the mine. Why, God had turned a scary situation into a blessing. With a gold mine, she and Mary and Lily and Harper would never have to worry about their welfare again. And it was a worry. They couldn't stay at the parsonage in Denver City forever.

She could buy a house, and the four of them could make a home. Wilson too. He had to be included in this. Mary was sickly with asthma. They could take care of her. And Harper was black. There weren't many opportunities for black women. Blacks were treated unfairly even though the war to free them had been fought years ago.

Suddenly she wasn't scared anymore. She should have known God would take care of them. With gold from the mine, the people she cared about the most would be secure. Instead of worrying about a bleak future, they would have plenty. She smiled, looking forward to the exciting and productive months that lay ahead. She would find a crew to work the mine. The diggings would pay their salaries. She would take care of Wilson—and notify Mary, Lily, and Harper of her whereabouts as soon as she found out for sure just where she was. Why, the kidnapping had been a blessing all along! She had to pinch herself. Gold!

She owned a *gold mine!*

Or she would, just as soon as she could get to an assayer's office and stake out her claim.

Wilson interrupted her plans. "What are you thinking about? Dreaming of being rich?"

"No. Well, yes, I suppose. I was just thinking of what we would be able to do with our earnings."

"My guess is we won't be doing much. You'll never get a crew to work here."

She stared at him. "Why ever not?"

"I watched the old prospector try to get men. They won't come. They're superstitious, and they think it's a bad-luck mine."

She laughed in relief. Bad luck? Superstitious nonsense. "They must have other reasons. He probably didn't know how to approach them—or more likely, he didn't have any business savvy. There are people like that. You can always find someone who needs a job. I'll find men to work the mine, and I'll make us rich in the process."

She closed her mind to Wilson's doubting smile.

Hefting a canvas knapsack over her shoulder, Patience started off before sunup the next morning, with Wilson in tow, to claim the mine.

Cutthroat, Randy Doddler, Shirttail Diggin's, Bloody

Run, Bladdersville, Gouge Eye, Humbug Creek, Red Dog, Tenderfoot Gulch, Lost Horse Gulch, Gulch of Gold, Mad Mule Gulch—there were a hundred and one gulches where her mine could have been.

And the closest town to Mule Head was Fiddle Creek.

What struck Patience when they entered town was that nearly every man wore a beard. Not one man in a hundred had a clean-shaven face. Some looked to have cut a swatch of hair from around their mouths so they could feed themselves more easily, but in general all the males looked alike: flannel shirts, heavy boots, trousers saturated with muck, and long, matted hair.

Stepping over ankle-deep ruts to cross the street, she stared at the large assemblage of masculinity. She jerked Wilson out of the path of a careening wagon. They had walked for forty-five minutes to reach the small mining community, but the weather had held. Frozen ground had not impeded their journey.

The town itself was an eye-opener. Tucked at the base of a foothill, the camp appeared on the surface to have no civilized refinements. A vast sea of tents sprawled at the base of the mountain, interspersed with crudely assembled buildings that looked to have been thrown together with rampageous zeal. Wagons were lined up, people living out of the back of them.

Traffic had no right-of-way, with many conveyances traveling right down the middle of the street. Patience yanked Wilson from the path of another careening wagon. Rude. The citizens of Fiddle Creek were downright rude!

The stench coming from the livery stable was crippling. Manure from hundreds of horses and oxen that freighted up and down the main street was piled high.

A round of six shots erupted from one of the nearby saloons, and patrons scrambled out of windows and doors in search of cover.

Gripping Wilson's hand tightly, Patience forged her way down the crowded sidewalk in search of the land office. Her eyes watered from the blend of odors of livery stable, chicken feathers, grimy cats and dogs, and unwashed humanity.

Wilson, wearing his Sunday best, made a face when his shoes made a loud clunking sound with each step. "I'm not going to like it here," he predicted. Pinching his nose between his thumb and forefinger, he hurried to keep up with her. "It smells as bad as the old prospector's socks in late August!"

"It'll be fine," Patience soothed, more concerned over how she was going to find the assayer's office than the odors around her. She must also send word to her friends in Denver City that she was well and happy, and that she had a gold mine!

Coming down the middle of the street was a small funeral procession. The bereaved walked hand in hand, grim-faced. Some wept openly. Stepping aside to allow the mourners to pass, Patience restrained Wilson, waiting while the small cortege stopped in front of a modest-looking house with an open grave beside it. A couple of sturdy-looking chaps gently lowered the casket into the ground.

The minister, a tall, sparingly built man with ruddy cheeks and a receding hairline, opened his worn Bible, and addressed the people. "Brethren, it is a sorrowful occasion that unites us this day. In this most solemn of hours we gather to pay our final respects to Sister Oates—let us pray!"

The minister's powerful voice washed over Patience.

She nudged Wilson, and they bowed their heads with the mourners.

"Heavenly Father, we ask that you look down on Sister Oates's family and her precious loved ones. Grant them the peace that passeth all understanding—"

With her head still bowed, Patience snuck glances at the crowd through lowered lashes. She noticed that one of the mourners began to examine the dirt he was kneeling on as the preacher droned on.

"He's not bowing his head," Wilson whispered.

"Shhh."

"Sister Oates was a kind and obedient servant, Lord! Those she leaves behind will take comfort in knowing that at this very hour she walks hand in hand with loved ones who have gone before her."

The mourner began to edge his way to the mound of fresh dirt piled high beside the grave, passing the word to the fellow next to him. *Gold!*

The preacher shot him a disapproving stare but continued. "Ashes to ashes, dust to dust . . ."

Whispers of "gold!" gained momentum throughout the crowd. First one man and then another started to paw the earth. The preacher, setting his Bible aside, gazed thunderstruck at the ground, then shouted. "Gold! You're all dismissed!" Dropping to his knees, the man of the cloth clawed the dirt, the solemnity of the moment shattered.

Shaking his head, Wilson watched the spectacle taking place. "It bears repeating. I'm not going to like it here."

Grasping him firmly by the hand, Patience crossed the street, glancing over her shoulders to watch the greedy frenzy. The casket was dragged out of the grave and moved to a different spot to allow for more digging.

To her dismay, she learned the wire line between Fiddle Creek and Denver City was down due to heavy snows. She could not send a wire informing her friends of her whereabouts.

"When will the line be fixed?"

The man behind the counter shoved his green eyeshade back and glared at her. "When will the line be fixed?" he mimicked. "If I've heard that question once, I've heard it a hundred times. I'll tell you, I ain't got no crystal ball, and the good Lord don't let me in on no secrets. So I don't know *when* it's gonna be fixed."

"Well, goodness, there's no cause to shout." Surely this was the rudest place she'd ever been. She left the telegraph office, intent on laying claim to the mine and getting home before dark. She'd wire Denver City the next time she came to town.

"Oh, dear," she murmured when she finally spotted the assayer's office a few minutes later and saw that the line was backed up clear to the street.

"It's going to take forever, isn't it?" Wilson said nasally, still holding his nose from the stench.

"A while, I'm afraid."

Taking her place at the back of the line, Patience looked around her, dismayed to see the recorder's office was every bit as chaotic as the streets. Yet she had no other choice but to wait. She had to claim the mine before greedy speculators beat her to it.

For more than two hours they stood in line, wedged between smelly old men who shouted and pushed and shoved and said awful things to each other.

Recalling the earlier conversation with Wilson who said that most men worked for the larger mining companies, she leaned forward to shout above the din to the man standing in front of her.

"What's going on?"

"New strike—big one, over near Poverty Flats!"

"Gold?" she asked hopefully.

"Silver."

As Patience's part of the line edged nearer the building's entrance, she heard male voices raised in a circuslike atmosphere. Timidly, she opened the door and stepped inside. A sea of men's faces turned to stare, then continued on with their conversations.

Around two o'clock her head began to pound. She glanced down when she felt Wilson yanking on the hem of her jacket.

"I'm hungry."

"It won't be much longer." She patted his head consolingly. It had been hours since they'd eaten a meager fare of cold bread and salt pork, but if she stepped out of line she'd lose her place and have to start over again.

"I'm tired, and my shoes are too tight," he complained. He sagged against her, visibly weary from the long journey and the extended wait. Patience was starting to wonder if she was doing the right thing. What if the mine *was* worthless? What if it yielded so little gold she would be forced to return to Denver City empty-handed? She couldn't bear the thought of coming so close to an answer for her and the other orphans and losing out. They depended on her, and she had promised God she'd always take care of them. This mine would help her keep that promise.

Here, in a strange town, with even stranger-looking men flanking her on all sides, doubts assailed her. If anything were to happen to either Wilson or her, there would be nowhere to turn for help. Loved ones in Denver City were worrying themselves into a stew—how was she going to let them know that she was okay?

A scuffle broke out and two hefty-looking men hauled the ruffians outside. She tensed when she overheard two men ahead of her talking.

"Silas Tucker will grab any unoccupied mines around here; you can bet on that."

"Tucker's a leech," the second man sneered. "Wouldn't be the first time he jumped a claim."

Patience moved Wilson closer. For over an hour she had been aware of a scruffy individual two places in line ahead of her. He was, without exception, the most tattered and torn man she had ever seen. He was a caricature of an old miner— unkempt red hair, filthy beard, the rim of his old brown hat disgraceful. What had once been a flannel shirt now hung in ragged scraps, covering most of his soiled trousers.

Her eyes meandered to his boots and found that they had more holes than leather. The man stood head and shoulders taller than the other miners.

"Look, Wilson," she whispered. "There's a man with hair the same color as yours."

Wilson's face screwed with disgust.

"Except yours is cleaner," she added.

"P!"

She patted his shoulder. "Much, much cleaner."

The man suddenly turned, his eyes nailing Patience.

With a hushed catch in his throat, Wilson stepped back.

For a moment Patience couldn't breathe. The stranger's arresting clear blue gaze captured hers. Caught off guard, color flooded her face, and she realized he knew she had been staring at him. For a moment she thought she recognized him; then she quickly dismissed the idea. She couldn't know him—she didn't know anyone in Fiddle Creek.

Yet recognition briefly flashed in his eyes, and he suddenly smiled. He was about to doff his hat when he must have thought better of it. Instead, he graciously bowed from his waist. "The boy is weary. Would you like to take my place in line?" His hand indicated their chaotic surroundings. "It won't help much, but some."

Moving Wilson protectively closer, Patience summoned her most charitable smile. "No, thank you. We'll wait our turn."

Conceding with a gracious nod, the man turned back to continue the wait.

The hands on the clock crept from three to four. Wilson reeled with fatigue, clinging to Patience's trousers like a wet blanket.

"Are we *any* closer?" he asked. She heard his stomach rumble conspicuously.

The line moved at a snail's pace. Men's voices rose and fell with anticipation and anger. The room was so hot Patience could hardly breathe. Loosening the top button of her collar, she took deep breaths, directing an evil eye to the man who kept dumping coal into the corner stove. It was hot enough to cure meat in the room, but the man didn't seem to notice. Every half hour, he stepped up and fed the black monstrosity another bucket of coal.

Patience had worked her way to within five places of the assayer's desk when she suddenly felt light-headed. Fighting the weakness that threatened to overcome her, she squeezed Wilson's hand tighter.

Wilson's glasses tilted askew as he sagged against her, catnapping.

Minutes ticked by. Sweat trickled down the small of Patience's back. Bringing her handkerchief to her forehead, she blotted perspiration, willing her eyes to focus. *Only four more,* she told herself. Then she could seek a breath of clean, blessedly cool air.

She was third in line when her knees buckled. With a whimper of despair, she was overcome with blackness.

Chapter Four

Patience felt herself being lifted, carried out the door. The cold air hit her like a blow. She gasped, reason returning slowly. She could hear Wilson calling her.

"P! Wake up, P! What's wrong with her?"

A deep rumbling voice answered him. "Got too warm, probably. It was hotter than July in there."

Patience opened her eyes to find herself lying on the ground, her rescuer kneeling beside her.

"Are you feeling better now?"

"Yes, thank you," she said, grateful for his help and recognizing the scruffy miner who had offered her his place in the line. He bore a striking resemblance to Sheriff Longer. . . . "It was so hot in there." She hoped her smile was properly apologetic to make up for her earlier exclusion. The miner had been exceedingly kind. "I'm sorry you lost your place in line."

He shrugged. "It doesn't matter." He studied her features intensely. "What about you?"

Sighing, Patience got up and readjusted her old hat. "I have to claim my mine tonight."

The man's eyes skimmed her trousers. "It's getting late," he said. "And the boy's hungry. Can't you wait until morning? The lines are usually not so long then."

"I can't." Patience took Wilson's hand, trying to comfort him. He was bone weary, and neither of them could go much longer without eating. "I have to get back in line."

"It will be dark soon."

For a moment Patience was tempted to tell the man he was being intrusive. She knew it was foolish to encourage conversation with a stranger—much less one so disreputable-looking. Yet he had been kind enough to help her. . . .

Sighing, she noticed that the shadows were lengthening. Soon it would be pitch-black. "I'm afraid I have to get back into line."

Studious blue eyes assessed her, and he dropped his voice. "Is someone watching you?"

She frowned, glancing around her. "No . . . why?"

"Just pretend we're discussing a claim," he advised.

She smiled at him lamely.

He glanced at the crowd in front of the assayer's office, then back at her. "Where is your mine?"

Loosening the buttons of the worn coat, she searched for a way to get rid of him. "Not far—Mule Head. Have you heard of it?" Getting a closer look at his hands, Patience was surprised to see they were strong and tanned. Why, he wasn't nearly as old as she'd first thought. No one to take care of him properly and hard living, she suspected when she studied his features beneath the scrubby beard.

He nodded. "I know where it is."

Relief flooded her. Maybe he knew something—something she should know. "Is it a good mine?"

"Depends on what you call good. It's haunted."

So, he'd heard the speculation. She supposed the ghost was common speculation around here.

She stood shivering in the mountain air, holding tightly to Wilson's hand. "I'm afraid rumors regarding the Mule Head have been greatly exaggerated." She paused when she saw him staring at her in an odd, almost embarrassing way. She touched her hair self-consciously, aware of her manly attire. "Is something wrong?" She was quite certain she didn't look her best—maybe her hairpins had come loose.

He glanced over his shoulder again, then back to her. "Are you all right?"

"All right?" She frowned. "I'm fine. Why?" For heaven's sake—why was he so worried about her health? The room was too hot—that's why she fainted.

Stepping closer, he lowered his tone. "It's me." He lifted the brim of his hat to allow her closer inspection. She stared at the red beard and ruddy complexion. Nothing. Whoever "me" was, she didn't know him.

Her frown deepened. Oh, dear. He was peculiar. A hundred men in the vicinity, and she attracted the addled one.

"Me." His tone turned a little sharp. "Take my arm and walk slowly away from the area. Once we're clear, I have a horse waiting. You don't need to be afraid."

She nodded blankly. Oh, *dear.* "Wilson," she called brightly. "Time to get back into line—"

The man reached out and grasped her by the forearm, suddenly propelling her in the opposite direction.

"Excuse me!" she bellowed, trying to jerk free of his steel-banded hold. Why the man was more than addled—he was deranged!

"P!" Wilson called, running to catch up. The miner threaded Patience through the teeming crowd.

"Let go of me this instant!" She managed to break the man's grip, incensed that no one was coming to her defense. What kind of men were these rowdies?

"Stop it! You're causing a scene." He latched onto her arm again and purposely marched her in the direction of the livery.

"You stop it!" She was making a scene big enough to alert anyone to her situation—but nobody seemed to notice. Men and women went about their business with barely a glance at the growing fracas.

"I'm trying to get us out of here without a fight," he muttered. "Will you please cooperate? You're just plain lucky I doubled back through Fiddle Creek today, or I would have missed you completely."

He didn't make a lick of sense. "Why would anyone fight over us?" She stumbled over her own feet and had to steady her balance on his arm.

He glared at her, shooting furtive glances over his shoulder. "Are your captors nearby?"

"Captors—?" Patience suddenly stopped in midtrack. Now she knew why he bore such an uncanny resemblance to Jay Longer. He *was* the sheriff of Denver City! He was her rescuer! But why was he dressed so—awful?

She voiced her shock. "Why are you dressed so awful?"

He glared at her. "I'm in disguise."

"Oh." Well, she should have figured that out. Of course he wouldn't ride into one of these rowdy mining towns with a tin badge on his chest. He was infuriatingly contrary but not stupid.

"Sheriff Longer, isn't it?"

He quieted her with a dour look. "I'm *trying* to get us out of here in one piece."

She drew herself up straighter, eyes narrowed. "How very

kind of you to come after me. There is no captor—the horse stumbled and landed on the kidnapper and I got away." She frowned. "Didn't you find the horse carcass and the man's body?"

"I found it, but I thought maybe the culprit was part of a gang and they still had you. I've been trailing you for days."

"Well, how nice," she said, and then straightened her hat. Turning to a wide-eyed Wilson, she said, "Wilson, Mr. Longer is Denver City's sheriff. He's been looking for me."

Wilson refused to warm to the stranger. "Hello," he mumbled.

Briefly Patience filled Jay in on the past days' events, the death of the old prospector, the mine, and Wilson's role in the strange circumstances. She said she was here to claim Mule Head and that she planned to stay for however long it took to get the mine producing gold. "Mary, Lily, and Harper will never have to worry another day about their future," she finished.

Longer took off his hat and swatted the brim on his dusty thigh, apparently unconcerned whether the material would hold together. Annoyance lined his weary features. "Denver City is twenty-eight miles from here; I know these parts as well as I know the back of my hand. Mule Head is worthless, Miss Smith—"

"Call me Patience." She didn't know why she was so charitable, but they couldn't keep calling each other by their last names.

He conceded, "Okay. Your mine is haunted, Patience Smith. You won't get one man to work it—let alone a crew of men."

Her face fell. "That's just plain not true. The part about the mine being haunted is silly rumor. I don't believe in ghosts."

"Neither do I, but the majority of folks around here do, and that's your problem. You best forget about staking a claim and come back to Denver City with me. Your friends are worried about you."

Patience could feel her dream crumbling, and she struggled to hang on. That mine was the only future she had. Go back to Denver City—to an uncertain life? His advice wasn't fair—not fair at all! She could find men to work the mine; she knew she could. The sheriff gave up too easily.

Stiffening her resolve, she turned and reached for Wilson's hand. "I'm sorry, Sheriff Longer; I don't want to be rude—" *like you,* she wanted to add but didn't—"and I truly appreciate your coming all this way to rescue me, but I don't need rescuing. I'm going to claim the Mule Head and work it, because it will give us a chance to have a future—a future we would not have otherwise."

With a curt nod in the sheriff's direction, she stepped back into line.

Women! Jay watched her flounce off. Stubborn, ornery . . . wouldn't listen to a blessed thing. A woman didn't have any business running a mine. Some men believed women were bad luck in a mine. If you asked him, women were bad luck, period.

Take this one. He had been looking for her in one mining camp after another, sleeping on the ground, spending restless nights, and then when he did find her, she brushed him off. Didn't want to go home. Going to work the mine and get rich.

Not at the Mule Head, she wasn't. He knew that mine.

Knew most of the mines in this area. Had worked some.
Even if she managed to file the claim—and she was just
bullheaded enough to do that—she'd never find a crew.
He wondered where she'd picked up the boy. Spunky kid.
He'd tried to protect her when she'd passed out.

Jay chuckled. Funny little guy. Doubled up his fists and
started swinging. Jay had held him at arm's length and let
him whale away until he'd run down. But he'd tried; he
had to give him that.

He watched Patience and the boy inch along in line.
They'd be a while yet. Probably getting hungry. Well, he
could do something about that. Satisfied they weren't in
any immediate danger, he sauntered off, searching for food.

Sheriff Longer was leaning insolently against the surveyor's
office, arms crossed, when Patience emerged two hours
later. Darkness cloaked the mining town. Lanterns glowed
brightly in the cold mountain air.

When the sheriff fell into step beside them, Patience
ignored him. She had filed her claim, and he wasn't going
to talk her out of working it. Nobody was going to talk her
into giving up. Too much depended on it. The other three
and Wilson. Four people who needed the security the mine
would give. She couldn't fail.

He didn't argue. They walked to the edge of the town in
stony silence. Once he reached into his pocket and took out
two warm biscuits stuffed with fat sausage slices, and handed
one to Wilson and one to her. Wilson tore into the food
like a ravenous animal.

She ate hers more slowly, savoring the first warm thing in
her belly all day.

"You're walking back to the mine tonight?" His voice broke the strained silence.

"I don't have a choice." She swallowed a bit of biscuit and meat. "I have no money for a room—even if a room were available." She hated to admit her immediate disadvantage, but there it was; she was flat broke and she had to go back to the mine.

"You're not going alone."

"I came alone—at least, Wilson and I came alone, and we had no trouble."

"You walked daylight hours, didn't you?"

She had to admit that she had. And that she was terrified to walk in the dark. So many ravines and gulches. One misplaced step and . . . she closed her mind to the dangers. She had responsibilities now—as Wilson's self-appointed guardian, she had to put on a brave face.

"You'd be better off waiting until morning," Longer said shortly.

"We'll walk a ways and then rest until dawn."

His eyes accessed her trousers and wool coat. "You'll freeze before dawn."

She didn't break pace. "I've survived overnight in a wedding gown, sir—besides, I brought extra clothing." She wasn't that green. The old prospector owned quite a few clothes, and she'd packed every one of them in the bag—and extra food and water, hidden along the trail.

"These mountains are treacherous if you don't know them."

A smile filled her eyes when she heard the hesitation softening his deep baritone. "But you do know them, don't you?" She wasn't sure why, but she knew he would help her. She wasn't foolish. For all she knew he could be dangerous *and* contrary under that scruffy façade; yet she

sensed that he wasn't. His outward appearance was a
well-executed ploy, but his eyes gave him away. Patience
saw a sense of nobility in them.

"You do know the mountains?" she repeated softly.

A muscle flexed in his bearded cheek. "I know them."

"Then I'm sure we could not ask for more capable assistance." Her pleas formed a soft vapor in the cold night air.

Glancing at the boy, he said quietly. "We'll need
lanterns."

"I don't have money to buy one," she reminded him.

"Wait here . . . and wrap that scarf in your pocket around
your neck. The temperature is dropping."

Patience took Wilson's hand, found a large rock, and sat
down to await the sheriff's return. She couldn't be rude,
and he had agreed to walk them back to the mine—sort of.
When he returned to Denver City he could assure the
others of her well-being and explain why she hadn't come
back with him.

So she'd wait—and accept the sheriff's kind offer of
help—if it killed her.

Jay returned half an hour later carrying two lanterns,
canteens, and more biscuits and sausage. "I've decided to
leave my horse at the livery. I don't want to take a chance
of the animal breaking a leg. We'll walk up the mountain."

Wilson asked for seconds on the biscuits and sausage,
stuffing the steaming fare into his mouth. They started off.
The moon rose higher. Wilson walked beside Jay now,
apparently satisfied he was more friend than foe.

Jay glanced at the top of the boy's head. Good kid, but
an odd little duck. "What's your name, son?"

Wilson swallowed, panting to keep up with Jay's long strides. "Wil . . . son."

"Wilson?"

He nodded, running to stay alongside.

"You good with your fists, Wilson?"

"Not very . . . but with a name like Wilson, I should be, huh?"

Jay let his lips curve in a hint of a smile. "Is that an English accent I hear?"

"Yes, sir. My parents were traveling from England when they died of the cholera. I escaped the disease. The old prospector found me three days after they died—I was hungry and quite a pitiful sight, I understand. I don't know if my name's Wilson—but that's what the prospector called me."

Jay shook his head. Rough break, but a common enough story in these parts. Life could be tough on kids.

"What was the prospector's name?"

"Prospector. Sometimes Mr. Old Prospector. Me and you have the same color hair; you notice that?"

"I noticed."

"I could almost be your boy, couldn't I?"

The sheriff's face hardened. "I don't have a boy."

"Well if you *did,*" Wilson insisted, "I could be him."

Not in a million years. Jay kept his eyes fixed straight ahead. His boy was lying in a six-by-three-foot mound next to his mother.

Chapter Five

It got dark early. That was what Jay hated about the mountains. He didn't mind the cold when he came to Colorado years ago, but he hated it now. Mexico—that climate suited him. Hot winds and long, sultry nights with strumming guitars.

Leaving Patience and Wilson in the dugout, he picked his way back down the mountain, trying to erase the boy's face from his mind. Wilson. Odd little fellow. Reminded him in a strange way of Brice. His son. He'd have been about the same age as Wilson. Seemed like when Jay had lost Nelly and his boy to the fever, he'd sort of lost himself too. Took a long time to come to grips with their dying. He'd wake up in the night and feel the horrible, twisting pain of knowing he'd never see them again—not on this side of heaven, anyway.

He'd been so proud of his boy, had looked forward to teaching him how to shoot a gun and saddle a horse. To be a man. A good man, the kind who would do right, a man who would be honest, clean, trustworthy. The kind of man he wanted to be but couldn't quite muster after Nelly died. He'd planned to teach Brice to fish and ride and hunt, too. Oh, he'd had plans for that boy. Big plans. And then the fever had swept their home, and he'd buried those plans with his wife and son.

Jay had lost something else that day: his trust in God. How could a loving God take Nelly and Brice and leave him behind with nothing but broken dreams and a black, blinding despair that had almost destroyed him? Oh, he still believed there was a God—you couldn't live in these mountains and not see his handiwork—but he didn't believe that God cared about people.

He'd learned the truth that day, standing beside an open grave and listening to the wind wailing through the pines and the preacher droning on about God's love. The truth came to him, driving through his grief, hardening his heart until it was like a lump of stone inside him.

God didn't care.

If God had any love or compassion for Jay Longer, he wouldn't have taken Brice and Nelly.

That was the truth, and you couldn't get around it.

He'd learned to hide the pain and push away the memories, but this boy Wilson had brought it all back. Jay realized now that he'd made a habit of avoiding young boys, afraid of letting himself get too close. Afraid to revive old hurts.

He'd tried to reason with his wife, pleaded with her to let him take her to the doctor when the fever overtook her and the boy, but she didn't believe in medicine. Had some foolish notion that trusting in doctors showed a lack of faith in God.

Nelly came from a religious family, probably the most religious people he'd ever known. Lived by a set list of rules. Sometimes he'd wondered whose rules—theirs or God's?

Mostly he couldn't find their rules in his Bible, and he'd searched. But they believed in them and lived by them.

Nelly had gone to an old herb woman who'd mixed up some kind of potion for her to drink. According to Nelly, it was all right to take the potion because herbs were natural medicine. He couldn't see it himself. Sure, herbs could be powerful medicine sometimes, but so could store-bought medicine. Seemed to him if God could use an old herb-doctoring woman, he could use a regular doctor. But Nellie had followed her beliefs and she'd taken her potion and she died. And Brice had died with her.

Nelly had been real stubborn. Just like Patience Smith. And now Patience had this fool notion of working the mine. No one could do a thing with her. Get a notion in her head and you couldn't budge it, and dreaming of gold was a powerful notion.

Since he'd been in Colorado Jay had seen more stupidity than he could shake a stick at. Some of it his. Yeah, he'd followed the gold dream, but not anymore. When it came to mines, he was a jinx. Still, it was amazing how some people responded to the mention of gold.

The boy looked downright scared. Couldn't blame him. The Mule Head should scare anyone in their right mind.

But the two would be all right overnight. The dugout was dry, and he'd made sure they had plenty of wood before he left. Come morning, Patience would start the process of hiring a crew, and she'd find out what she was up against. She wouldn't stick around long after that.

Jay would bide his time. Let her learn the hard way. He could force her to go back to Denver City with him, sling her across his horse and haul her back, but she had a temper. He'd seen plenty of flashes of it. Twenty-eight miles would seem like a hundred-mile ride with a spitfire like that. He remembered a piece of Scripture from the book of Proverbs: "It is better to dwell in a corner of the housetop, than with a brawling woman in a wide house." Solomon had, what—about six or seven hundred wives? Jay bet the old king knew a lot about brawling women.

He was on the right track. Let Miss Patience Smith see what she was up against, and she'd beg him to take her back to Denver City.

He tried to think of more pleasant things as he walked, but he couldn't get Patience's face out of his mind. Odd, since he hadn't thought about a woman since Nelly's death. Not for any length of time. Seemed like he couldn't get interested in a female after Nelly; he'd just drawn into a shell and stayed there. Nelly had been so sweet and so pretty, so eager to please him in everything except where her beliefs were concerned. And in the end, her beliefs had killed her.

They'd married young, sort of growing up together. Life had been good then. When Brice was born, Jay had held the two of them in his arms, his heart filled to bursting with love.

Maybe they'd have died anyway, even if he'd gotten them to a doctor. No way of knowing. If only Nelly had loved him enough to listen, to forget the rules for once, to trust him enough to seek medical help.

He suddenly lost his footing, stumbling.

Quickly righting himself, he concentrated on the trail. *Watch it, Jay; you can't fall and break your neck. . . .*

Who'd care? he thought, laughing outright now.

Sure, Jenny would be upset, but she'd get over it. His kid

sister didn't know where he was, let alone worry about him.
Hadn't kept track of him for years. She was in Phoenix
being a dutiful wife to her husband, good old reliable Joe.
Together they had respectfully produced three strapping
heirs in less than four years. Pop was probably real proud
of them.

"And he'd consider me a flat-out disgrace," he acknowledged.

Loose rocks gave way beneath his heavy boot as he edged
the steep incline. If he fell and broke every bone in his
body, there'd only be one man who'd care.

That, of course, would be Mooney Backus, the man who
held his gambling debts.

How much did he owe Mooney now? Twenty-five
hundred dollars. A small fortune—one he didn't have.
Sheriff's pay didn't cover his former insanity, the years
following Nelly's death.

Years ago—when he'd believed in a caring God—he'd
have been worried about owing a man money and then
suddenly finding himself unable to meet his debt. Yes sir,
there'd been a time when he'd have stayed up nights trying
to figure out how to repay the money.

And gambling would have been the last thing on his
mind. But when God stepped out of Jay's life—the day God
took Nelly and Brice—Jay's responsible thoughts ceased.

Back then he'd been honorable. Honorable and full of
himself.

But no use crying over spilled milk. He had no one but
himself to blame for his problems; he could easily have
become a town doctor. Pa was a physician, and by the time
Jay turned sixteen he'd helped deliver half the babies in the
territory and even helped Pa when he cut out bullets and

sewed up men's faces. If doctoring hadn't suited him, he could have married Mary Porter. Mary's pa wasn't exactly a pauper. The old man would have given him fifty acres of prime farmland—no, more like two hundred and fifty—in order to spare his daughter the agony of spinsterhood. But that wasn't what he'd done.

No sirree, not Jay Longer. Not the brash twenty-year-old who had life all figured out. He'd married his true love, pretty Nelly Briscoe, whose family lived on a neighboring farm, and like so many other misguided fools, the two had started out for Colorado to claim their fortune. He'd sunk every last penny he had in a gold mine that had produced nothing.

Absolutely nothing.

Not particularly bright of him, but when a man had gold fever he wasn't thinking straight.

From the day James Wilson Marshall discovered the first gold nugget in a ditch that channeled water from river to sawmill, gold had enriched and ruined men's lives. That afternoon of January 4, 1848, forty-five miles east of Sutter's Fort in Sacramento Valley, changed the course of history.

And put a fair-sized dent in Jay's life.

But that was neither here nor there. Pop had given up on Jay's ever taking over his doctor practice; Mary had been spared spinsterhood when she married the depot clerk, Pete Wiler; and any day now, Jay would be dead.

Mooney Backus wasn't long on patience. He'd been after Jay to pay off his debt for over two years now. Jay was running out of excuses and was tired of avoiding Backus's thugs, Red and Luther.

He laughed, wondering what the good folks of Denver City would say when they found out their sheriff was a wanted man. Not by the law but by something more deadly.

Four days ago, Backus had delivered an ultimatum by wire. Jay had exactly two weeks to come up with five hundred dollars. Which had a lot to do with why he wasn't in a hurry to get back to Denver City. If Mooney wanted him, he'd find him, but no sense making it easy for him.

Jay caught himself again as his boot slid in the loose dirt, the rocks spilling down the precipitous incline. The trail started to blur. Shaking his head, he tried to focus on the path. Cold seeped through his senses, and the moon barely shed enough light to walk by. He'd stayed at the mine longer than he should have, stacking wood and making sure the girl and kid were settled. There was a hundred-foot drop on either side of him. One slip, and he'd save Mooney the trouble of coming after him.

Concentrating now, he slowed his pace. The wind whipped his frayed coat. His hand came up to hold his battered hat in place. A lone coyote howled at the moon. He rather liked this disguise, might even keep it to throw Backus's men off his trail.

One moment he was walking, and the next he felt himself hurtling down the mountainside. Panic-stricken, he tried to catch himself, but he was too far gone. He tumbled end over end, arms and legs flailing wildly.

Bile came up in his throat and he choked, hitting the ground hard. Sliding, he snatched for a handhold, his life flashing before him. Miraculously, one of his hands snagged something and latched on.

Silence closed around him. He lay, afraid to move a muscle, panting, praying that whatever he held on to would continue to support his weight.

A coyote yelped, its cries fading into emptiness.

Using his free hand, Jay slowly felt around, determining

that he was on the edge of a mine shaft or maybe a deep precipice. His scraped and bleeding fingers explored the uneven ground. Sweat beaded his forehead. He touched the small outcropping of rock he was lying on.

He was afraid to risk even the slight movement needed to yell. Besides, no one would hear him. Not here on this remote mountainside.

Flat on his back, he watched a cloud drift across the moon, temporarily obscuring it. Snowflakes started to swirl. A cold wind buffeted the hillside.

Jay lay motionless, his eyes fixed on the sky. Nothing he did lately worked out.

"P, I *am* thankful for food, but I don't like turnips," Wilson reminded Patience the next morning. "Especially not for breakfast!"

No longer than they'd been together, Wilson had decided he liked P. Liked the way she smiled—and she was kind. She didn't yell or cry or act like a baby even though he knew she was scared.

Animals prowled the mine site, growling with hunger. Once last night, Wilson had heard something big lumbering around outside—a bear, he suspected. A big out-of-sorts grizzly. It sniffed around for a long time. Patience heard it—he knew she heard it—but she pretended to be asleep, although he could see the blanket quivering over her slim frame.

He didn't blame her. The boards the old prospector had nailed over the mine entrance and the heavy door over the dugout kept out most four-legged intruders, but a grizzly would be hard to stop.

"Turnips are good for you—and we can be thankful that

the old prospector laid up plenty of store for the long
winter."

This morning she'd discovered the small root cellar adja-
cent to the mine, stocked full of potatoes, turnips, beans,
butter, and salt pork—"enough to see a small army through
the hard months," she'd exclaimed. You'd have thought
she'd hit the mother lode the way she carried on. She got
more excited when she discovered the old cow. Even tried
her hand at milking and did as well, or maybe better, than
the old prospector had done. It looked like she was settling
in for a long spell. Probably he shouldn't have suggested
working the mine. She had the fever now, and it would be
hard to discourage her.

Sighing, Wilson quietly set to work eating.

Patience let her mind pleasantly drift, and she contemplated
all the things they could do now that she owned a gold
mine! Wilson needed shoes, and she needed a new
dress—maybe even two! And, oh, what she could do for
Mary. She could rent—no, *buy*—larger quarters for the
millinery, and for Harper she could buy Mrs. Katskey's café
so the grandma could devote all her time to raising her
young grandson. Harper would have income for the rest of
her life.

Then she would buy a big house—big enough for Mary and
Harper and Lily and her and Wilson to live in comfortably.
Oh, it would be so grand—they would be a family, a real
family, with Thanksgiving dinners and plum pudding and lots
of oranges and peppermint-stick candy at Christmastime.

The mine's proceeds would mean that an exceptionally
bright young boy could attend college and have all the

things his parents would have wanted for him. The orphanage had supplied life's necessities for her, as long as she was young, but the headmistress made it clear that once Patience reached adulthood she was expected to provide for herself. Well, she had tried her hand at becoming a mail-order bride. That had fizzled, but God had given her another chance.

Wilson reached for his glass of milk. "Will we live here in the dugout?"

"We'll have to—I'll have to oversee the mine." She'd managed to stake a claim to the Mule Head before news of the prospector's death reached other materialistic would-be miners. Maybe they could build a cabin. She didn't fancy living underground like some burrowing animal.

Wilson peered back at her through his bottle-thick spectacles. "Mining is hard work, P—"

She didn't mind the shortened name, but she'd reminded him that she shouldn't be so lenient since she was his elder. Nodding, she took a bite of potato. "We'll hire strong men to do the work. At least eight or ten."

The boy sighed. "The old prospector said that wasn't possible. All the men in this area have jobs, and besides, they're afraid to come near Mule Head."

"Nonsense. You're talking about the ghost again, aren't you?"

"How do you know it's nonsense? Just because you've never seen a ghost doesn't mean they don't exist."

She stared at him. "I asked you once before. Have you ever seen the ghost?"

He squirmed, turning red in the face. "I'm not saying what I've seen, but I do believe it might be a mistake to be overly confident. Whether you believe in ghosts or not, the men do. They won't want to disturb a 'haint,' as they call it, and they might not want to work for a woman."

Patience glared at Wilson. "It was your idea to claim the mine. Why are you trying to discourage me now?"

"I've had time to think, and I do believe we might be taking on more than we can handle."

She sighed in exasperation. "So I should let someone else have the mine? Do you really think I'm going to do that? Stop coming up with reasons why this won't work. We've claimed this mine, and we're going to work it, and we're going to be rich. I already know what I'm going to do with the money."

This wasn't just about her. It was a chance to do something for others. Jay Longer couldn't see that, but he was a rigid, arrogant . . . ole goat. God would help her help Mary, Harper, and Lily. After all, he'd brought her here.

Wilson sighed. "I've never thought it wise to spend money you haven't received yet. We have a long way to go before we see any monetary compensation."

Patience sent him a reprimanding glance. "Wilson, where *did* you learn those big words?" He was eight going on forty. She didn't know where all that wisdom came from, but at times he seemed the adult, not her.

Wilson shrugged. "I have a flair for English."

Grinning, she reached over and tousled his flamboyant thatch of carrot-colored hair. In many ways he *could* be Jay Longer's son, not only in looks but in stubborn persistence. "With all that money we'll even be able to buy you some new glasses."

"That would be nice. The old prospector didn't have money to be throwing around. He said I was lucky to have

any." He stabbed a turnip with his fork and stared at it.
"Can I have a dog now? The old prospector strictly forbade
pets. He said they ate too much, and barked and left stuff in
the yard he was always stepping in."

"Sure, but no more than one—too many mouths to feed."

Taking a bite of bread, he frowned. "I wouldn't be
counting my nuggets yet if I were you."

Her brows lifted. "And why not? We own our own gold
mine."

"Well, I don't know," he contended patiently. "I'm only eight,
but I sense we're in over our heads here. I realize you don't want
to hear about that, but who will do the work? I'm telling you,
the old prospector couldn't find anyone to help him."

"But I can get help. Once I set my head to something, I
usually achieve the end result. At the orphanage, if anyone
wanted anything done, they'd come to me."

Wilson's eyes returned to his plate. "You can be so naïve,
dear friend."

They continued eating breakfast, letting the subject drop
momentarily. Finally Patience looked up again. "Are you
really suggesting that we desert the mine? that I go back to
Denver City?"

"How old are you?"

"It isn't proper to ask a lady's age."

"I'm sorry. How much do you weigh?"

She'd sooner tell her age. "Wilson!"

"What funds have you set aside for your welfare?"

"Well, none . . . " Her words wavered when she saw him
shaking his head. "I lived in an orphanage before coming to
Denver City, where I was supposed . . . to be . . . a mail-order
bride." She paused, worrying her teeth on her lower lip.

"Homeless and broke." When she was about to argue,

Wilson continued. "I'm homeless and broke too, and I'm only eight years old. It's nothing to be ashamed of—just a small nuisance."

She slid to the front of her chair. "Don't you see? Our situations make it even more imperative that we work the mine. We don't have any other choice. I can take you back to Denver City with me, but to what? I don't have a home—Mary, Lily, Harper and I are living with Pastor Siddons and his wife, and the house is fairly bursting at the seams. Listen, Wilson—" her eyes pleaded for understanding— "maybe the Lord will shine on us and we'll unearth a vein of silver. That's even better than gold, isn't it?"

"Silver would be better, but a good gold vein is capable of producing a handsome profit," Wilson mused.

Patience leaned in closer. "Then let's do it. Let's ask the Lord to bless our efforts, and let's do it."

"Most assuredly." He slid a piece of turnip into his mouth, momentarily gagging. He continued. "There are still a few small problems."

"What?"

"You don't know how to mine, I'm too little, and Gamey's ghost won't let anyone in the mine."

Smiling, Patience continued eating. "There is no ghost, and there's enough gold here to make our wildest dreams come true."

Taking a drink of milk, Wilson sighed. "Logic isn't your strong suit, is it?"

The first warming rays of the morning sun woke Jay. He flexed his feet, feeling like one solid block of ice. Turning his head, he gauged the width of the ledge on which he lay.

It protruded maybe six inches past his body. He shuddered. Lucky for him he had landed here. Now he had to do what he could to get out of this fix.

He reached up and grasped an outcropping of rock, carefully pulling himself to a sitting position. His body ached from various bruises and scrapes, and he felt stiff from the cold. Tilting his head back, he squinted up, relieved to find that the top of the ledge was only about nine or ten feet above his head. He was a good six feet tall. If he could find handholds, he could possibly get out of here.

Easing to his feet, he avoided looking down. By standing on his tiptoes and reaching up as far as possible, he managed to grip a small ledge. Inch by inch he pulled himself upward, scrabbling for toeholds. He tried not to think of the stabbing pain in his shoulders and the way the rocks scraped his hands raw. A few more inches and his groping hands caught a tree root. He tested its strength, not sure if it would hold his weight, but it held firm.

His head crested the top of the ledge. He grabbed a slender bush, hauling himself up. His shoulders were over the rim, now his waist. He scrambled forward on his belly until he lay full length on top of a smooth boulder. Sun warmed his shoulders and he breathed deeply, knowing he would live.

After a few moments, he got to his feet, stumbling a little in his haste to get off this mountain and find shelter and warmth. As he strode down the trail, he tried to ignore the thoughts that troubled his mind.

All through that long, lonely night, when he wasn't sure if he'd live or die, it wasn't Nelly's face that had filled his dreams. It had been the stubborn, irritating image of Patience Smith.

Get a grip, man. Give the lady enough rope and she'll hang herself.

The thought wasn't all that disagreeable. Yet it was, and for the life of him, Jay couldn't understand why. Until Patience was kidnapped, his life had been going smoothly; no problems—other than bad debts. He kept to himself and encouraged others to do the same. He'd eaten steak and potatoes, slept on clean sheets, and propped his feet in front of a roaring fire every night. He resented having to chase a mulish woman over the hillsides. Resented the dickens out of her.

If that was the case, why did he have to remind himself three times a day that what he was doing was a job, pure and simple? Patience Smith didn't factor into the picture.

Actually, this woman was more trouble than she was worth, and the sooner she got this get-rich notion out of her head, the quicker he'd be back home in his own bed.

Well . . . he grinned. Maybe he'd just hurry Miss Smith's reasoning process along a little bit. The thought of steak and potatoes and a warm bed was powerful motivation for a man who hated the cold.

Not to mention the dark.

Chapter Six

Before the sun topped the ragged summit on the crisp January morning, Patience stepped out of the dugout and took a deep breath of mountain air. Confronted with magnificent beauty, she clasped her hands in awe of Colorado's snow-covered peaks silhouetted against a flawless blue sky. Icy tendrils hung in long, glistening blades off craggy ledges.

Searching for the proper term to describe such breathtaking beauty, she found none. Yellow pines, Douglas firs, and blue spruces covered the mountainsides. Just below the timberline, hardy bristlecone pines, gnarled by the constant winds, dotted the land. And the aspens—their magnificent trunks were resplendent beneath a layer of fresh snow.

On the lower slopes, mule deer browsed on nuts and lichens. Elk and bighorn sheep leapt among the crags at higher elevation.

How could she describe such splendor—such grandeur—when she told Mary, Lily, Harper, and Ruth about her adventure? How could she find the words to define the simplicity—the marvelous beauty that God had made? The

troubles they had experienced had drawn them together
until they were as close as sisters. They were the family
she'd never had. When the mine began producing, Patience
was going to bring the three single women here and let
them experience the sights for themselves.

Sighing, she breathed deeply of the pine-scented air. Her
friends would be so worried about her. She'd go into Fiddle
Creek today and try again to wire them or ask around and
see if perhaps someone planned to travel to Denver City
soon. She thought of the mine she now owned. *Lord, I'm
not greedy. Really, I'm not. It's just that we need that gold.* It
was difficult to be a single woman out here, or anywhere
for that matter. There weren't many jobs available. If she
could get this mine producing, none of them would ever
have to worry again.

She sighed. She'd claimed her mine over two days
ago—but Jay hadn't returned.

Worry nagged her. Had he gone back to Denver City
without her? Would that audacious man just *ride off* like that
without saying good-bye? She was conscious of a flash of
disappointment. Flustered, she tried to ignore the emotion.
Why should she care what Jay Longer did? He was nothing
to her. Wasn't likely to ever be important in her life. Sure,
he was a big healthy specimen of manhood. Nice to look at
too—or would be, if you cleaned him up and put some
decent clothes on him.

They'd gone nose to nose in Denver City, and thinking
back, Patience remembered that he had a very nice nose.
A very manly nose indeed, but he'd always been aloof, not
talking much or paying her any attention. She realized now
that she—along with every other single woman in town—
had been miffed at his conspicuous lack of interest.

He was obstinate too. Trying to take her away from
Fiddle Creek by discouraging her efforts—although she
tried to tell him she could get a crew. This was her only
chance to make a future for herself, and she had a lot of
people depending on her.

She kicked a rock out of her way, hoping he hadn't left
the area yet. She hated to admit it, but she liked him. Was
even a little attracted to him, although she wouldn't ever
want him to know it. She was hoping he would help her
hire a crew before he returned to Denver City.

Hands on hips, she focused on the mine's boarded
entrance, determined not to be beaten by her circumstances.
Sure, there were problems she hadn't considered, but problems were meant to be solved, weren't they? And the ghost?
The Good Book said not to acknowledge superstitions.

Sitting down on the stoop, she sighed. Surrounded by
God's glorious work, Patience found it hard to be pessimis-
tic about the future.

The Mule Head wasn't that bad. Why, in the time it took
to say, "What am I doing here?" she'd have the mine operating at full speed.

Ghost or no ghost, the men in Fiddle Creek would
welcome new employment opportunities. The big companies couldn't offer the caring, family-oriented workplace she
intended to give her crew. Wilson's college nest egg would
be growing—

Feathers! Who was she kidding? The living conditions
were deplorable. Vile, dirty, cold, horrible . . . and lonely.
So very lonely.

She'd be lucky to hire a monkey crew if the Mule Head's
reputation was as bad as Jay seemed to think it was.

Patience got up, went into the dugout, and closed the

door. Rubbing the goose bumps on her arms, she hurried to the fire.

"Wilson!" She eyed the tuft of russet sticking out from beneath the blanket. She swung a pot of water over the flame to boil. "Rise and shine! We have a lot to do today!"

"Freezin'," Wilson complained in a muffled voice from under his covers.

"Get up, slug bug! Sun's up!"

A jumbled thatch of reddish hair poked out of the blanket, followed by a pair of disgruntled eyes. "I'm stiff as a poker."

"We'll have to do something about that draft," she agreed.

"Draft!" Wilson exclaimed. "It's more like a cyclone whistling beneath the door." Throwing the blanket aside, he stared at his feet. "I'm crippled," he announced.

"No, you're not," Patience assured him cheerily. "Your feet are just cold." She stirred oats into the pot of boiling water. "The circulation will return once you're up and around. Hurry now—we have a crew to hire!"

Wilson watched her as she fixed breakfast. "Are you going into town today?"

"I thought we would." Her first visit to Fiddle Creek had been focused on filing a claim. Now she was anxious for any tidbit of information, however small, regarding the mining town. For instance, did they have a school? She'd been thinking that if she was going to work the mine, Wilson would need proper schooling. He also needed to be with children his own age. He'd probably been with adults most of his life, and he needed youthful, carefree days. The good Lord knew Wilson had seen few of those.

Besides, she would be too busy working to teach him. She had to set up a household, hire a crew—oh! There were so many things to be done!

Breakfast finished, she went outside again to check the weather. It had snowed last night. The door opened behind her and a tousle-headed Wilson stepped out, snuggling deeper into a fur-lined coat. He squinted against the sun's glare on the fresh snow.

"If you're planning to hire a crew, most of the bigger mining companies have taken over. In order to have their families with them, the men settle for an hourly wage now."

Patience's brows lifted. "Then we'll pay our crew hourly."

The boy shook his head. "I've been thinking, P. The old prospector thought silver was more profitable."

"Silver?"

He nodded, shuffling through knee-deep snow to reach her. He stopped, took a big sniff, and then wiped his nose on his coat sleeve.

She frowned. "Don't wipe your nose on your sleeve, Wilson."

"But it's dripping."

Patience remembered that he had mentioned silver earlier. But gold! Now gold was always gold and surely profitable.

It was still fairly early when Patience and Wilson walked down the mountain. Approaching town, she searched for any sign of Jay, but he wasn't around. Yet she couldn't make herself believe that he'd actually left her and Wilson here alone. He was pouting; wasn't that what men did when they didn't get their way? She bet Jay Longer was a big pouter. Her attention was diverted by the schoolhouse. She hadn't noticed the building the day she claimed the Mule Head.

"There's the schoolhouse."

Wilson shrugged his shoulders. "I've never been interested in academics. The old prospector said I had enough schooling to use words no one could understand. I didn't need any more."

Patience was aghast. Not need schooling? Of course he needed to go to school. She realized that she could probably be considered Wilson's guardian. At any rate, she had taken on the responsibility of looking after him, and if she had anything to say about it he would go to school. Even at the orphanage, she had received an education.

"Of course you need to go to school. We'll check into it this morning."

"P, I don't want to go to school! I want to stay with you."

"Wilson, you need schooling. How do you expect to get ahead in the world without it? You'll always be at a disadvantage with people who are more educated."

Wilson screwed up his face in outrage. "I've been told I'm exceptionally smart for my age. I don't think many eight-year-old boys could outthink me."

"Probably not, but you won't be eight years old forever, and all of those people who are sitting in school and learning from books will soon know more than you do. Knowledge is power, Wilson. Never forget that. Besides, the Bible says we are to study to show ourselves approved."

Wilson peered at her over the tops of his spectacles. "I do believe God was referring to studying his Word, not arithmetic."

The schoolhouse was a one-room affair of plain boards weathered to a soft gray. Patience noticed Wilson eyeing the building with distaste.

He looked up at her. "This is a waste of time. Someday I'll be grown, and then no one will make me do anything I don't want to do."

He followed Patience up the steps and inside. Nine pairs of eyes stared at him. He stared back. Patience stiffened with irritation. Look at him. He'd already decided the other students wouldn't like him and he wouldn't like them. He shuffled a little closer to the door, and she took a tighter grip on his collar, thinking he was probably considering making a run for it.

The young teacher with plain features introduced herself, greeted them warmly, and had the children bid Wilson a hearty welcome. He mumbled a reply.

The schoolroom was dimly lit and drafty. Twelve student desks, the teacher's platform, a blackboard, and a large potbellied stove crowded the interior. Along the back of the room, heavy coats, knit hats, and warm mittens haphazardly hung on pegs. Nine pairs of children's galoshes and one pair of adult's formed muddy puddles along the wall.

Miss Perkins smiled. "We're just about to work on our geography, Wilson. Please take a seat."

"Geography," Wilson whispered to Patience, "my *worst* subject!"

"You're welcome to stay and visit the class this morning," Miss Perkins invited Patience.

"Thank you," she said. "I can't, but I will another day."

"*Psst*. Four eyes—over here!" a big kid in the third row jeered.

Placing her hands on Wilson's shoulders, Patience gently steered him to a seat close to the blackboard.

"Can you see clearly from here?"

Removing his glasses, Wilson wiped a film of steam off

the lenses with the handkerchief Patience had stuck in his pocket earlier. Hooking the earpieces back over his ears, he squinted up at the blackboard. "I can see."

"Good." Patience squeezed his shoulder reassuringly. "I'll be back to walk you home." Leaning closer to his ear, she whispered, "Don't be nervous; the first day is always the hardest."

Wilson nodded, his eyes glued to the colorful world map covering the blackboard.

"Geography," he muttered. "And on my first day too."

The first person Patience saw after leaving the school was Sheriff Jay Longer, leaning against the front of the mercantile and looking more disreputable than ever. Her heart threatened to pound out of her chest.

He tipped his hat. "Morning, Miss Smith."

Swallowing the monstrous lump suddenly blocking her airway, she said, "Mr. Longer."

"This your first trip to town after filing your claim?"

"Yes, it is." *And none of your business.*

"Planning to hire a crew?"

"Yes, I am." She tilted her chin, meeting his eyes. "That's exactly what I'm going to do."

"You're not going to have any luck." He grinned. "Might as well give it up now and come back to Denver City with me."

The palms of her hands itched to wipe that grin off his insolent face. What right did he have to interfere? "I appreciate your staying around to look after me, but as you can see, I don't need your help. Why don't you go back where you belong and leave me alone?"

He straightened, towering over her. "Number one: I'm not staying around to look after you. I'm just not in any hurry to leave town. Number two: I'll go back when you're ready to go with me. I told Dylan and your friends I'd bring you back, and that's exactly what I plan to do."

"*You* plan? What about *my* plans? Aren't they important?"

"Not to me. Go ahead and try to hire a crew. See how much luck you have, and when you fall on your face, look me up."

She drew herself up to her full height, blistering him with a look she hoped he'd not soon forget. "That day will never come. I'll go back to Denver City when I'm ready, and I won't need your help getting there."

He calmly adjusted his hat back on his head. "All right. I'll leave you alone. You go your way and I'll go mine."

She firmed her lips. "That's fine with me."

He bowed mockingly from the waist. "Me too."

"Fine."

"Fine."

He strode away and she glared after him. *Ill-mannered bore.* Who did he think he was? She was so tired of men pushing her around. First Tom Wyatt and now Jay Longer. She had one more reason to make the mine pay. If she could strike it rich, she would never have to put up with an arrogant, insolent man again.

"Your best bet's to post the work notice on that thar board, lady."

Patience thanked the elderly prospector and walked on. She tacked her notice on the public-information board. She had carefully compiled the handbill while Wilson ate his breakfast. It read:

Wanted: Men willing to work for competitive wage.
Must be honest and hardworking. Age no factor.
Dinner provided. Contact Patience Smith, proprietor
of the Mule Head.

She stood in front of a nearby saloon, waiting for takers.
Returning to the board at 11:26 A.M., she rewrote:

Wanted: Anyone willing to work. Wage negotiable.
Two square meals a day. Contact Patience Smith
(woman standing in front of the saloon), proprietor
of the Mule Head.
P.S. Thank you.

Men came and went, pausing in front of the board long
enough to read the advertisement. One or two glanced in
her direction. Several laughed. One even snorted.
But not one approached her about the job.
At 1:43 P.M. she marched back to the board and
scrawled:

Hello? Anybody out there? I am willing to pay
above-average wages, expect you to work no more
than forty hours a week, and promise to provide three
delicious meat-based meals a day.
What more do you want?
Patience (the woman who's been standing in front
of the saloon for hours now!), proprietor of the Mule
Head.

By 2:35 P.M. sheer desperation set in. Pacing back and
forth, Patience observed Fiddle Creek's male population
with mounting resentment. What was wrong with these

people? There had been no fewer than two hundred men who had read that handbill and walked away. Family men—men she suspected could certainly use the money.

She had been as generous as projected funds allowed. She wasn't made of gold. What more did they want?

"Might as well save your energy. Ain't nothin' you're offerin' likely to entice 'em, miss."

Patience glanced over to see the elderly prospector who'd spoken to her earlier sitting on the sidewalk steps, whittling. Jay leaned against the hitching post, passing the time of day.

"Is *everyone* employed?" she asked. "Doesn't *anyone* in this town need a job?"

"Nope." The old man leaned forward and spat. Wiping tobacco juice on his coat sleeve, his eyes returned to the small deer he was carving. His crippled hands worked the wood slowly and lovingly. The carved figure was intricately fashioned with delicate details.

Stepping around Jay, Patience came over to sit beside the man. She watched him work for a moment before she spoke. "That's very nice. Have you been carving long?"

The old man spit another reddish stream. Wiping his mouth on his sleeve, he nodded. "Pert near all my life."

"You're very good at it." She'd never seen an image so lifelike. The doe's supplicating eyes immediately drew her in.

"He sells his work," Jay observed.

Patience lifted her eyes coolly.

"Ain't no one gonna work your mine," the prospector predicted.

Patience's thoughts unwillingly returned to the problem at hand. "The men can't *all* have jobs."

"Nope, lot of 'em looking for work. But they don't wanna work for you."

What was wrong with her? she wondered. She hadn't been in town long enough to make enemies.

The old man held the carving out to study it. "Well, it ain't *you* exactly. It's the mine."

"Mule Head?"

"Yep. Gamey O'Keefe won't let no one come near it."

"Oh—Gamey O'Keefe. I should have known." She glanced at Jay.

He held up his hands in protest. "I didn't say anything."

"He didn't say a thing," the miner confirmed. "Didn't need to. Gamey's ghost is living in your mine."

"Oh, that's nonsense. You mean to tell me that grown men would actually refuse to work for me because they think the mine is haunted?"

"Yep." He spat again.

"Feathers."

He looked, frowning. "What's that?"

"What's what?"

"That thar *feathers*. You a cussin' woman?"

"That's *her* way of cussin'." Jay grinned.

"Oh, my . . . no," Patience stammered. She could feel her face burn and she wanted to throttle Jay Longer for telling tales. If *feathers* was offensive, she hadn't been told. "I wasn't being vulgar. *Feathers* means nonsense, empty talk . . . you know."

"No, cain't say as I do. Never heared the term before. Thought feathers were something you found on a bird or duck." He smiled. "Rumor has it that you come from Denver City. They talk like that over there?"

"Well, some do—but I don't think *feathers* is especially prevalent." The orphanage housekeeper favored the term, and Patience had latched onto it. She eyed Jay, who seemed to be enjoying her discomfiture. The big brute.

"Yeah? Well, it's a new one on me," the miner confessed.

Patience watched while he painstakingly shaped the carved animal's hind leg with a knife blade.

Drawing her knees to her chest, Patience rested her chin, watching the men come and go, their incredulous laughter getting on her nerves. The old prospector's clothes she was wearing were three sizes too big for her, and she had to roll up the coat sleeves to use her hands. "Do you believe in ghosts?"

"Ain't never seed one, but I allow they could be some."

"Well, apparently everyone around here thinks there are." She sighed. "I have a problem."

"Yep, guess you do."

"I'd say," Jay added.

Patience shot Jay a warning look that said *You're not in on this conversation, mister.*

"What should I do?"

The old miner looked thoughtful. "Hard to say. Rumor also has it you have to work the mine. You need the money, bad."

Patience snorted. *Rumors* certainly spread fast in these parts.

"Heared tell thar's some Chinymen over at Silver Plume. They might help ya."

"How far is Silver Plume?"

"Oh . . . day, day-and-a-half ride from here."

"A *hard* day-and-a-half ride," Jay confirmed.

A day-and-a-half ride! Patience didn't own a horse, and she couldn't leave Wilson alone.

The old miner seemed to read her thoughts. "I got a jenny. She ain't pretty, but she'll get you there."

"It isn't that—I don't care what the animal looks like. It's the small boy I'm looking after. I can't leave him unattended."

"Wilson? The boy's old enough to take care of himself, ain't he?"

"Do you know him?"

"Seed him around with the old prospector."

"Wilson is sensible, but I wouldn't leave him alone," Patience said. She noticed Sheriff Longer didn't come to her rescue. Well, good. She wouldn't have accepted his insincere help anyway.

"Well, ole Widow Noosemen will help you out." The old miner held the carving out for final inspection. "She'll look after the boy till you git back."

"I can't pay her anything for her services."

Handing Patience the carving, the old man smiled. "That's all right. Widow Noosemen's service ain't worth nothing, but she'll see to the boy."

"Ole Widow Noosemen," Wilson groaned. He and Patience walked up the mountain late that afternoon. "She smells funny!"

"I'll only be gone four days, Wilson. That old miner Chappy Hellerman told me there are some Chinamen in Silver Plume who might be willing to work. I've already spoken to Widow Noosemen, and she has agreed to let you stay with her until I get back."

"But, P—"

"No *buts*, Wilson." Patience hated to disappoint him but there was no other way. "Widow Noosemen is very nice, and I'm grateful for her kindness." The widow did reek of snuff, but she adamantly refused Patience's eventual offer of money, saying it was her Christian duty to help out. "You know I've tried everything I know to hire workers, but no one wants to work for me. Maybe if I go far enough away, I'll find *someone* who's never heard of the Mule Head."

Wilson huffed and puffed, climbing higher. "How you gonna get there? Walk?"

"No, Chappy has graciously offered to let me borrow his mule."

"Aw, rats."

"I'm sorry; that's how it is. I'll be back as soon as I can. With any luck, we'll have our crew, and maybe some nice Chinaman will even teach you to speak Chinese."

"Aw, rats. What about Jay? Can't I stay with him?"

"Absolutely not! And don't ever mention his name to me again."

"You mad at him?"

Patience bit her lower lip, deciding if she couldn't say anything nice about the sheriff she wouldn't say anything at all. So she kept quiet.

As they trudged up the incline, Wilson bombarded her with all the logical arguments against staying with Widow Noosemen he could think of: someone might steal him, he might get hurt, he could fall off the mountain and no one would ever find him, an elk could eat him, he could lose his glasses and never see again, Widow Noosemen could beat him.

But in the end, Patience held her ground. First light tomorrow morning she was going to Silver Plume, and Wilson had to stay with Widow Noosemen.

Things would have been a whole lot simpler if Sheriff Longer wasn't deliberately making her situation harder. It wouldn't *hurt* him to watch Wilson, and it sure wouldn't kill

him to help her hire a crew. He had seen they had plenty of
firewood and fresh water, and she had thanked him for that.
But then he just left her alone. She wouldn't have thought it
of him. A knight in shining armor he wasn't.

She stifled a grin. A knight in shabby clothes, maybe.
She'd never seen a man so raggedy. His shirt would surely
come apart if you washed it. Still, there was something solid
about him. But if he hoped to soften her up by leaving her
alone, he was wasting his time. She owned this mine, and
she planned to work it if she had to do it all herself.

Jay watched Patience and Wilson leave town and start their
ascent up the mountainside. He'd kept an eye on her all
day. A rough miner's camp wasn't any place for a pretty
woman like Patience Smith.

Pretty, *aggravating* woman like Patience Smith. Seemed
every time she failed, she just dug her heels in a little
deeper. Now she was going to try her luck in Silver Plume.
If he had any sense, he'd go on back to Denver City and let
her fish or cut bait. But somehow he couldn't do it. It
wasn't in him to leave a woman in a dangerous situation,
and the Mule Head was no place for a woman. He'd just
saddle his horse and follow her to Silver Plume.

But she'd never know it.

Chapter Seven

Who'd ever have believed news could travel so fast! Even the Chinese had gotten wind of Gamey's ghost. Week two flew by, and Patience still didn't have a crew. Jay Longer was still hanging around, goading her to go back to Denver City. Well, she wouldn't. Not as long as there was a breath of hope to get the mine up and working—albeit the breath was getting a mite ragged.

Brave words, and she tried to believe them, but she was getting discouraged. Worse, sometimes she got so downhearted she even cried, and she wasn't a crying woman. She'd always been the type to pull up her socks and go on. "Crying won't mend no britches," the matron at the orphanage used to say, but it seemed like Patience just couldn't help it.

At first she had been so excited thinking about how she could take care of her friends back in Denver City. She'd even made plans for Wilson, wanting to help him get a good education, more than he could receive in a mining camp. She had been so certain that God had led her to the

Mule Head, but now she had doubts. How could she work a mine if she couldn't even get a crew?

She tried to keep Wilson from knowing how discouraged she got, but she knew he noticed sometimes how red and swollen her eyes were after she had cried at night when he was supposed to be asleep. Well, she'd have to think of something. Somehow there had to be a way to get a crew together. If God wanted her to work the mine, he would lead her to a solution.

Lifting an egg out of the skillet, Patience called Wilson again. "Hurry up! Breakfast is getting cold!" She sliced bread and her mind raced with a new plan.

Women. That's where she'd go. Fiddle Creek women enjoyed an uncommon amount of independence. Miners, it seemed, were starved for the fairer sex, so women were revered and seldom hampered by propriety.

The town ladies were mostly shopkeepers' wives who enjoyed certain refinements within their own social realm. They might welcome a break in their monotonous routine. After all, a woman could mine gold just as easily as a man. Patience would just go to the women, explain the problem, and offer to pay them a man's wage to help her.

Of course, they wouldn't be able to work the mine forever, but they could at least get the work started. They had little else to occupy their time but a few frivolous activities that Patience had prudently avoided by saying her obligations to the mine prevented her from joining in the fun.

During her recent journey to Silver Plume she'd witnessed an incident that left her both amused and sad. A woman's bonnet had been found lying in the middle of the road. No one seemed to know how it got there, but it caused quite a stir among the miners. Three or four of them had nabbed the saucy little hat with its ribbons, bows, and laces and erected it on a maypole in the center of town.

Their shenanigans turned into a near riot. The other men, looking for an hour of diversion from the cold streams and damp mines, poured into camp to join in the fun.

The bearded, booted roughnecks were so hungry for female companionship they staged an impromptu dance around the bonnet, joking and laughing as they took turns dancing with the lovely "Miss Bonnet."

Patience had watched the good-natured fiasco, wondering if Jay Longer was as eager for female companionship. Her thoughts surprised her, and she wondered why she'd thought them in the first place.

She'd seen Jay in Silver Plume, but he'd steered clear of her. Now, what had he been doing in Silver Plume the same day she was there? Drawing her knees to her chest, she grinned, admitting that with a little cleaning up the handsome sheriff of Denver City would be downright interesting. She had never seen eyes so remarkably blue or hair more fiery red or a chest so broad and manly.

She couldn't imagine why he kept himself so distant and—unhappy. He looked to be in excellent health—too thin, perhaps, but a few good meals would remedy that. He had no zest about him, no anticipation for life. He was a man with no purpose other than to drag her kicking and screaming back to Denver City.

Wilson's voice jerked her back to the present. "Couldn't we wait until it warms up?" he complained, decidedly disgruntled about being pulled from his bed before daylight.

"Just eat. We have to hurry."

He cracked one eye in the direction of the door. "It isn't even day yet, is it?"

"Just barely. Now hurry and eat, grouch."

Directly after breakfast, they set off. "You'll be a little early for school, but I want to be the first one at the mercantile this morning," she explained. They descended the narrow trail. She didn't want to miss talking to a single woman. The moment the school bell rang, the mothers would head for the store to exchange the latest gossip. This morning she planned to be there waiting for them.

"I don't like school, Patience. Nobody likes me," Wilson complained, his feet hurrying to keep up with her. "The girls talk mean to me, and the boys call me Four Eyes and Bat Boy."

"Bat Boy?"

"Yeah, 'cause I'm blind as a bat. Butch Miller tried to make me eat bugs yesterday."

"Why?"

" 'Cause that's what bats eat, P."

"The moment we start making money we're going to get new glasses for you," she promised. He needed stronger lenses—these lenses were barely adequate. Yesterday he'd bumped into the door and bloodied his nose, and she knew it was because he couldn't see clearly.

"Why do I even have to go to school? You could teach me at home."

"I have a gold mine to run."

"No, you don't. You're trying to get someone to run it for you. Once you do, then you can teach me at home, *hmm,* P? Then I won't have to put up with Butch Miller anymore."

"I can't do that, Wilson. Money will be extremely tight, and I'll have to work no matter who I get to run the mine." She gave him a quick hug. "Besides, it'll do you good to be around children your own age. You'll make friends. The others will warm to you."

"They won't. They're mean. Butch Miller took my sandwich yesterday and threw it down the privy hole. I was hungry all day."

"Did you tell Miss Perkins?"

He looked aghast. "No! Butch would've creamed me!"

Oh, Patience wished she knew how to fight! She would teach Wilson how to hold his own against bullies like Butch Miller! She caught herself, knowing that the Good Book said to turn the other cheek—but there were some folks you had to allow for, and it sounded like Butch was one of them.

"If Butch Miller takes your sandwich today, you tell Miss Perkins, you hear?"

Wilson sighed. "I can't."

"Well, for heaven's sake, why not?"

" 'Cause he'll just take my apple too."

After depositing Wilson on the school steps, Patience went straight to the mercantile, hurrying up the steps so lost in thought that she slammed into Sheriff Longer, almost knocking herself off balance. She grabbed at him instinctively.

His arms went around her, breaking her fall. He grinned down at her. "You in a hurry this morning?"

She was all too aware of his nearness. When he made no effort to release her, she placed her hands on his chest and pushed him away. "I'm sorry. I should have been watching where I was going."

"Don't apologize. It's always a pleasure running into you."

She flushed, remembering the way she had clutched at

him. "I thought you would've gone back to Denver City. You do still have a job there, don't you?"

He shrugged. "I'd be in Denver City right now if you weren't so bullheaded.

She stiffened. "I am merely taking care of business."

"And it doesn't concern me?"

"That's right."

His expression softened. "Look, Miss Smith, you've done your best, but it isn't going to work. You aren't going to find a crew. Give it up and go home. You're fighting a losing battle."

She looked up at him, near tears. "You don't understand. I can't quit. You're a man. You can't know what it's like to be alone with no money, no job, no home. Well, that's what it's like for me and for Mary, Lily, and Harper, and for Wilson too. That mine is our only chance. I have to make it pay."

She pushed past him and entered the mercantile.

Jay stared after her. Now why did she have to go and get womanly on him? He could handle it as long as she was as prickly as a hedgehog cactus, but he'd seen tears in her eyes, and now he felt like a heel. He walked off with a sinking feeling that he was going to hang around Fiddle Creek and the Mule Head a little longer.

Using the money Jay had left her, Patience bought a half pound of sugar, three apples, half a pound of tea, and a spool of white thread before the women started to arrive.

The more she thought about her new plan, the more she warmed to it. Women working in the Mule Head. Not only would they enjoy the added income, they could also take pride in the fact that they were lending a sister a helping hand, and she doubted few, if any, believed in ghosts.

One by one the women came into the store, their conversations ranging from diaper rash to peach butter. When the most recent gossip, innuendoes, and rumors were adequately *ooh*ed and *ahh*ed over, they started to browse.

Patience approached each one singly, striking up a friendly conversation. "Hello! My name is Patience."

"I don't know anybody."

Patience blinked. "Pardon?"

"I don't know anybody to work your mine."

"Oh—well, thank you." Patience moved to the dry-goods table, still looking over her shoulder. "Hello! My name is—"

The woman sorting through the bolts of calico never looked up. "Patience."

"Yes." Patience smiled. "I'm the new owner of—"

"Mule Head."

"Yes, that's right, and I'm—"

"Looking for a crew."

"Yes—do you—"

"Know anyone who'll work for you?" The woman laughed. "No."

"Nice talking to you."

"Hello, my name is Patience."

"So nice to meet you."

"Have you ever considered a job outside the home? The pay is good, and it can be arranged for you to be home when school lets out."

"I have a job: five kids and a lazy husband."

"Yes, but haven't you ever wanted to stretch? Do something on your own?"

"No. Never."

"Nice visiting with you."

"I'm Patience Smith—"

The young mother turned and smiled. "I know, dear. Welcome to Fiddle Creek."

"Thank you. I was wondering if you could possibly help me?"

The young woman's smile never lost its vigor. "I'm afraid not."

Patience frowned. "You don't know what I want."

Lifting a spool of ribbon, the woman waved to the clerk. "I'll take two yards of the lavender, Edgar!" She flicked a glance over her shoulder. "Nice talking to you."

"The same, I'm sure." Patience moved on.

"Think about it. The pay is excellent, and I'll arrange to have you home before your family even realizes you're gone. You don't believe those silly ghost stories, do you?"

"Certainly not!"

"That's what I thought. The moment I saw you, I said to myself, *Patience, this is an intelligent, hardworking woman whom you would be honored to call an employee.*"

"Well, thank you. I certainly would try to be."

Patience's smile lifted. "Then you'll help?"

The lady gave her an affronted glare. "Do I look like I've lost my wits?"

Snatching up a tin of peaches, Patience moved on.

Coming out of the store several minutes later, Patience blew her bangs out of her eyes and sighed.

Jay leaned against a hitching post, whittling. She shot him a disdainful glance and walked past him, her chin in the air. She could hear the thud of his boots following her. Why wouldn't he go away and leave her alone?

"No luck?"

She stopped and turned to face him. "You know what kind of luck I had. It turned out just the way you said it would. I guess that makes you happy?"

He frowned. "Not exactly."

She stared at him. "What does that mean?"

"I admire someone who doesn't have enough sense to give up, but you're fighting a losing battle. These people have a thing about the Mule Head. You'll never get anyone to work there."

She stepped closer, looking up at him. "You could help me if you would."

He shook his head. "No, ma'am. I'm not a miner. I'm a lawman."

"Then go back to Denver City and do your job."

"Right now my job is taking you back where you belong."

"I belong here." Her eyes locked with his, challenging him. "If you'll help me hire a crew, I'll cut you in on the profits."

He removed his hat and slapped it against his thigh. "What is it about *no* that I'm not conveying to you?"

His eyes, electric blue, burned into her. His hair glowed in the sunlight. She fought an urge to brush her fingers through it. What was she thinking? This . . . oaf infuriated her!

She gripped her hands behind her back. "I'm staying. Go

on back to Denver City. You found me; that's all you were supposed to do. Tell my friends I'm all right, and I'll come when my business here is finished."

He opened his mouth, closed it, clapped his hat back on his head, turned, and walked away.

Patience stared after him, feeling suddenly lost and alone. She looked up to see Chappy sitting on the porch steps, whittling.

"Hire a crew?"

"No." She glanced in the storefront resentfully. "They must all think I'm a fool."

"Well—" the white-haired prospector calmly inspected the hummingbird he was carving—"I wouldn't feel too bad. I could have told you they wouldn't be interested. Women are considered bad luck in a mine."

"I've heard." She crossed the wooden planks and sat down beside him.

"Known men to set fire to a mine if a woman's been in it."

"Why, that's mad."

"Might be, but folks up here are a mite set in their ways."

"Well, I guess it doesn't matter." Patience leaned back, soaking up the sun. She didn't have the slightest idea what plan four was. "The women didn't want to work anyway."

"Got their hands full taking care of the family."

"Seems that way."

He chuckled. "Don't know much 'bout miners, do you, sissy? Or men."

"Nothing," Patience admitted.

"Well," he said, a foxy note creeping into his voice now, "you ought to learn. A pretty little thing like you will be wanting to take a husband someday. Might need to know what he'll be looking for."

"And what might that be?" Patience asked, not really interested. From what she could tell, the only prerequisite a woman needed to catch a man around here was that she was breathing.

"Well now, the Frenchies think it's got something to do with a woman's legs."

"A woman's legs."

"Yep, the dark-haired girl with a large leg will get fat at thirty and lie in bed reading novels until noon."

Patience looked back at him, sneering.

"The brunette with the slender limbs, now she'll worry a man's heart out with jealousy."

Patience's gaze moved to her wool trousers.

Chappy examined the bird's progress. "Now, the olive-skinned maid with a pretty rounded leg is sure to make a man happy. The blonde woman with big legs will degenerate by thirty-five into nothing more than a pair of ankles double their natural size and afflicted with rheumatism. The fair-haired woman will get up at the crack of dawn to scold the servants and gossip over tea."

"So, a man wants the olive-skinned maid?"

"No, the light, rosy girl with a sturdy, muscular, well-turned leg is the one men want. But if he's lucky enough to find a red-haired little gal with a large limb he'd better pop the question quick as he can." The old man's eyes twinkled with devilment.

"What about a redheaded man? Do the same rules apply to him?"

"You know any redheaded men?"

"Maybe," she answered evasively.

There were only two in camp: Jay Longer and seventy-year-old Webb Henson.

"The short lady should have a slender limb, and the tall lady should possess an ample one." He handed Patience the finished bird. "Think you can remember that?"

She nodded. Of course she could remember that, but she couldn't for the life of herself see that the observations held any credibility.

She walked back to the mine, fighting tears. At least no one could see if she cried way out here. She wouldn't give them the satisfaction of knowing she felt like giving up.

And there was Wilson. He'd been brought up right, you could tell that. His parents must have been good people. But the old prospector probably hadn't been a proper influence on the boy, and he was exposed to a rough element in the mining camp. A boy needed a man's influence, a godly man's influence. Although where she'd find that kind of man in Fiddle Creek, she couldn't imagine.

Her thoughts turned to red-haired Jay Longer. He seemed like a good enough man, but godly? Not that she could see, but then prayer could work miracles. She might pray for him; surely God would understand she wasn't asking anything for herself, although he was surely a decent man. She climbed toward the mine, with her thoughts of the sheriff for company.

Chapter Eight

P had a problem. Wilson wasn't supposed to know it, but he did.

He might be only eight years old, but he had a big mind. Almost old—really old—adultlike sometimes.

And his adultlike mind told him Patience had a problem.

She'd done a good job hiding it, but she didn't fool him. He saw how red and swollen her eyes were every morning. And she blew her nose a lot lately. She kept saying she was coming down with a cold, but if that were so, she'd already have gotten sick.

No, Patience couldn't fool Wilson; she was worried. Worried sick because she couldn't get anyone to work that ole mine—and Jay Longer wasn't very friendly. Wilson suspected P would like for the sheriff to be friendlier.

She'd gone everywhere there was to go, done everything there was to do, talked to anyone who would listen, but nobody wanted to work for her. Nobody liked ghosts. Some didn't believe there was such a thing, but others only shook their heads and said they didn't want to take a chance on running into Gamey if he was in the mine.

Wilson walked to school with a heavy heart. P said it was okay for him to walk by himself this morning. He appreciated that. He liked it when she treated him like an adult. She did most times, except lately, when she couldn't think of anything but ghosts. And maybe the sheriff—only she got mad when he mentioned that man. Called him pigheaded and . . . something else. He couldn't remember what, but he didn't think Jay would like it.

Wilson didn't know if he believed in ghosts.

Maybe he did; he wasn't sure.

Patience wouldn't be having such a hard time getting workers if it wasn't for the rumor. If he were a man and P asked him to work in the mine, he'd do it—whether he believed in ghosts or not—because P was nice. And even better than that, there were some things a man just ought to do.

Swinging his dinner pail, Wilson made his way down the mountain. He bet that sheriff would work in the mine. He didn't know why P hadn't asked him to.

Hunching deeper into the coat lining, Wilson pretended he was smoking a cigarette. The crisp, cold air formed a perfect vapor for his favorite make-believe game. He played it every day when no one was looking. When he grew up, he was going to smoke for real. Smoke and cuss and spit tobacco and look mean, because that's what men did, only P would never let him. She said a boy wasn't to live that way, that God frowned on smoking and cussing and spitting tobacco and looking mean—well, she hadn't said anything about looking mean, but if God didn't like the other things, he probably didn't like anyone looking or acting mean.

Exhaling, inhaling, exhaling, inhaling, out, in, out, in. Wilson watched the air take on fascinating shapes. It was easy to play like he was smoking because it was freezing cold. Colder than kraut—though he didn't know why he was thinking about kraut. He hated the stinky stuff.

His foot struck something and he stumbled, nearly pitching face first into a snowbank. He caught himself in the nick of time.

His face brightened when he spotted the sheriff coming up the hill, walking toward him.

"Jay!" he called, happy to see a familiar face. He hadn't seen the sheriff in a long time. "What're ya doing?"

When Jay didn't answer, Wilson veered off the path to visit.

~

Jay watched Wilson trotting toward him. He looked closer to see if Patience was with him, but she wasn't.

Irritating brat. Look at him—scrawny, red hair; wearing bottle-thick glasses that make him look like a hoot owl.

"Hey, Jay? You got a minute to talk?"

"I guess so." Not that he wanted to talk to the boy. He didn't; he was just killing time until Patience came to her senses. Once that happened, he, the girl, and the child would be on their way back to Denver City in the blink of an eye.

"Why haven't you been back to see us? P misses you."

Nosy kid. "I don't have time for visiting. Got things to do."

"Like what?"

Jay glared at him. Someone needed to teach this boy some manners. It wasn't polite to ask questions like that. Besides, he couldn't think of an answer. He'd not been all that busy, but that was his business. He had a reason for not going back to the mine. That stubborn woman would have him working for her if he wasn't careful.

"I don't have to discuss my affairs with you."

Wilson cocked his head to one side, appearing to think about this. "No, I suppose not. Are you doing something you don't want anyone to know about?"

Jay bit back the word he wanted to say. "No, I'm not doing anything I need to hide. Didn't anyone ever tell you not to ask questions?"

"Yes, all the time. But how will I learn anything if I don't ask?"

"You're liable to learn more than you want to know if you do."

"I don't see how that would be possible," Wilson said, after giving the matter some consideration. "I'd think it would be difficult to learn too much about anything."

Jay smothered a sigh. What could you do with a boy like this? You couldn't talk to him, for sure. Hard to talk to someone who had an answer for anything you said. Kid acted odd too. Hard to tell if he was all there or just being obnoxious.

He was going to be a handful when he grew up. A mining camp was no place for him. Patience meant well, and someone had to see to Wilson's needs, but the boy wanted a man's influence. A man's firm hand. But he wasn't that man.

Apparently aware of Wilson's close scrutiny, Jay growled. "Shouldn't you be somewhere, kid?"

"I'm walking to school by myself this morning. P said I could."

"You better hurry along—you're going to be late."

"It doesn't matter. I only go because P makes me. I hate

school." When the sheriff didn't answer, Wilson continued. "Want to know why I hate school? Because the kids don't like me."

"Have you done something to make them not like you?"

"No, honest." He hadn't done anything—not that he could remember. He sure hadn't thrown Butch's sandwich anywhere.

"Yeah, well, that happens. Don't worry about it; it'll work itself out." Jay pulled the collar of his wool coat tighter. "You better run along."

"The girls talk mean to me, and Butch Miller steals my sandwich every day."

"And you let him?"

Wilson made a *humph* sound. "I can't *stop* him."

Rubbing his shoulder, Jay looked away. Sunlight danced off the heavy layer of early morning hoarfrost.

Wilson suddenly thought about P and all the trouble she'd been having. Why, he bet she had forgotten to ask Jay to help her run the mine! Excited now, he realized how he could make P happy! He'd take Jay home with him; that's what he'd do. He'd surprise the smile right off P!

Wilson sized up the sheriff's muscular frame and decided he was *strong*. Strong as a bull. Fit as a fiddle. Tight as a drum, and all that other stuff people always said. He'd make a good gold miner.

He could mine a bunch of gold and then P wouldn't cry herself to sleep; she wouldn't cry anymore, period, because the sheriff would be around every day and she would like that.

Wilson wasn't a fool. He knew he'd have to be pretty crafty to trick Jay into coming home with him. The man would be a good worker, all right, but it seemed like he

didn't like work. He frowned a lot—and he got mad sometimes, though Wilson could tell Jay tried to hide his anger
as much as he could.

Wilson noticed that the night he'd brought him and P up
to the mine. Maybe that's why P forgot to ask him to help
her: she knew he was a testy sort.

Jay was probably a little uninspired because P wouldn't
go back to Denver City with him. Even Wilson knew that
men preferred the women to mind.

Well, he'd just have to fool Jay into going home with
him. Once he was there, P would see that he was strong,
and she'd remember that she hadn't asked *everyone* to
work the mine: she hadn't asked the sheriff. She was good
about talking people into doing things they didn't want to
do. She called it tact, but Wilson called it plain ole brow-
beating.

But Wilson liked his idea a whole lot and decided to
follow through with it. "Jay?"

The sheriff looked up. "Yes?"

"I'm not feeling so good." Wilson clutched his stomach.
"I'd better not go to school today."

Jay frowned. "What's wrong with you?"

"My stomach hurts."

"Well, go back home."

"Okay." Wilson made it sound like he didn't want to go
home but he guessed, since Jay said it, he ought to obey.
"You'd better walk me home, huh, Jay?"

Wincing, Jay glanced down at him. "You know the way
back."

A ray of sun glinted off the rim of Wilson's glasses. "I'm
feeling kind of dizzy. I can't see straight." He held his head
for effect.

Jay shifted to the opposite foot. "You'll be all right—it's not far."

Grabbing his middle, Wilson bent double. "Noooo, I think you're going to have to walk with me, Jay, because I'm *real* sick."

"Wilson—"

"Really sick, Jay. Honest."

Jay shifted his stance, annoyed.

"Yeah—please don't tell P!" It was a white lie; the old prospector had said only the black ones counted.

"You have to come with me. P'll be mad if anything bad happens to me."

"Look, kid, I didn't take you to raise."

Wilson peered up at him. "You don't want me to walk home by myself, really sick, do you?"

Actually, Wilson didn't think Jay cared one way or the other, but he was beginning to suspect he didn't have a choice. *If I'm sick, he'll have to walk me home.*

"All right, let's get it over with."

Wilson's face lit up. "You'll do it? You'll walk home with me?"

"I said I would. Let's go."

"Okay. Just a minute." Wilson motioned for him to lean over.

Eyeing him warily, Jay refused to comply. "What?"

"Lean over."

"Lean over? Why?"

"Just lean over."

Jay hesitantly bent over.

Wilson set to work sprucing him up. "Do you have a comb?"

"A comb?" One eye cracked open. "Do I look like I have a comb?"

No, he sure didn't look like he had a comb. He didn't look like he'd ever *seen* a comb. "Never mind, I'll use my fingers." That's what P did.

Wilson carefully fluffed Jay's hair and knocked the crumbs out of his scraggly beard. He had to get the sheriff more presentable or P wouldn't hire him. She didn't like messiness, especially bad messiness.

Knocking dust and twigs off the back of Jay's coat, Wilson took his handkerchief out of his pocket, spit on it, and was about to wash Jay's face when a big hand with curly red hair on the knuckles stopped him. "Don't even think about it."

The sheriff could've used a full bath, but Wilson knew he wasn't smart enough to fool him into that. He'd just have to make sure Jay stood downwind of P.

When Wilson finished, Jay didn't look any better. He could've used a lot more attention, but this would have to do.

The sheriff returned his critical look impassively. "What are you doing?"

Wilson shrugged. "Nothing."

"Obviously you're trying to accomplish something."

"No, I'm not." He grinned. "Wanna stay for dinner? P cooks turnips real good." If he stayed for dinner that'd give P more time to remember to ask him to help her work the mine, plus the two of them just might take to each other.

"I'm not staying for dinner."

"Well, you can think about it."

"I'm taking you to the mine; then I'm leaving. You don't look sick to me."

"What does sick look like?" If he knew, Wilson could fake a lot sicker, but for now he'd have to just look puny.

"Okay." Turning, he walked off, casting a sly look over his shoulder to make sure Jay followed.

Patience stood in front of the mine, watching Jay and Wilson approach. They stopped before her, and it only took one look to see that Wilson was up to something. She just didn't know what.

Jay nodded. "Miss Smith."

"Mr. Longer." She could be just as polite as he was.

"The boy's sick. I brought him home."

"Really?" She looked at Wilson, who was winking frantically. She hid a grin. Sneaky little kid. All right. She'd play along. "Thank you for bringing him. It was very nice of you. It will be lunchtime soon. I can whip something up in a jiffy. Won't you join us?"

Jay wouldn't look at her. "No, I'd better be running along."

"There's peach cobbler for dessert."

He looked at her, a curious expression in his eyes. "I don't get much home cooking."

"Then we'd be really happy to have you join us." She turned and went back inside before he had a chance to refuse.

Jay entered behind Wilson, apparently uncomfortable with the situation. Patience busied herself throwing together a hearty dinner, letting Wilson play host. Thank goodness she had fried a chicken last night and saved the leftovers for today.

When everything was ready, she motioned for them to take their seats. Jay started to reach for a biscuit, but she stopped him. "First we say the blessing."

"Oh, sure." He bowed his head, flushing.

Patience folded her hands. "We thank you, dear Lord, for this food we're about to eat and for all of your blessings.

Thank you for sending Sheriff Longer to be with us. Lead
him to do what is best for all of us. And bless our work in
the mine, Lord, and we'll give you the praise. Amen."

No harm in giving the Lord some suggestions.

Wilson echoed "amen," and Jay followed, sounding
reluctant. His eyes were accusing when he looked at
Patience, but she merely put on a sweet, innocent smile.
Sweet was always good.

Jay thawed perceptibly under the influence of cold fried
chicken, biscuits and gravy, and two helpings of peach
cobbler. By the time they finished eating, he was laughing
and teasing Wilson. His manner toward her was a combina-
tion of suspicion and deference.

She did her best to be charming. He only pokered up
once when she asked for advice about opening the mine,
but she tried to look like a helpless, admiring female,
although it almost choked her to do so, and he relaxed.

He went outside with Wilson while she cleared the table
and fixed the rest of the chicken for him to take home with
him, although she could certainly have used it herself. As
she tidied up, she hummed a satisfied little tune. Jay Longer
would help them; she could feel it in her bones.

That Wilson was positively a genius.

Chapter Nine

Toward dark, Patience rinsed the last supper dish and laid it aside. With a tired sigh, she recalled how the sheriff had eaten like a hired hand—a very underfed hired hand. His tall frame could use a few extra pounds—the kind a family man carried with pride. It was a treat to cook for someone other than herself and Wilson.

Of course she had seen right through Wilson's ploy. It had taken very little persuasion for her to talk the sheriff into staying for dinner. After dinner, Wilson's usual robust health returned, and he pressured his new friend into a game of stickball.

Stickball turned into mumblety-peg. The sheriff showed Wilson how to hold the knife just right, so that with a flick of the wrist he could stick the blade into the ground. Watching from the dugout doorway, arms crossed, Patience decided she hadn't known how many different ways a knife could be thrown.

Later in the day she looked out to see the tops of two red heads, one big and one small, disappearing over the hill. Seemed the fish were biting.

She grinned, grateful Jay was spending time with the child. Wilson needed a man's influence—and Jay, it appeared, needed a small boy's adoration.

Late in the afternoon, the two had returned toting an impressive string of trout, which she rolled in cornmeal and fried for supper. It had turned out to be quite an extraordinary day.

Jay Longer was anything but ordinary. Normally she would have thought twice about taking up with someone who cared so little about his personal appearance, but Jay had been different in Denver City. Always clean shaven and his clothes freshly laundered and neatly pressed. During both dinner and supper he proved to be an interesting conversationalist, and his table manners were impeccable.

She wasn't entirely certain yet of the role he'd play in her life, but she knew he had one.

One really did have to wonder what lay beneath Jay's defensive facade. It might be interesting to find out. There hadn't been much opportunity for getting acquainted with men at the orphanage, so one might say she was inexperienced. She'd seen enough of male behavior at Fiddle Creek and Denver City to suspect there was more to Sheriff Jay Longer than he chose to reveal.

The way he got along with Wilson seemed to be more than just an adult spending time with a child. He *enjoyed* playing games with the boy, and the sight of the two of them wandering off to go fishing had been downright heartwarming. Judging by the looks on their faces when they returned, she had felt that just being together had filled a need in each of them.

And what about her? She had needs too. She had watched Glory and Ruth fall in love and get married, wondering if she would ever find someone with whom to build a life. Sitting at the table with Jay, listening to him talk and watching him tease Wilson, had revived those feelings. No matter how many times she tried to pretend she wasn't interested in Jay Longer, she couldn't deny the truth. She was attracted to the man. He would ride away someday, back to Denver City, and she would miss him. Too much.

She would have liked for him to stay and visit longer, but he seemed uncomfortable with the notion. The moment he swallowed the last bite of fish, he had bolted for the door like a jackrabbit.

Hastily downing the last of his milk, Wilson ran after him, explaining over his shoulder that the sheriff was going to teach him how to tie trout lures. He had returned alone at dark, tired but happy.

Maybe Jay would find her more interesting if she had something important to talk about or if she wasn't so stubborn and agreed to go back to Denver City. He was a man who honored his word, and he'd promised Dylan to bring her home safely. Well, she would eventually return to Denver City, and the girls would sit up all night talking about their newfound fortune. That thought alone kept her going, because everything else about the situation appeared hopeless. No crew; no gold. She had to find help—and quickly—or circumstances would force her to abandon the mine. She couldn't bear to even think about that.

Emptying the dishpan, she wished she had a book to read. Always after supper at the orphanage she read—stories about Calamity Jane, Deadwood Dick, and Kit Carson. When she tired of dime novels she'd pretend to be Meg in *Little Women* by Louisa May Alcott.

She loved them all.

Untying her apron, she laid it aside, then knelt beside Wilson's pallet. He was fast asleep, exhausted from his busy day. Lifting a stockinged foot, she gently tucked it beneath the blanket.

Gazing down on his cherubic features, Patience was once again overcome by doubts. Was she doing the right thing? Colorado, for all its beauty, was a harsh land. Maybe too harsh for a child. They had been here over three weeks, and she had yet to find one man or woman willing to work for her. Emotions surrounding the mine shaft ran high and were coupled with deep-seated suspicion. It was useless to try to persuade the residents of Fiddle Creek there were no such things as ghosts. Years of skepticism and unexplainable events surrounding the mine had convinced them otherwise.

Last night she had found the old prospector's Bible under the cot and read to Wilson. Hoping to dispel any notions about ghosts, she had pointed out that ghosts, as we call them, were not mentioned in the Bible, probably because God knows they don't exist.

She read to him about Jesus on the cross, hanging between two thieves. Taking advantage of the chance to do a little teaching, she brought out the fact that one thief mocked Christ. The second thief believed in him and asked to be remembered when Jesus came into his kingdom.

Although she had read the printed words many times, they still had the power to thrill her: "Today shalt thou be with me in paradise."

"You see, Wilson, God has prepared a place for our spirits to go when we die. We can't interfere with God's plans and decide we'd rather stay on earth and hang around where we used to live, having fun scaring people.

"Gamey's spirit went to either heaven or hell when he

died. He didn't have the opportunity to stay in the mine. We aren't given that choice. God created us, and he is in control, in this life and the life to come."

Wilson had looked serious, reflecting on what she said. "I guess that has to be right. The Good Book doesn't lie."

"No, it doesn't. We can trust what it says." She had closed the book, relieved that at least she had provided sound principle for her decision to stay.

But Wilson, with his inquisitive mind, had had another question. "What about all the strange things that happen in the mine? How do you explain them, P?"

Patience had no explanation for the strange goings-on Wilson had related: cold gusts of air coming from nowhere, strange lights seen in the shaft, falling rock endangering the lives of anyone who ventured deep into the tunnel. Nothing unusual had happened the few times she'd ventured into the shaft—no odd cave-ins or peculiar lights or bizarre singing—none of the various incidents people claimed had happened.

Restless now, she moved to the door for a breath of fresh air. A full moon bathed the mountain. Loneliness gripped her. She had been alone few times in her life. The orphanage had always been full and rowdy; then on the long journey out west she didn't have a private moment.

Leaning against the doorsill, Patience thought about Missouri and the life she'd left behind. She had been content there—comfortable. And she'd thought that by coming to Colorado she would become a wife and eventually a mother. Now, here she was in the Rockies, the sole caretaker of a small boy—friends miles and miles away. If she couldn't find anyone to work the mine, what good would it do for her to stay? She couldn't work it herself. She knew nothing about mining.

Her mind drifted to the other girls, and she was consumed with guilt. Mary had to be worried sick, and the others just plain worried. She'd tried to send them word, but the telegraph line was still down. It took forever to get anything done out here. Men would rather seek their fortunes in the mines than work at anything so mundane as repairing telegraph lines. Mail service was erratic, taking weeks to deliver, if it got through at all. For the moment, there was no way to let them know she was all right or to tell them about her quest to prosper them all.

A twig snapped and Patience's hand flew to her heart.

A deep voice came to her from the shadows. "Didn't I tell you to keep your door shut at night?"

"Sheriff?" She shaded her eyes against the bright lantern rays. "I thought you had gone."

"Sorry, didn't mean to alarm you." Jay stepped from the shadows, removing his hat. "The name's Jay."

Calling him by his first name didn't feel quite right, but maybe in time she could get used to it. *Sheriff* did seem awfully formal. Opening the door wider, she smiled. "Would you like to come in and warm yourself by the fire?"

"No, thanks. I just wanted to make sure Wilson was all right."

Now why was he making up excuses? He had to know Wilson had pulled a fast one on them. The boy was no more sick than she was, but the funny way her pulse leapt at the sound of the sheriff's familiar voice made her realize she didn't care why he was still there. She was just glad that he was.

She nodded. "He's fine—doesn't seem to have a trace of whatever was ailing him on the way to school this morning."

"He's okay, then. Figured I might have worn him out this afternoon."

"Oh . . . yes." She smiled, meeting his cool direct gaze. "He's sound asleep."

An awkward silence hung between them.

Why, the man was lonely! She smiled, reaching for a wrap hanging on a peg next to the doorway. "He was asleep two minutes after his head hit his pillow." Stepping outside, she closed the door, settling the woolen shawl around her shoulders. They causally fell into step. "I'm glad you decided to come back."

"It got dark on me—I decided to bed down close to the mine."

They walked for a while, she mindful of his company, he mindful of hers.

Twisting the brim of his hat in his hands, the sheriff appeared to be searching for a mutual topic. "Nice night. Not so cold," he ventured.

Pulling her shawl closer, Patience gazed at the overhead star-studded canopy. "You think so? I haven't been warm since I got here."

"It doesn't get cold in Missouri?"

She grinned. "Oh, yes—it gets cold in Missouri. Ever been there?"

"No." He glanced up to study the sky. "I've heard that it's pretty, though."

"Very pretty—especially in the fall. The leaves turn magnificent reds and ambers and golds. In the spring, bright green grass carpets the hillsides, and yellow jonquils and forsythia pop out. Summers are hot and humid with savage thunderstorms, but then fall rolls around again and you forget all the things you don't like about Missouri weather.

Suddenly you find yourself thanking the good Lord for seeing you through another year."

The edge was gone from the silence now; she liked that.

"I wanted to tell you . . . you're a good cook," Jay said. "Haven't tasted fish that good in a long time."

She felt her cheeks grow hot even though the wind was brittle. "Just plain old fish and corn bread. Nothing special."

He touched her elbow, directing her around an outcropping of rock shooting up through the uneven ground. She decided she liked his gentle pressure on her arm—manly, persuasive, without being intrusive.

"Been here long?" she asked.

Jay shrugged. "Few years."

"I assume gold brought you here?"

"No." He smiled, his tone lighter now. "Actually, it was a train, but I came in search of gold."

"Oh." She laughed, relieved to discover he had a sense of humor. At times she would have guessed otherwise.

A cloud shadowed the moon, and the wind picked up. She drew closer into the wrap, wondering why she'd left a warm fire to walk a rocky ground with a man who opposed her at every turn.

"Warm enough?"

"Fine, thank you. And you?"

"Fine." His eyes skimmed the dark clouds. "Snow before morning."

"It seems it snows every night."

The conversation started to lapse.

"You're sure you're not too cold? We can go back," Jay offered.

"Really, I'm fine. Thank you."

"The 'quarters' warm enough?"

She laughed, recognizing the tongue-in-cheek tone. "Well, actually, there's a crack at the bottom of the door big enough to throw a moose under. We're losing a lot of heat."

"I'll take a look at it tomorrow. Meanwhile, stuff a blanket in it."

"In the door?"

"In the crack."

"Oh . . . thanks. I will."

They walked to the edge of a precipice and stood staring across the snow-covered landscape. Ragged summits draped with snow jutted upward in the light of the passing moon.

"So, you're doing okay?"

"Sheriff—"

"Name's Jay."

She glanced up at him. "Do you really want me to call you Jay?"

"That's my name."

They stood for a few minutes more, their breath making frosty air vapors. She wondered how much longer it would be before the sheriff ordered her back to Denver City. Had news of her failure to hire a suitable mine crew exasperated him? Would he now demand that she go back? She supposed he reasonably could; she had failed—that was pretty common knowledge. Without the mine's proceeds she'd couldn't hold out any longer. The old prospector had laid in a good supply of food, but firewood was running low, and she couldn't seem to chop enough to keep up with the demand. And there was still plenty of winter left on this remote mountaintop.

"You were saying?" Jay prompted.

What had she been saying?

"I asked if you were doing okay, and you said—"

"About to say I was, but that isn't the truth," Patience admitted. She didn't know how he'd feel about her confiding in him, but she had to talk to someone. Even an enemy was better than no one.

"Something wrong?"

"I can't find anyone to work the mine; but then, you know that, don't you?"

To his credit, his tone held a note of humility. "I don't stick my nose in other people's business, Miss Smith."

"If I have to call you Jay, you have to call me Patience. Smith's just a name they gave me at the orphanage. I didn't know my last name. None of us did, except Mary; her last name is Everly."

His expression softened. "Does it bother you, not knowing your last name or who your folks were?"

"Some," she admitted. "I'd like to have known my parents, but then, I guess who you are isn't as important as what you are. I try to live in such a way that no matter who my folks were, they wouldn't be ashamed of me." He looked stricken. She had touched a nerve somewhere. Best leave the subject. "Please, call me Patience."

That would be hard for him, she knew. *Patience* was too personal, and the last thing he wanted was to get too personal. She had known that from the moment she'd set eyes on him.

"You do know why no one will help me, don't you?" she asked.

"I know why." His gaze fixed on a distance point, and she could see his jaw firm.

She sighed. "Well, you did warn me the mine was haunted."

"That I did."

"But you also said you didn't believe in ghosts."

"I don't, but everyone else does. That's the problem."

Gazing at the mountain, she said softly, "I'm in trouble, Jay. I've been everywhere, tried everything, and I can't find one single person willing to work for me. You know what happened in Silver Plume. The Chinamen just laughed at me. Even they had heard of the Mule Head."

A wry smile touched the corners of his mouth.

"Then I got this bright idea to ask the townswomen to work in the mine."

His grin widened, and she figured he'd heard about that too.

"They thought I was crazy. I didn't know women were considered bad luck in a mine." Sighing, she leaned back, staring at the moon darting in and out of clouds. "Guess I shouldn't be burdening you, but I don't know who else to talk to—Wilson's tired of hearing about my problems. The old prospector's food supply won't last forever. I have to get that mine operating."

When he didn't respond, she glanced sideways, silently praying that he wasn't laughing at her. That would greatly upset her. "What would you do?" she asked.

"Me?" He laughed. "You're asking the wrong person."

She cocked a brow in disbelief. Since when was he shy about offering his opinion? He'd been pretty verbal before—now she really needed some common sense. "You've worked in mines, haven't you?"

"I've staked claim to several, but as you can see, my success has been limited."

"Perhaps you're too modest."

"Perhaps I've been skunked one too many times."

"But you know a lot about mining."

"Not a lot."

"But some—you know what needs to be done."

He looked away. "I know enough to recognize when it has me whipped."

"Feathers—nonsense," she amended quickly. Their eyes met briefly in the moonlight. "You're not the kind of man who gives up easily. You've nearly driven me *crazy* ordering me back to Denver City. I cannot imagine that something like a little old mine would intimidate you."

"No disrespect intended, but you couldn't know that."

"I am an excellent judge of character."

He found that amusing. "Trust me. You're wrong about this one."

"Why don't you work the mine for me?" He was strong, capable, and knew about mining. "I'll hire you to run the mine. You can operate it any way you see fit."

"I'm afraid not. I am gainfully employed—sheriff of Denver City. That's my home and I like it that way."

She had seen no indication that he had a permanent home—here or in Denver City. He seemed more like a man who hung his hat on a different peg every night.

"I could make you rich."

"Rich," he scoffed. "That notion's for fools and dreamers. Not interested. I appreciate the offer and I regret your circumstances, but I'd be of no use to you." He pulled his threadbare jacket closer around him. "We need to go; wind's coming up stronger."

Patience turned to face him. "I beg you to reconsider. You must have come here with a dream. Apparently, that dream hasn't worked out. I'm offering you a second chance."

He looked down at her, and for one crazy moment she

saw something akin to anticipation flash in his eyes; then it faded just as quickly.

"Another chance, Jay Longer, to realize your dream." She pointed to the mine. "Right now, the Mule Head's got me whipped. I'm asking—no, I'm *begging*—you for help. You don't believe in ghosts. You said so yourself. So that shouldn't stop you. Work the mine for me. Half of whatever gold it yields will be yours."

"Miss Smith . . ."

She lifted her hand. "My name is Patience, and I mean every word of what I've said. If you'll supervise the work, half of whatever the mine yields is yours."

He turned away. "I don't want your money."

"It wouldn't matter if you did." She took his chin and turned his face back to meet hers. "I'm desperate. See? My only hope to offer Mary, Lily, and Harper a future is buried in that shaft. The *only chance* Wilson and I have is that mine."

"The mine could be *worthless*. Most likely is," he argued. *"Will be,* I can assure you, if I work it."

"Maybe, maybe not. We won't know until we try. Think about it: more gold than you've ever dreamed about. Another chance. A fresh start. A probability to realize your dream."

For a moment, hope flickered in his eyes.

"If you can't find anyone to work the mine, what makes you think I can? I haven't got the best record in this area. Other miners have seen me fail—not once, but several times. No one would take me seriously even if I attempt to run a crew."

Patience was relying on instinct now, but instinct told her she was on solid ground. "Because you're a man who doesn't want to give up his dream, and I believe in you."

"Believe in me?" he jeered. "Why would you believe in

me? I've done nothing to deserve your confidence. Sorry, I can't help you." He turned and started to walk away.

"Say you'll think about it," she called, refusing to give up. He could do it. She knew he could.

"Sure, I'll give it some thought."

"And you'll let me know?"

Lifting his hand aimlessly, he dismissed her. "Sure, sure, I'll let you know."

Chapter Ten

Snow drifted from the sky in thick, wet flakes, piling up onto the crude building Fiddle Creek called a hotel. The primitive structure, which sat on a hillside overlooking a deep ravine, was joined side by side, sharing a common wall with the other buildings. Elegant it wasn't.

Jay's rented room was about the size of a clothes closet with one dirty window. A rough bedstead made of planks dominated the small space. A mattress and pillow stuffed with dried meadow grass discharged a rustling sound when lain upon. An old blanket, a washstand with a chipped bowl and a fragment of a mirror above it, and a bar of claybank soap topped off the dismal setting.

Crawling off the bed, he reeled to the washstand. Fumbling for the tin pitcher, he dumped the contents over his head. Shuddering, he threw back his hair in an effort to minimize the icy jolt. Grabbing a towel, he buried his face in the cloth, trying to block out the morning light.

Catching his image in the mirror, he bent closer. A stranger stared back at him. Long dirty hair, matted beard, bags beneath his eyes. Not a pretty sight. Maybe it was time for the disguise to go. He hadn't seen Mooney's thugs around in a while.

For no particular reason Patience came to mind. If things had turned out differently he might have fallen for a woman like her. She was pretty, smart, spirited. There wasn't a woman in Fiddle Creek who could hold a candle to her.

She had spunk. He used to like that. Nelly had spunk . . . and warmth and compassion. He'd seen the way Patience fought to assemble a crew. Even watched her become the laughingstock of Fiddle Creek. He'd turned his back on the unkind remarks, closed his ears when they ridiculed her perseverance, but he still admired her. Maybe a little too much.

A smile creased the corners of his mouth. What a pair the two of them would make. She refused to give up; he gave up too easily.

Pounding sounded at the door. Spinning around, he dropped the towel.

"Open up, Longer! We know you're in there!"

Mooney's thugs. Red and Luther. They'd caught up with him.

Snatching his trousers off the hook, Jay hopped on one foot, trying to get them on, his eyes searching for his boots.

"Longer!" The racket got louder. "Open up!"

Jay dropped to his knees, frantically searching under the bed. Where were his boots?

Grabbing his shirt off the chair, he yanked it on, all the while gravitating toward the window, hoping it wasn't far to the ground.

Lifting the window sash, he managed to throw a leg over the sill before the door splintered in half. Two beefy characters rushed into the room, snaring him by the shoulder before he could jump.

"Not so fast, Sheriff!"

They spun him around and a fist slammed into his stomach, then another. Red backhanded him across the face. His bottom lip split, and he tasted blood.

A well-aimed kick found its mark, sending him sailing across the warped floor. Yanked back to his feet, he felt a meaty knuckle connect with his nose. A swift knee smashed to his groin, followed by a right hook to his chin.

A left, then another fast right, and the floor came up to meet him. Sprawled flat on his back, Jay stared up at the double images floating above him.

"Mooney's gettin' impatient," a gravelly voice reminded.

"Yeah, he wants his money."

A boot smashed into Jay's rib cage, knocking the wind out of him. Rolling to his side, he teetered on the brink of unconsciousness.

"It ain't nice not to own up to your debts."

"Yeah, it ain't nice, Sheriff. How many times you got to be told that?"

A sharp blow to Jay's back sent an excruciating pain spiraling up his left shoulder.

"This is your last warning. Either pay up, or you're a dead man."

Turning, the two thugs stalked out of the room, slamming what was left of the door behind them.

Shifting to his back, Jay squeezed his nostrils to stem the stream of blood gushing from his nose. He lay for a moment, trying to clear his head.

As his vision gradually returned, he spotted his boots, crammed upside down on the bedposts. *Nice,* he thought. *Now I find them.*

Patience answered the knock at the dugout door later that morning to discover the sheriff, hat in hand, standing there. For a moment she didn't recognize the stranger before her. He was cleanly shaven, freshly bathed, his hair fresh cut, and he was wearing a new red flannel undershirt under a blue woolen shirt, jeans tucked into new leather boots, and a brand-new hat. Only the color of his hair remained the same—fiery red.

Jay Longer had transformed himself back into one fine-looking, respectable-appearing man. The conversion nearly took Patience's breath away.

He also had a humdinger of a shiner, a deep slash across his right cheekbone, and a wad of cotton stuck up his right nostril.

"Morning, P."

"What in the world happened to you?" Taking his arm, she pulled him into the dugout and shoved him into a chair. Grabbing a dish towel, she wet the end and went to work cleaning away the remnants of blood circling his cuts.

He seemed awkward with her sympathetic clucking. His thoughts were as transparent as his wounds. It was bad enough she had to see him this way. It was bad enough he had to show up here at all, and he sure didn't like her making a big fuss about it.

She stepped back, planting her hands on her hips, frowning. "Have you been fighting?"

"No, ma'am, I haven't been fighting. Unfortunately, I never threw a punch."

Taking the towel out of her hand, he laid it aside. "Patience, I've come here to say something, and I'd appreciate it if you let me get it said."

Relaxing, she waited. "All right."

"This is no place for a good-looking, single woman. It isn't safe. I'm surprised you haven't had trouble before now."

Good-looking? He thought she was good-looking? Or was he just saying that to sweeten her up and bring her round to his way of thinking?

She scowled at him. "Save your breath. I'm not leaving."

Jay sighed. "Please don't be like that."

"Like what? Don't you talk down to me."

"I'm not talking down; I'm talking sense. You can't get a crew. These people are too superstitious to go down in that shaft. It's not going to happen. You may be sitting on a fortune in gold, but it won't do you any good if you can't get at it."

"But I can get the gold if you'll help me."

"Would you just listen? This is no place for either of us. Give it up, P. Let's go back to Denver City. We'll take Wilson with us. If you insist on staying here, you'll just cause grief for both of you."

Patience sank down in a chair and stared at him, willing him to understand. "I can't leave. It's not that I want the money for myself. I have too many others depending on me. Lily isn't robust. She's not able to do heavy work. Harper's black, and you know what that means. People treat her like she's not a real person with feelings and needs. There's no future for her. Mary is sickly, and Ruth and Glory are married, so I guess you wouldn't say they're dependent on me, but I'd help them if I could, and now there's Wilson."

Jay shook his head in frustration. "You're not leaving, are you?"

"That's what I said. I can't."

"You won't."

"I guess it means the same thing. Either way, I'm staying."

He sighed gustily. "All right. I'll make a deal with you. I'll give you two weeks to see if we can find a crew."

"We? You'll help me?"

"For two weeks only. If we don't get a crew by then, you'll go back to Denver City with no argument. Agreed?"

She pursed her lips, staring at him. Two weeks wasn't a lot of time. Still, it was more than she had expected. She held out her hand. "Agreed."

God would help them; she knew he would. He wouldn't have brought her this far to abandon her now. She had no idea where they would find a crew. If they didn't, she would have to keep her part of the agreement and go back to Denver City. In her heart, she refused to think of that possibility.

"Then you will work the mine for me?"

"I'll run the crew for you."

"Oh, thank you so much!" He still had to find a crew willing to confront Gamey O'Keefe's legend. Until the mail got started regularly, by the time she could get a letter to the others, she'd probably be on her way home with a trunk full of gold.

"Run the crew," he stressed. "I don't intend to work in the mine. And you have to know, Patience. I lost my faith five years ago. God doesn't figure into my life anymore, so don't be spouting things like 'God will take care of us' or 'God is good; he'll provide,' because he doesn't provide and he's got a strange way of showing his goodness. I don't want you to cram religion down my throat. Do we understand each another?"

He had been deeply hurt, she realized. And he blamed God. But he hadn't said that he didn't believe in God. Somewhere in his tortured mind he must still have a seed of trust, or else why would he say, *"He's got a strange way of showing his goodness"*? To admit that meant he still believed in God. And if that was the çase, Jay needed healing, not censure.

"Do we have an understanding about your faith?" he asked.

She nodded, thinking they really didn't, but she needed him on any terms. "What about a crew?"

He looked away, his gaze rather sheepish, she thought. "I know where I can put one together."

"I've asked everyone," she warned. "I even borrowed Chappy's mule and rode to Silver Plume, but to no avail."

"I know all about that, but there's one place you haven't tried. There's a female work camp over near Piety Hill. I think I can arrange to have the convicts work the mine."

"Women? Women are bad luck in a mine." If she'd heard that once she'd heard it a hundred times in the last week. Gamey's perceived ghost *and* women would be a dicey match.

He gave her a long-suffering look. "You really think our luck can get any worse?"

She frowned. He had a point. "Who do you have in mind?"

"Moses Malone. She and several other women were working a worthless claim over at Piety Hill before they were arrested for murder. Rumor has it they shot a couple of prospectors and jumped their claim. But they say they didn't do it."

Patience swallowed, aware her eyes were as wide as doorjambs.

"I can't say for certain, but I think I can pull strings and get the women released to my custody during the day. If you don't have any objections, I'll talk to the warden this morning and see what I can arrange."

"Objections? Of course I don't have any objections."

Murder. Moses Malone and her cohorts may have shot two miners. Was she that desperate?

The answer came more swiftly than her opposition. She'd do anything to secure the others' future. If that meant hiring cutthroat murderers to mine the gold—as long as Jay oversaw the operation—then she was going to count blessings instead of doubts. "How soon do you think the women can start?"

"I'll have to see if I can pull this off first." He stood up, looking as though he had something more to say.

She met his direct gaze. "What?"

"You should know . . . Moses and her crew are tough cookies."

Patience stood and gripped the edge of the table for support. "I suspected as much. Other than murder, how bad does it get?"

"You name it. They're no church choir."

Women convicts. How reckless was she? Pretty much that reckless.

"Will I be endangering Wilson?" She wouldn't jeopardize Wilson's safety for any amount of gold.

"The women are loners. They'll keep to themselves."

"Do they know about the mine?"

"About the ghost?"

"Yes . . . him." Gamey O'Keefe.

"I don't know anyone around these parts who doesn't," he conceded.

Sighing, Patience lifted her hand to her temple. It was sink-or-swim time, eat or be eaten. She'd stake her life on

the fact that there was no ghost, but would anyone else?
"I'm desperate. Do whatever it takes to get them."

He nodded. "This brings me to the next question. What can you afford to pay?"

"Nothing at the moment, but I'll match any wage around once the mine is producing." If there was no gold, she was sunk. Wilson said the old prospector buried his diggings in a coffee can. She had already dug up half the hillside, and she hadn't found anything but the bones of a dead animal. She had a mental image of herself lying faceup, brains in a puddle beside her, when the disgruntled convicts rode off with empty saddlebags. Shuddering, she shook the thought away.

"Not good enough," he stated.

"Well . . . " She started to pace the tight quarters, anxious now. "I don't know. What can I offer?"

"That depends on your funds."

"Nonexistent. I had a paltry amount saved over the past few weeks when I helped Mary and Harper in the millinery, but as you're aware, I left town rather unexpectedly and didn't have an opportunity to pack." She wasn't being facetious, merely truthful. "I'm counting on that mine to contain a lot of gold."

He shook his head. "Fools. Men and women are fools when it comes to gold. What happens if that hole is nothing but a dry vein?"

"I'll face that when it happens," she said. "I'm willing to put my trust in God, Jay. Some folks believe in ghosts; I believe nothing coincidental happens to those who trust their life to God."

He pointed at her sternly.

She changed the subject, aware she had already violated

their agreement. "What about you? You can't keep walking to the mine every morning. It's at least a forty-five-minute walk each way, and we'll work daybreak to sundown."

"There's a miner's shack half a mile from here. It isn't fancy, but I can bunk in there."

Walking to the door, he opened it. "You know we're going to have to hit the mother lode."

She nodded. "I'm praying—" she stopped—"I think we will." Otherwise she was as good as on her way back to Denver City.

He returned her gaze. He appeared competent and self-assured—a far cry from his former self. What had happened to Jay Longer? A miracle? He said he didn't believe in miracles, but maybe God had jerked a knot in his backside. A big ole painful knot.

"Jay?"

"Yes?"

"What made you change your mind?" He'd been so adamant about not taking the job—insistent that she return to Denver City. He was still sheriff—still negligent in his obligation to take her back, with or without her consent.

"I need the money."

She knew it took a good deal of courage for him to admit that, though she'd rather that she was the reason he was staying. Smiling, she said quietly, "Then I guess you'll want to get started right away."

Nodding, he turned to leave when she added, "I want you to know I don't care why. I'm just glad you're doing it."

He looked up, his gaze meeting hers. "Don't be; I'm no bargain."

She hoped something deeper than a smile shone in her eyes now. "Isn't that for me to decide?"

Chapter Eleven

B_{ut}, Patience! It's only a chicken! He won't
eat much!"

"Wilson, take the rope off that chicken's neck and turn
him loose immediately!"

"You *said* I could have a pet," Wilson reminded sullenly.

"One pet, Wilson, not an entire zoo." Balancing the wash
basket on her hip, Patience sidestepped a raccoon, a squirrel,
two rabbits, a stray hound dog with its ribs showing, and a
rooster. The child had tied ropes around the animals' necks
and staked them to the ground in front of the dugout.

Wilson was suddenly adamant about acquiring yet another
pet. "He lays eggs!"

"*He* does not lay eggs."

Wilson bent over to examine his latest acquisition.
Straightening, he called back expectantly. "He can wake
us up!"

"Turn that rooster loose." Jamming a clothespin in her
mouth, Patience marched to the line to hang the wash out
to freeze-dry. All she needed was another mouth to
feed—even if it was a chicken's!

She realized she was on edge this morning. Jay had been gone for over twenty-four hours. He said he'd be back by dark, and she stayed up long into last night, waiting to hear if he'd hired a crew. She wanted to believe he was a man of his word, prayed that he would come back, yet doubts colored her faith.

Why should he be concerned about her and Wilson? He was a full-grown man, and he probably didn't want to be bothered with an eight-year-old boy and a headstrong young woman.

Her heart told her that, and yet she'd lain awake most of the night listening for his footsteps. Toward dawn she accepted that he wasn't coming.

The rooster set up a terrible squawk, and Wilson slipped the rope off his neck and set him free. Feathers fogged the air and the bird ran around in circles, flapping its wings and screeching. In a burst of energy, it charged Wilson, sending him shrieking toward the dugout.

The remaining animals scrambled for cover, but their tiny legs jerked from under them as the ropes around their necks yanked them to a screeching halt.

"You're going to get spurred!" Patience called out. Wilson raced headlong around a bush hounded by a reddish white blur.

At the height of the ruckus Jay arrived, followed by a group of women, all carrying picks, axes, and shovels.

With an exclamation of relief, Patience dropped the wet shirt she was about to hang back into the basket and ran to meet him. She was so relieved to see him that it took concerted willpower to keep from flinging herself headlong into his arms. She deliberately slowed her steps. The odd assortment of humanity approached.

"Hi," Patience greeted him.

Jay swept off his hat. "Morning."

Wilson rounded the bush again, the rooster bearing down on him hard.

"The trip over to Piety Hill took longer than expected," Jay apologized. "And it wasn't easy to talk the warden into our plan."

She smiled gratefully and said, "I'm glad you're back." Her eyes switched to the women, and she swallowed. A church choir they certainly weren't.

"Patience Smith, Moses Malone," Jay introduced.

Patience recoiled. She faced the rawboned Indian woman who looked mean enough to fist fight a weasel. Dressed in men's boots, faded overalls, and a heavy bearskin coat, Moses Malone's squat, two-hundred-pound, five-foot-plus frame was intimidating.

Moses' eyes coldly skimmed Patience. "Heard you're looking for someone to work your mine." Her voice was whiskey-deep, her hair cut with a butcher knife. The uninspired salt-and-pepper locks hung in dirty strings below the flaps of a dingy, yellow wool hat. Her features were ageless. She could have been thirty or sixty.

"Yes," Patience said, unhappy about the sudden squeak in her voice. "I understand you might be interested?"

Moses' eyes roamed over to the small shaft. "Might. For a price. A third of the profits."

Patience's gaze shot to Jay. "A third?"

"A quarter," he corrected. "That was the agreed amount."

Patience's mind was busy trying to add and subtract. Half to Jay, a quarter to Moses . . . that left a quarter for Patience and Wilson. Not exactly the fortune she'd envisioned, but enough, if the mine proved generous.

Moses locked eyes with Jay in a silent duel. After a while she turned and said over her shoulder, "A quarter of the profits."

The women, having exchanged a series of harsh looks, nodded.

A quarter of the profits. They'd gone for it. Patience released a breath she hadn't realized she was holding.

Moses turned back to address Patience. "You know about me and my crew?"

"Yes . . . somewhat."

"Couple of prostitutes, bank robber, an ax murderer. And I'm just plain mean," Moses said.

Patience nodded. Definitely not your typical mining crew.

"Got any problem with that?"

"No—" Patience swallowed— "ma'am."

"Longer says we work for him."

Patience glanced at Jay. "He's the boss."

Wilson rounded the bush a third time, flinging his arms and screeching.

The convict threw him a practical glance. "The boy has a rooster after him."

"I know. One or the other will eventually give in." Patience grinned. "How soon can you start?"

"Tomorrow."

"Thank you—tomorrow it is." Money would be coming in now; Patience thought her troubles were over. "I'll have breakfast waiting."

"We fix our own breakfast." Moses' gaze drifted again to the mine.

Holding her breath, Patience wondered if she knew about the ghost.

"We use our own equipment."

That was good, since Patience didn't have any. "All right."

Eyes still fixed on the Mule Head, Moses pledged, "If there's gold in there, we'll get it."

Patience didn't doubt that. This woman was downright scary.

When Wilson raced toward him, Jay reached over and plucked him up by the collar, and the rooster shot past.

At daybreak the next morning Patience's crew arrived. The women convicts looked like fifty miles of bad road.

When Patience asked to be introduced to the other women, Moses told her they were there to do a job, not to socialize. Names didn't matter. Folks called them shady ladies, and Patience could do the same if names were important to her.

Armed with their picks, axes, shovels, and lanterns, the women went to work. Day one passed without incident. At dusk the women came out of the mine and snaked their way back down the mountain, trailing Jay, who had stood guard over the mine entrance all day.

Neither Patience nor Wilson was allowed inside the mine; they could tote water and Jay would ferry it to the workers. When the women emerged, black-faced from the mine, Wilson was allowed to visit with them briefly but Jay kept him in sight.

Patience watched the strange assemblage go, wondering how the day had gone, but she wasn't brave enough to ask. If *they* encountered the likes of Gamey O'Keefe, *he* would have been the one to vacate the mine.

After they left for the day she ventured into the mine, curious as to what they were doing. She walked cautiously over the rough ground, lifting the lantern high to help her avoid rubble. Fresh pick marks showed where the women had worked. She shuddered, thinking of spending all day in this dark and damp place. Although she searched the walls diligently, no golden gleam caught her eye.

Suddenly a low moan came from nowhere and everywhere, swelling in intensity. Patience backed up, moving as fast as she dared toward the exit. The sound ebbed around her, bouncing off the walls, and then died away.

She stumbled out of the mine, trembling so hard she almost dropped the lantern. Sinking down on a nearby boulder, she thought about what she had heard. She didn't believe in ghosts, but a few more experiences like that and she might start to.

Day two dawned. The women returned. After a short meeting, Jay dispersed them into the mine. His gaze touched Patience's briefly before he turned and walked away. As far as she knew, he entered the mine only to dole out water.

She sensed he avoided contact with her, and she wondered if he disliked her faith or her optimism. Both seemed to disturb him. Was he playing games with her— letting the mine prove her wrong? Was he hoping for defeat—for a dry vein—so he could take her back to Denver City without a quarrel? She'd done everything she knew to make him feel comfortable around her. She'd cooked food and put it in his saddlebag so he would find it at the end of day.

She'd racked her brain trying to come up with interesting things to talk about and, although she still wore the old prospector's clothing, she tried to be clean and well groomed, but at times she wondered if the fine-looking sheriff even noticed.

Day three came and went.

Day four.

Jay showed up each morning to issue the women their orders. By sundown he disappeared again, and Patience and Wilson spent another cold night huddled before the fire. Not one word was mentioned about gold. Not one single word.

Sighing, she shook out a rug, praying that gold would soon be found.

Jay Longer—and Denver City—were beginning to look good to her.

During week two, placer deposits, small hollows in the streams near the dugout, began to show up. Gold dust, flakes, and nuggets were found scattered throughout the sand and gravel downstream of the Mule Head.

"That's encouraging, isn't it?" Patience exclaimed when Jay told her the news that evening.

"It's going to take a lot more than flakes and dust to meet the payroll," he warned.

"Still, it's encouraging." She smiled expectantly. "Maybe we're getting somewhere."

"Maybe, but the old-timers say the easiest way to find gold is to get a burro and turn it loose."

Taking three browned loaves of bread out of the oven, she set them on the table to cool. "A burro?" She laughed. That's all she needed, another animal to feed.

"Laugh if you want, but there's been many a prospector who's hit pay dirt because of his donkey."

"Now what could a donkey possibly have to do with finding gold?"

Jay took off his hat. "Whiplash Johnson tells the story about how his donkey got away from him one afternoon. When he finally caught up with it, the animal was standing next to an outcrop of gold."

"Jay," she chided, wondering if he really believed such exaggerated claims.

"Go ahead, laugh. Spineless Jake Henshaw swears his mules ran away, and when he found them they had taken shelter from a storm behind an outcrop of black rock. While Jake waited for the storm to blow over, he got to looking around, and what do you think he found?"

"Gold."

"Not right away. He chipped a few samples out of the rock and talked a friend of his into having them assayed. Know a lot of men who've found water, gold, and silver with a dowsing rod."

She gestured to the simmering pot of stew she'd just taken off the stove. "Stay to supper? There's plenty."

"Thanks, not tonight."

"There's fresh butter," she tempted. It would be so nice to have adult company at the table tonight. Wilson sometimes thought and talked like an adult, but he was still an eight-year-old. Although Jay had already taken the shady ladies downhill, he had come back to work awhile longer.

"No, I need to be going."

Patience wasn't going to let him see her disappointment. "Maybe next time."

He nodded. "Maybe next time."

You will stay next time, she added under her breath as the door closed behind him.

"Apple pie?" she called from the doorway the following night.

Jay glanced up. He'd taken to honing knives while he stood watch over the women convicts.

"It's just coming out of the oven!"

"Don't much care for apples," he called back. "They give me the hiccups."

She frowned. *Peaches next time.*

"Biscuits and rabbit?" She stood in the doorway the next evening, shading her eyes against a fading sun.

Jay glanced up from his work. "Fried?"

"Boiled—with dumplings."

"Like my meat fried. Much obliged, though."

Sighing, she closed the door.

"Hot biscuits and honey!" she sang out the next night.

Getting to his feet, Jay dusted the dirt off his pants. "Give me a few minutes to wash up."

"Take as long as you like!" She burst into song and closed the door with her backside. "Wilson, pick up your shoes! We're having company for supper."

Chapter Twelve

Thanks to a late January storm that night, the snow was so deep the women couldn't make it up the incline, but they were back the following morning. Mining the Mule Head was exasperatingly slow. Only a few small nuggets came out of the shaft—hardly worth counting.

"Boy, this is hard work, huh, Jay?" Wilson, standing behind a crouching Jay, rested his elbows on the sheriff's shoulders while Jay checked the day's work.

"Pretty hard," Jay agreed absently. He tightened his grip on the knife handle and shifted a blade.

"Wilson," Patience reached to pull him off Jay's back. "You come back to the dugout with me and let Jay work."

Jay gave her a smile. "He's all right. Go bake those apple pies."

"Are you sure?" she asked. "I know he can be inquisitive—"

"He's fine."

Smiling, Patience patted the boy's shoulder, then turned and walked off.

Wilson settled more comfortably against Jay's back. "You smell better'n you used to."

"Thank you."

"You don't stink or nothin'."

"I appreciate that."

"And you look better. I didn't like your beard."

"Well, I guess I needed a change." He looked at Wilson briefly. "You could talk the leg off a table—anyone ever tell you that?"

Wilson nodded and went back to the subject. "Your face is cleaner this way," he explained. Shifting his stance, he squinted thoughtfully. "Jay?"

"Yes?"

"If a word is misspelled in the dictionary, how would we ever know?"

"I'm . . . not sure."

"Well, then—" Wilson frowned, thinking—"why do they call it 'after dark' when it's really 'after light'?"

Jay turned to look at him. "Shouldn't you be taking care of your animals?"

He shook his head. "And why do we wash bath towels? Aren't we clean when we use them?"

"You'll have to ask Patience." Jay stepped farther into the mine, holding a lantern aloft.

Wilson trailed behind. "What're you doing now?"

"Cleaning a crevice."

"Why?"

"Because a little piece of gold might have been over-looked."

"Gold?"

"Yeah."

"We found gold already?"

"Not in any quantity yet."

"But soon, huh, Jay?"

"I hope so."

"How much gold is in the crevice?"

"I don't know if there's any, but we clean them once we've worked an area. It's called coyoting."

"Coyoting?"

"Yeah, coyoting."

"That's a funny name."

"Yeah."

"How come?"

"How come what?"

"How come they call it coyoting?"

"I don't know. They just do."

"Who calls it that? Moses?"

"Moses, and other miners."

"How come?"

Jay paused, cocking an ear to the wind. "Listen, I think Patience's calling you."

"Uh-uh. You *said* I could stay and keep you company—long as I don't ask a bunch of questions."

"I said that?"

Wilson viewed Jay charitably through his thick lenses. "Aw, you're just teasing again, huh, Jay?"

"Yeah, only teasing, Wilson."

Wilson followed the tall sheriff deeper into the shaft.

"How come you're in the mine this afternoon? You don't like to come into the mine, huh, Jay?"

"I'll only be here a few minutes." Wilson could already hear the sheriff's breathing quicken. The sheriff didn't like

the mine, Wilson knew that, but he didn't know why. P
said it was because he'd worked his own mines for five years
and had gotten real discouraged when he didn't hit gold.

"You afraid of the ghost?"

"No, Wilson, I'm not afraid of the ghost. I don't believe
in ghosts, and you shouldn't either. Ask Patience to read
you what the Good Book says about the supernatural."

"She already did." Wilson felt a sense of relief. He really
liked Jay, and he wanted Jay to like God more. "You believe
in God, huh, Jay? Everybody with a lick of sense believes in
God because what's the alternative? If you don't believe in
God and you die and then there is a God, then—"

"Haven't you got something else to do?"

"Oh." Wilson caught himself. He was talking too much.
Jay didn't like a lot of kid racket. He'd said so—lots of
times.

"Are you sure Patience isn't calling you?"

Wilson listened for a moment. "No, she's not. Honest.
Where's Moses?" Wilson had taken an instant liking to the
convict. Although Patience forbade him to get in anyone's
way, Wilson still managed to sneak in a daily visit when the
women came out of the mine. Moses told him stupid jokes,
like what do you get if you cross a dog with a chicken?
Pooched eggs. Or, why are skunks always arguing? Because
they like to raise a stink.

Moses was funny—and nice, even sharing part of a fish with
him for lunch one day. She didn't cook it, but Wilson ate it
anyway because he didn't want to hurt her feelings. But, boy,
he'd spat and spat and spat on the way back to the dugout.

He didn't like them other convicts much because they
never talked to him. Just Moses was nice.

"Moses went home," Jay said.

"How come?"

Holding the lantern higher, Jay inspected a heavy beam. "Because it's time for her to go home. Didn't you see me walking the women down the hill?"

"No." Wilson shook his head. Switching subjects abruptly, he launched into a review of his day. "Thursday Matthews almost ate lunch with me at school today, but she changed her mind and said she was going to eat with Prudy Walker, but *maybe* she would eat with me on Monday, or maybe on Friday. She'd have to think about it."

"Well, maybe she will," Jay mused.

Wilson sighed. "Who knows? Women are a mystery to me. She thinks I talk too much."

"Can't imagine that." Jay swung a heavy rope onto a rock ledge.

"Do you think P's a mystery?" Wilson could tell Jay a thing or two about P—like how she cooked all the things the sheriff liked most, and only baked pies Jay liked, and how she was always opening the dugout door to see if she could spot Jay. She'd always say she was checking the weather, but Wilson knew the weather didn't change that often—just Jay's whereabouts.

"P thinks I talk too much too." He didn't think Jay was listening to him. The sheriff's breathing was more pronounced now—like he could hardly breathe and he was real nervous or something.

"Did you know my parents died when I was a little boy? The old prospector found me, and since he didn't know anything else to do, he brought me home with him."

"You told me that, Wilson. I'm sorry."

"You've worried about that, huh?"

Jay shot him a tired look.

"Oh, it's all right. I'm not sad anymore. P says Mama and Papa are up in heaven, singing with the angels and walking on streets of gold. That's nothing to be sad about, huh, Jay? P says they're real happy, and we shouldn't wish them back. That would be selfish of us."

"She's usually right, kid."

Wilson cocked his head cagily. "You think P's pretty?"

Slipping the blade of his knife inside a crack, Jay pried a piece of quartz loose. "She's okay."

"She can cook good, huh?" He'd seen the way Jay enjoyed her meals, and the funny way he looked at her when she wasn't looking back. Outright stared at her twice, he'd noticed. He didn't think Jay was supposed to be looking at her that way, all warm and soft—the way the cat looked at a bowl of cream—but there was still a lot Wilson didn't know about men and women. Just a whole lot.

A smile lifted the corners of Jay's mouth. "She's a good cook."

A thump at the back of the mine suddenly diverted Jay's attention. Halting the discussion, he cocked an ear, listening.

"What?" Wilson whispered. "You hear something?"

"Shhh," the sheriff warned, listening intently now.

A low rumble centered at the back of the mine. Dirt and loose rock showered down through the cracks of uneven timbers.

Wilson coughed. "What's happening, Jay?"

"Come on, son." Taking the boy's hand, Jay started propelling him toward the shaft opening.

"What's wrong? Is it the ghost?"

"Keep walking, Wilson." Glancing over his shoulder, Jay

moved the child swiftly back through the mine. Bedrock showered down on them, hindering their progress. The ground vibrated, and walls started to crumble.

"Run, Wilson!"

Breaking into a sprint, Jay impelled Wilson toward the mine entrance. A loud roar followed on their heels as they burst clear of the shaft.

A thunderous explosion rocked the ground, and dirt and rock came crashing down. Dust obliterated the fading twilight. The entrance to the mine was sealed shut.

Clasping Wilson tightly to him, Jay seemed shaken by the unexpected onslaught of destruction.

Swallowing hard, Wilson squeaked, "We must've made Gamey O'Keefe mad."

Jay snapped. "It was a cave-in—a cave-in, Wilson. Nothing more."

For a moment Wilson stood transfixed, afraid to move a muscle. When he couldn't stand the silence anymore he finally said, "Hey, Jay?"

"Yes?"

"Knock, knock."

"Is this another one of your silly jokes?"

He nodded, eyes fixed to the sifting dust still pouring out of the hole. "Ahab."

"Ahab who?"

"Ahab to go home now."

Jay stared at the obstructed mine. Like he'd said, it was just a cave-in, all it could be, but what had caused it? The timbers were sturdy; he'd checked them himself. That noise had sounded like an explosion, but how could anyone set off an explosion inside a mine without blowing themselves up with it?

The timing was suspect too. After the women had gone home. Of course, he was in the mine with the kid, but no one knew that. He didn't want to think someone deliberately blew up the mine, but he wasn't convinced the cave-in was natural. There was one other alternative he didn't want to think about.

Gamey O'Keefe's ghost.

Chapter Thirteen

Patience finally knew what hades was like; she'd lived five weeks in it.

"Why?" she agonized. She stood beside a pale-faced Jay, viewing the latest catastrophe.

"It just happened, P!" Wilson was still visibly upset over the experience. "Jay and I were just talking, and all of a sudden we heard this funny noise and Jay said, 'Run, Wilson!' and I did!"

Patience looked at Jay expectantly.

He shrugged. "I don't know what happened. The timbers were shored up properly. I checked them myself." Kneeling before the pile of rubble, he examined it for color.

Patience closed her eyes, heartsick. It would take *days* to get the mine running again. "Now, what?"

Jay's eyes firmed with resolution. "We dig."

It took all of them—shady ladies, Patience, and Jay—working twelve-hour shifts to extricate the rubble from the mine entrance. The front section of the tunnel had collapsed, and after days of digging, they managed to clear the biggest part of rubble away from the opening.

It was challenging, backbreaking labor. The women swung picks, axes, and hammers, sweating like men in the cold temperatures.

Even Wilson did his part when he got home from school, lugging heavy buckets of water from the stream to slake their thirst.

Jay labored steadily, working alongside the women, giving orders when needed, a strong back where necessary.

Patience wasn't surprised by his quiet leadership. It was just one more facet of him that intrigued her.

She had a growing need to prove her own worth, but by the end of the week, she realized she was no match for his strength.

He discovered her late one evening sitting outside the dugout, trying to conceal her emotions. "What's wrong?" Concern filled his voice, and he knelt beside her. "Are you sick?"

"No, of course not. I just needed a few moments alone, that's all." With all the activity and confusion lately, heaven knew she'd had little of that.

"Are you sure?"

She shook her head, smiling. "I'm fine, honest."

"Wilson sick?" Jay turned to peer over his shoulder, where the boy was forcing worms down his latest acquisition, a blackbird with an injured wing.

"No, Wilson is fine. We're both fine," she insisted. "I just wanted to be alone."

"What then?" he asked, exasperation filling his demand.

Sighing, she turned her hands over, revealing the huge watery blisters covering her palms.

"Blisters?"

She nodded. "I don't know what to do for them."

Reaching out, he gently took both her hands in his. "Why didn't you say something sooner?"

She gazed back, biting her lower lip to keep it from trembling. "I've . . . never had . . . blisters."

"Well, you do now." He smiled at her, and she immediately felt better. She hadn't known he knew how to smile. The realization did wonders for her flagging enthusiasm. She suddenly missed Mary, and Harper and Lily even more. They would have tended her injuries, sat and talked for hours, sipped tea, and encouraged her with Scripture. Why was she holding so tightly to what increasingly looked like a worthless pipe dream?

"Where's the old prospector's salve?"

"I didn't find any."

Bending, he lifted her into his arms and calmly carried her down to the stream.

Wilson, sitting on his heels, looked up and saw Jay disappearing over the hill carrying P. Dropping a grub, he sat up straighter. "Hey! What's the matter with P?"

"She's got blisters!"

"Oh." Sinking back to his heels, he crammed another worm into the bird's mouth. "Blisters. I get 'em all the time."

Kneeling beside the stream, Jay dipped Patience's palms into the icy runoff. The crystal-clear liquid bubbled and danced musically over the jagged rocks. Leaving her momentarily, he returned carrying a tin of salve Moses kept in a leather rucksack.

Liberally coating her palms with the thick ointment, he gently bandaged them with a layer of clean, white cloth.

Patience watched him tend her wounds, gently as he would a child's. Something akin to love stirred within her heart.

When he was through, he continued to hold her hands cupped in his. "Better?"

Nodding, she smiled, embarrassed he'd had to take care of her again. First fainting at the survey office—now blisters. He undoubtedly thought she was a world-class weakling. "I'll bet you think I'm something—crying over some silly blisters."

He put the lid on the salve tin and stuck it back into the sack. "You'll need to change the bandages twice a day."

Patience was determined to hide her swelling frustration with him. The moment he sensed he was getting too close, he retreated into a shell. Was it just her, or women in general, that frightened him?

"Will you be working the mine tomorrow?" she asked. Now that the entrance was passable again, there was a lot of work to be done.

"Moses can handle it."

"I suppose. But because of all the delays, I thought you might be working with her."

She thought it was strange that Jay rarely entered the mine. He did so only at the end of the day, and only long enough to review the women's work.

"That's Moses' job."

She squirmed to look at him. "Yes, but if you were working too, it would go faster."

They had already lost a week, and she couldn't imagine what he did with the rest of his time. He vowed that he didn't believe in ghosts, but something kept him out of the mine.

"I agreed to run the crew for you," he said. "You agreed to the terms."

"Well, feathers! What's wrong with going into the mine?"

"I don't want to. Moses and her crew can bring the diggings out, and I'll work the sluice boxes—day and night, if necessary, but I'm not going into the mine any more than I have to. I've had my fill of mines, Patience. Five long years of wasting time digging for gold, and I'm not doing it again."

"Of all people, Jay Longer, you would be the last person I'd think of being a quitter," she fussed. "Whoever heard of a foreman of a mining crew refusing to enter the mine?"

He turned away, seemingly unaffected by her scorn. Apparently she could think whatever she liked. He'd agreed to oversee the mine, not to work it.

"A quitter!" Patience taunted in a surprising spurt of annoyance. "Quitter, quitter, quitter!" She was going to replace his apathy with enthusiasm if it killed her!

Springing to their feet, they butted noses.

"You're calling *me* a *quitter?*"

"Yeah, a big one."

His eyes glittered dangerously.

Hers flashed in resentment. "You don't scare me, Jay."

"I could if I tried."

"Truth is, you are a scaredy-cat." Their gazes locked in a poisonous duel.

"You don't know what you're talking about."

"Then tell me why you won't go into the mine," she goaded.

"Because I won't. That's all you need to know."

"No, it isn't. I want to know why you won't go in there. You are afraid of ghosts, aren't you?"

"I am not."

"Yes, you are!"

They were shouting now.

"One of us has to be in there," she reasoned. "We can't let Moses do all the work."

"That's why she has a crew."

"I'm hurting, Jay. I can't hold out much longer without paying the crew, and I haven't found enough gold to meet the payroll. Work will go faster if you're in there helping. That's what I'm paying you for."

"No," he contended. "You are paying me to run the crew."

She had a fit of stubbornness. "Then I'll just have to try to help—get in everybody's way, because I don't know anything about gold mining!"

Bending from the waist, he politely gestured for her to be his guest.

She whirled, her anger exploding. "You *are* a sissy."

"Think whatever you like."

He was about to walk off when she reached out and latched on to his coattail. "All right," she relented. Her gaze shifted to the mine—she was beginning to hate the thing. It was a curse! "I'll help, but you have to give us more guidance. You know gold mining inside and out, Jay. What are you not telling us?"

His tone was gentler now. "I've told you all I know. Gold mining is a gamble, Patience. You win some and lose most of the others. Give up this idea you're going to get rich. Let me take you back to Denver City, where you can enroll Wilson in school and get on with raising the child. This mine is never going to produce anything."

The time for honesty was at hand; Patience knew it, yet she continued to fight the inevitable. "There is more to your story. Tell me why—if you truly don't believe in the supernatural—*why* are you being so stubborn?"

Stripping his hat off, he beat the dust from it, his face a stained mask.

"Jay?"

"All right! I'm claustrophobic."

She gasped. Terminally ill. She knew it. The first man she was ever interested in, and he was dying.

"Oh, Jay . . . how long . . . ?"

A muscle flexed tightly in his jaw. "Four and a half years."

Four and a half years. So little time left for a man who was still young and vital.

"I'm so sorry," she murmured, prepared to do anything to make what time he had left bearable. "When did you find out?"

He glanced up. "Four and a half years ago. At first I didn't know what was happening. Every time I went into a mine I felt like I was suffocating."

"Oh," she soothed. *A horrible lung disease.*

"One day it got so bad I blacked out. My partner hauled me in to see a doctor, and that's when I learned the truth."

Her heart ached. *Consumption.* "It must have been dreadful."

"No. Embarrassing."

She gazed back at him, longing to cradle him in her arms. God love him; he was so brave—so sensitive. He was dying, and *he* was embarrassed.

Meeting her stricken gaze, he suddenly frowned. "Patience?"

"Yes?"

"Do you know what *claustrophobic* means?"

Patience felt faint. She needed to be strong in his hour of need, but she was hampered by a delicate constitution. "No," she admitted hesitantly, hoping he wouldn't find it necessary to go into detail.

"It means a fear of tight places. It's a relatively new term in medicine. I was fortunate enough to be diagnosed by a young doctor who had recently completed his training in Boston and knew of the latest medical advances."

Nodding in total understanding, she sighed benevolently. That would make the grave even more dreadful.

Cupping her chin in his hand, he said, "I am not dying. I *faint* when I'm in a mine because I have a fear of being closed in."

It took a moment for his words to register. When they did, Patience was giddy with relief. *"That's* what's wrong with you? You're afraid of tight places?"

He looked away. "Isn't that enough?"

"Well, all you had to do was say so," she chided. "Then you're *really* not afraid of ghosts?"

"Afraid of Gamey O'Keefe?" He laughed. "No."

"While we're on the subject, who *is* this Gamey O'Keefe?" She'd heard the name until she was sick of it, and yet she hadn't the faintest idea who he was.

Jay's gaze pivoted to the shaft. "A long time ago Gamey and Ardis Johnson both laid claim to the Mule Head. Seems Gamey stole the mine from Ardis while Ardis was gone into town for supplies and . . . other pursuits."

"Other pursuits?"

He looked away. "Other pursuits."

"Oh," she said, getting it.

"The story goes, O'Keefe was trying to bluff Ardis and the sheriff off the property when he blew himself up."

"How did he do that?"

"The stories vary, but apparently it was a blunder on O'Keefe's part. Some say he never intended to kill himself, only to trick Ardis."

"But if Gamey was dead, the mine would have returned to Ardis."

"It did, but from that day on, no one has been able to work it. Legend has it, O'Keefe's spirit lives in the mine and isn't about to let anyone near his gold."

Patience laughed. "That's absurd. And now Gamey is supposedly in the mine, aimlessly roaming around?"

"Worse. The legend is that he's locked in the Mule Head forever."

She glanced back to the mine. "I don't believe a word of it."

"Others do."

She crossed her arms, thinking of the agony she'd gone through to hire a crew. "People can't conceive that this 'ghost' has been blown out of proportion—that it's only silly folklore that's been passed from one miner to another. No one's thought to question whether or not it's just a figment of someone's highly active imagination?"

"It looks that way."

"Feathers."

His brows rose a notch.

"Rubbish," she amended. Turning away, she muttered, "Fiddle Creek men are a disgrace." She glanced over her shoulder protectively. "Present company excluded."

Scooping up the leather rucksack, Jay followed her up the hill.

"How do you figure?"

"They've left a bunch of *women* to do their work."

Chapter Fourteen

Patience lingered in the door of the dugout and watched the activity going on at the mine. Wilson spent most of his afternoons hanging around in the way, and even though she scolded him and so did Jay, he was so fascinated with the work and with Jay he couldn't stay away. His assortment of animals was growing too. Where on earth did the boy find all of his pets and how did he catch them?

She hadn't been back to Fiddle Creek lately. Seemed as if she had so much to do here, and like Wilson, she didn't want to be away for very long. She thought of Mary, Lily, and Harper and felt guilty. She should make a greater effort to send word to them, maybe find someone going to Denver City who could carry a message, but it seemed that the longer she stayed away, the more remote her old life became. Right now, she was content to see Jay every day, cook for him and for Wilson, and look forward to the times they spent together talking. They were sort of like a family—a real family, something she knew little about.

She knew her way of thinking was dangerous. Jay Longer wasn't interested in her that way. He was just being friendly, and as he had made clear, he was only working the mine because he needed money. Her needs were secondary. She had learned a lot about mining since they had started working the Mule Head. Of course there was a lot she didn't know, but she was gaining in knowledge every day.

Jay said the Mule Head was a lode mine. Once the diggings were brought out they were scooped into long flumes and sent to the bottom of the mountain. There they were washed in sluice boxes—long troughs, sometimes in several sections, from fifty to one hundred feet long, designed so water could run through them. Riffle boxes, which had false bottoms with cleats to arrest the flow of water and mud, were used to let the gold and heavier particles sink into the shallow boxes. Most of the equipment was in good condition from the old prospector's time, and Jay had repaired the rest.

It was excruciating, backbreaking work, but Moses Malone and her crew didn't seem hindered by their gender. Two of the women stood beside the sluice boxes with hoes and shovels, keeping the dirt stirred up. The residue washed down the trough. Two more women shoveled in material at the head of the sluice, while yet another pair hauled dirt from the mine in wheelbarrows.

Patience ceased trying to help; she only got in the way. But she could cook, toting large pails of food and piping hot loaves of fresh-baked bread to the mine daily. To vary the menu, she fried pans of rice with tomatoes, onions, and chili powder; baked pans of beans flavored with salt pork and thick, rich molasses; made crusty brown peach pies from canned peaches, and piping hot skillets of cinnamon-fried apples. She stayed busy trying to find something new to add to the menu—not that it was appreciated as far as she could tell.

The shady ladies consumed the meals without comment.

Patience wandered over to where she could sit on a boulder and look at the grandeur of the mountains. She'd never seen anything so beautiful. A couple of the women pushed a wheelbarrow of dirt out to be processed. Again she thought of the dark interior of the mine. If Tom Wyatt had had his way, she would be working in his mine right now, with no hope of escape. So would Harper and Lily. Mary might not have survived the rigors of digging for gold. Patience lifted her face to the sky, watching an eagle riding the air currents, thankful she was free to sit in the sun and enjoy God's creation.

Wilson came to join her. "P?"

"Yes, Wilson?"

"I've been going to school for some time now. Do I have to keep on with it?"

"Of course you do. Why?"

"Well, it seems like you and Jay could teach me all I need to know. Jay's real smart, P; don't you think so?"

"He's smart enough." So where was he going with this?

"I've been thinking. I don't believe I want to go to college. I want to be a lawman like Jay. He gets to do lots of exciting things."

"Like working in a mine? Do you think he finds that exciting?"

"Well, maybe not that, but he gets to carry a gun and hunt for bad men, and I don't think you need much book learning for that."

"What's the real reason you don't want to go to school?"

"I don't like being inside all day. The old prospector never made me stay inside. I could do anything I wanted to do, and he never complained."

"It isn't good for us to do just what we want to do. Life is mostly made up of doing what we *don't* want to do."

Wilson thought about this, his face screwed up in concentration. "That doesn't seem fair to me. You like Jay, don't you, P?"

"Of course I do; he's a good friend."

"Friend, huh? I was hoping for more than that." He seemed disappointed.

"Friendship, Wilson. Leave it at that."

"All right, if you say so." He sighed and picked up a broken branch to use for a walking stick. "Well, I guess I'll go explore for a while."

Patience watched him walk away, probably looking for a pretty rock or another animal he could claim for a pet. She thought about his last question. Yes, indeed, she *did* like Jay Longer. Maybe more than she should. But that wasn't anything she could admit to Wilson, because she was fairly sure Jay didn't care that much for her.

The next day was Sunday, and the women didn't work. Jay hadn't shown up either. Patience and Wilson sat on rocks in the sun, dressed in heavy coats, having an early morning worship service. The silence seemed almost unnatural after the daily clatter of mining activity.

Patience read slowly and with reverence: " 'I will lift up mine eyes unto the hills, from whence cometh my help. My help cometh from the Lord, which made heaven and earth.' Isn't that beautiful, Wilson? The psalmist never saw our mountains, but somehow he knows how we feel about them. God's creation is so wonderful."

"Did God make these mountains?"

"Yes, he did."

Wilson pointed to a small pinecone. "Did he make that cone?"

"Yes, that too."

"He does good work, doesn't he?"

"He does very good work. And he made us, in his own image."

"And he made Selmore and all of the other animals all different. God's so amazing, P. Sometimes it just takes my breath away to think about it."

"Mine too, Wilson. He's truly an amazing God."

They sat in silence for a few minutes, before Patience closed her Bible. "What do you want to do today? We can take a walk down the other side of the mountain, or go fishing, or I can make a pan of cinnamon rolls and we'll just be lazy the entire day."

Wilson didn't appear to be listening. "Someone's coming. Maybe it's Jay."

He ran toward the trailhead, coming to an abrupt stop when two burly, unkempt men came into view. Wilson backed slowly toward Patience.

She got to her feet, conscious of the isolation of this spot and her own inability to protect herself and Wilson against intruders. The old prospector's gun was in the dugout, but she had no idea how to use it.

"Howdy, ma'am," the one with the dirty blond beard said, revealing teeth stained brown with tobacco juice. "Jay Longer here?"

"No, he isn't here." She was furious at the way her voice trembled.

The one with brown hair and beard, wearing a grimy tan shirt, narrowed his eyes at her. "We was told he hangs out here."

Patience stiffened. *Hangs out here?* How dare they speak to her like that? "Neither Jay Longer nor anyone else *hangs out* here." Her hand shot out to clamp over Wilson's mouth, just as he started to speak. She didn't like the looks of these men. Whatever they wanted with Jay, they'd get no help from her.

The blond grinned. "If you see him, pass on a message: Red and Luther's looking for him. We got some unfinished business to take care of."

"If I see him, I'll tell him." Anger held her voice steady. "Good day, gentlemen."

The brown-haired one, Luther, nodded. "We'll be back. Maybe stay and visit a little while next time." His eyes skimmed her with disrespect.

After another look around the clearing, they turned and strode back down the trail. Patience, her knees gone weak, collapsed on the boulder, sighing in relief.

Wilson stood beside her, his eyes wide. "What did they want with Jay?"

"I don't know, but I don't think they were friends of his."

"Do you think they'll come back?"

"I hope not."

Wilson stood a little taller. "Don't you be afraid, P. I won't let them hurt you."

She was touched by his evident sincerity. "Thank you, Wilson. I appreciate that."

But if they ever did come back, she needed a plan of action. She had felt too helpless in this encounter. It was foolish to think she and Wilson could fight off two thugs like Red and Luther, but they might have to make the attempt. She needed to find something to use for a weapon.

Patience glanced up that afternoon when Jay came into the dugout. She smiled, relieved that he seemed to be more comfortable with her lately. He stayed for every meal now.

"Hi!"

"Hi."

"Seen any ghosts today?" It was getting to be a standing joke between them.

"Nary a one."

She hadn't told him about her experience in the mine. She wasn't sure she ever would. The passage of time had dimmed the fear she had felt. Probably it had been the wind howling through the old mine shaft. The wind could play tricks on you. She wasn't going to tell him about Red and Luther either. After thinking about it, she had decided they might be passing through and wouldn't come back, and she didn't want to say or do anything to make Jay leave.

"Finding any gold?" she asked.

"Nothing to get excited about."

Jay poured water into the wash pan and scrubbed up for supper. "Something smells good." He scooped water with his hands and flushed the grime from his face.

"Slumgullion," she verified. *Poor man's hash,* the orphanage cook used to say.

"It would be nice to have some fresh meat," she mused. They'd had very little the past few weeks. Just a few rabbits and a deer roast someone had given her last time she was in Fiddle Creek. Fresh vegetables were unheard of, and fruit was scarce as hen's teeth, unless you were fortunate enough to get a few cans of peaches in Fiddle Creek. She gave thanks every day for the old prospector's foresight. She couldn't believe how much food he'd managed to stockpile. Next summer she was going to plant a garden, a big one, and can everything she raised.

Jay blindly fumbled around the washstand, and she slapped a towel in his hand. Lifting his head, he smiled. "Thanks. I'll see if I can scare up some for you."

She smiled, happy to see the way his face had filled out lately. "Fresh venison or a plump, wild turkey would be delicious."

Taking the lid off the skillet, she stirred the hash. "I was just thinking how grateful I am that the mine isn't in Dawson City. Have you heard what's going on over there?"

"They say things are pretty crazy." He pulled out a keg and sat down. She took a pan of bread out of the oven and sliced it.

Jay seemed to deliberately turn his eyes in the other direction.

Setting the bread on the table, she brushed a lock of stray hair from her eyes. "You know what I heard the last time I was in town?"

"What did you hear?"

"I heard that picks and shovels are going for twenty-five dollars apiece in Dawson City. Nails, ten dollars a pound; flour, seventy-five dollars a sack; a can of tomatoes, eight dollars. Salt's worth its weight in gold, and eggs are two dollars apiece. Can you imagine?" She wouldn't be able to survive a day!

"They say the miners are paying the prices. Chappy Hellerman was telling me the hay is running five hundred dollars a bale nowadays."

"How is Chappy?" She hadn't seen the old prospector around the last time she went into town.

"He's staked a claim over near Cherry Creek. Word has it he's found a few good-size nuggets."

When she handed him a slice of warm bread, their hands touched. Her gaze fixed on his. "There's blackberry jam if you like."

"Thanks. I'll wait until you make biscuits again."

Her eyes seemed hesitant to move on, her breathing imperceptibly more shallow. "Guess I should call Wilson. Supper's getting cold."

"He's just outside the door. I had to cut the rope on the skunk. Wilson was upset, but if his luck ran out, you wouldn't be able to live with the smell that close to the dugout."

"You did the right thing. I've told him as much." It was a miracle the skunk hadn't turned on them already.

Don't you dare look the other way, her eyes admonished. *Is your lack of interest because I'm a burden to you? Not only did I defy your order to return to Denver City, but I have a small boy to raise. Do you dislike children? Are you afraid of responsibility?*

Then again, maybe it isn't indifference I see in your eyes, only idle curiosity.

"Butter?" she asked.

Jay looked away first. "Thanks."

The door flew open, and Wilson burst in on a draft of cold air, dragging a lynx on a leash. "Hey, guys, look what I just found!"

Patience and Jay bolted toward the door, scrambling over each other in their haste to clear the room.

Overturned kegs and the pan of bread clattered to the floor as they darted through the open doorway.

Chapter Fifteen

Don't *ever* do that again!" Patience, still shaking from the encounter, scolded Wilson. "You're going to get somebody killed!"

"But P, he's not very big! He wouldn't hurt nobody—and now you've gone and let Jay scare the cat off with a gun. It's not fair! You said I could have a pet, but then you get all excited when I try to bring one home."

"It was a *lynx*, Wilson. A wild animal. He has to hunt for food. When he grows up, he doesn't know that you're not his supper."

"I could train him. He likes me a lot! When he grows up, he won't be mean, honest. I'll teach him to be nice!"

"You can't keep him."

"Well, *feathers*," Wilson said disgustedly.

Patience gasped. "Wilson!"

"What?"

"Where have you heard such language!"

Wilson peered up at her. "You say *feathers* all the time."

"Well, don't say it again. And while we're on the subject, young man, your attitude is terrible lately!"

"Butch says worse things. He says really bad words when he throws my sandwich down the privy. He says, 'Say good-bye to your behind because it's going down the privy next'!"

"Wilson! Stop that this instant!"

"Privy is bad *too? Nothing* suits you lately!"

Patience started off in a mad huff toward the door. "Get into the house. I'm washing your mouth out with soap."

"Soap!" Wilson wailed.

"Yes, soap!"

"I won't say *feathers* again, I promise!"

"I know you won't, young man!"

Wilson whooped and kicked and yelled when she caught him by the ear and marched him straight into the dugout.

Feathers, indeed!

They were sitting at the supper table the following night when Wilson swore again. Patience's fork clattered to her plate. She glared at the child, her pupils large.

Silence seized the room.

Jay lowered his head, staring at his plate.

" . . . please?" Wilson added when the air started to palpitate.

"What did I tell you about using that kind of language?"

Wilson tried to think. *What* language? He'd asked for the beans! "What's wrong with saying—"

"Wilson!"

"That's what Butch calls them."

Shoving back from the table, Patience motioned him to the sink.

"What? What'd I say *now?"* The boy's pleading gaze shot to Jay.

Jay refused to look up.

Latching onto Wilson's ear, Patience hauled him to the sink, verbally castigating Butch Miller every step of the way. "You're turning into a common, foulmouthed hooligan!"

Patience opened the door and looked out to see the frost-frozen ground glittering under a full moon. Plagued by remorse, she stared at the small figure swathed in a heavy blanket sitting on the log, his revered pets gathered about him for support.

Emotion formed a tight knot in her throat. She was such a failure. "But Lord, I'm trying to be a good influence," she whispered, consumed by the need to talk to someone who understood. Anyone.

Maybe she was too young to raise Wilson properly. She didn't know the first thing about nurturing a child; that was all too apparent. In the past, she had relied on Mary's and Ruth's insight; now there was no one but herself to lean on. And her wisdom was running on empty.

Settling a coat around her shoulders, she stepped outside the dugout and closed the door.

Moonlight lit her pathway as she strolled to the log. When she approached Wilson, she was met with a frostier reception than the cool February night.

Undeterred, she sat down, nodding hello to the pets. A raccoon stared back with inquisitive eyes.

One by one she acknowledged the other animals' presence. "Hello, Edgar, Pudding, Jellybean, and of course a good evening to you, Selmore." She sat for a moment, enjoying the night.

Wilson refused to look at her.

After a while, she reached over and pulled him onto her lap. He was getting awfully big for such an action, but he wasn't too big yet.

He set up an indignant protest but she held him firmly to her until he gradually relaxed. They gazed at a sky ablaze with stars. Just the two of them, the way it had been for a while now.

"Bet you can't find a big fat cow."

Studying the sky, Wilson solemnly pointed to a cluster of odd-shaped clouds. The orphanage cook had played the nonsensical game with the girls from the time they were infants. The frivolous diversion never failed to win a smile or mend an unintentional slight.

"Bet you can't find a skinny pig."

Patience's eyes searched the sky studiously. "How skinny?"

"Real skinny."

After a while, she pointed to a configuration of stars just to the left of the Milky Way. "There, the scrawniest pig in the whole universe."

"No, it isn't."

"Yes, it is."

"Bet you can't find a fish wearing a hat."

"What kind of hat?"

"A *miner's* hat."

"Too easy." She pointed out a clump of stars to the right of the moon. "Right there, plain as day. A silly-looking fish wearing an even sillier-looking miner's hat."

"The kind Moses wears?"

"Even sillier."

Giggling, they played the game a while longer. The moon climbed higher in the winter sky.

Wilson snuggled deeper into her warmth. "I'm going to

try and do better. I'll never say *feathers* or that other word and *beans* again." Sadness touched his voice now. "I miss the old prospector."

Resting her chin on the top of his head, Patience hugged him tightly. "I know, Wilson. I miss my friends in Denver City too."

"Sometimes it's hard to remember what the prospector looked like," he admitted. "I think real hard about him, but sometimes I just can't see him."

"Maybe if you didn't think so hard, you might see him."

"What *did* he look like, Patience?"

Patience recalled the old man. "Well, he was about medium height, sort of skinny, with white hair and a beard. His hands showed he'd worked outside." She thought hard. "His nose was a little bit crooked."

"I remember that," Wilson exclaimed. "He broke it when he slipped and fell and hit his nose with his shovel."

"He must have been a good man," Patience said.

"Yes, he was," Wilson agreed. "I don't know what would have happened to me if he hadn't taken me in. I was so scared when he died, but then you came and it was all right again."

"God sent me, Wilson. He knew we needed each other."

"He always knows, doesn't he, P?"

"Yes, Wilson, God always knows."

They sat for a moment, recalling happier times.

"Wilson, I'm sorry I've been so hard on you lately."

He sighed. "I don't mean to say bad things."

"I know you don't. You know the Good Book tells us not to take the Lord's name in vain."

"*Feathers* is taking the Lord's name in vain?"

"No, but it is a mild form of cursing, and we shouldn't do it. I know I'm guilty of saying *feathers* myself when it would be better to just say yes or no. I think we'll both have to work on watching our language more carefully."

Wilson was immediately repentant. "I'm sorry. Butch says bad words all the time."

"Well, maybe no one has told Butch that he shouldn't. The Lord says we are in the world but not of it, and that means we are to be especially aware of what we say and do."

"But sometimes we mess up, huh, P?"

"Many, many times, but that should only make us try harder to be the very best that we can be."

Wilson thought about that for a while. "Jay messes up sometimes."

"Yes," Patience whispered conspiratorially. "Sometimes he does. Real bad."

"But he's getting better. He's nicer now than he used to be; why, he even shaved off his beard so's he wouldn't get snot in it anymore."

"Wilson, there you go again. Your language is slipping."

"Well, that's what *he* said."

She laughed, hugging him. "Well, I agree he is getting much better than when we first saw him at the land office."

"You knew him before, huh?"

"Just barely." Patience knew *of* him—had seen the handsome sheriff in Denver City a few times, even tangled with him on occasion, but he'd always kept to himself.

"Maybe he just needs someone to take care of him, huh?"

"Yes," she said softly. "Maybe he does."

"He's a real good worker."

She felt good about the work even though Jay contended mining was a waste of time. Any day now they would hit pay dirt, and then he'd know he'd been wrong. She shivered, thinking about the looks on the other girls' faces when she handed them each a sack of gold. She felt encouraged at the rate of progress. And there hadn't been a breath of whisper about any ghosts. She had proven that the rumors were just silly superstition that had abounded for over thirty years.

"Very good worker," she admitted. "We're lucky to have Jay helping us."

"Why doesn't he like to go into the mine?"

"Because he has something called claustrophobia, which means he's uncomfortable in closed places."

Neither spoke for a moment.

"How 'bout we ask him to marry us?" Wilson suggested.

Patience blinked. "Marry us?"

"Yeah. You like Jay, don't you?"

"Yes," she admitted. "I like him a lot." She liked him more than a lot, and every day the attraction grew. But he didn't seem to notice that she existed except for the day he had bandaged her blistered hands. At times he seemed almost afraid of her—afraid to look at her or talk to her.

"Well, I think he likes you too, so why don't we just keep him? He doesn't have a home, except that old deserted miner's shack. I bet he'd like for us to marry him."

"Well, I'd like to think he'd like that, but I don't think he would."

"Why not?"

"I think he's used to living alone. I think he likes it better that way."

"Want me to ask him if he likes us or not?"

"No! Under no circumstances are you to ask him that, Wilson."

"Why not? He always answers whatever I ask him. He's real good about that." His face brightened. "I'll even ask him if he wants to marry us, how about that?"

Scooping him off her lap, she hastily stood up. "It's late. You need to be in bed."

She helped him gather his pets, and together they herded the animals back to the dugout.

Ask Jay to marry them. Patience blanched at the thought— but she couldn't say the idea was entirely objectionable.

Jay had left to take the shady ladies home, and Patience was surveying the plot where she planned to plant a garden come spring, poking at the frozen ground with an old hoe she'd found. Produce she could raise would help with expenses and be better than anything available in Fiddle Creek. And she wanted a supply of stuff for the root cellar. Maybe a good variety of root vegetables. Like Wilson, she wasn't all that fond of turnips, but they beat nothing. Squash, onions, carrots, potatoes, even late cabbage would keep for some time. A well-stocked root cellar was like money in the bank.

Wilson came running. "P! Those men are back."

She turned around in time to see Red and Luther approaching. She waited, gripping the hoe in front of her like a gun. "What do you want?"

"Now, is that any way to treat company?" Red asked. "We might get the idea you're not glad to see us." He winked at Luther.

Luther moved a little closer. "Where's Jay Longer?"

"I don't know where he is." Which was the truth. He was somewhere between here and wherever he left the shady ladies, but she had no way of knowing where, and she had no intention of telling these thugs anything.

"Don't give me that," Red snarled. "You know where he is, all right, and you're going to tell us."

Patience noticed Wilson approaching with his most recent pet in his arms. A magnificent black-backed rooster with golden head and neck feathers and a tail of rich bronze. His large comb was a deep scarlet.

The men ignored the boy, concentrating their attention on Patience. Red spat a stream of amber juice, which missed her foot by two inches. "Stop giving us the runaround. We're here to see Longer. If you tell us where he is, you won't get hurt."

"You're threatening me?" Patience didn't try to keep the scorn out of her voice. "I have nothing to say to you."

"All right," Luther said. "You had your chance. What happens next is your own fault."

When he took two steps toward her, she jabbed the hoe handle hard into his midsection. He bent double, holding his stomach, and she slapped him across the back with the wooden handle.

Wilson flung the squawking, scratching rooster straight at Red's head. The man tried to ward off the angry bird, which only infuriated it more. Luther, still doubled over, tried to scurry toward the trailhead, with Patience behind him, whacking him across the seat of the pants with every step. The rooster flogged Red, jumping high in an attempt to spur him. The two men fled down the trail with Wilson hurling pinecones after them.

The rooster strutted back, crowing lustily. Patience held out her hand to Wilson. "Shake, partner."

Wilson placed his hand in hers. "We make a good team, don't you think?"

"A very good team."

"Do you think they'll come back?"

"I doubt it. Their kind only fight people they think can't fight back. They got more than they anticipated here."

And if they did come back, she would be ready for them.

Patience hefted the kettle of hot water and added it to the wash pan. She was still trembling inside from the unpleasant encounter, but she had to wash her hair. The cloud of brunette locks now fell below her waist in heavy waves. It had been over a week since the last good scrubbing, and if she hurried she would have time to wash it before Jay got back for supper. The dirt kicked up by the mine kept her constantly scratching her scalp. Colorado in winter wasn't the ideal time for hair washing, but she couldn't stand it any longer. Occasionally Missouri would have a nice spell during the winter, and that's when the girls really bathed and groomed themselves. Otherwise, they washed from a pan of hot water and simply brushed dust out of their hair.

She worked up a good lather, then rinsed it well, her mind still troubled by the two strangers. What had those two men wanted with Jay? It could be for no good—that was certain. She would die before she'd let them know that Sheriff Longer was here. Blinded by soap and water, she groped for a towel. She thought she had placed one within easy reach before starting the worrisome project.

Someone placed the towel in her hand, and she dried her face. "Thanks, Wilson."

"I'm not Wilson."

She lowered the towel to see Jay grinning at her mischievously. "Oh, I thought you were taking the shady ladies home."

"I did. I'm back."

"Yes, I see." She toweled her hair, thinking how awful she must look with her hair wet and hanging down her back. Taking a seat in front of the fire, she began to brush the tangles out with long flowing strokes. Jay watched, his intense blue eyes centered on her.

"Did the work go well today?"

"For a change. No problems so far."

"Find any gold?" She fell back on the old joke.

"As a matter of fact, we did find a small vein."

"Really?" She stopped brushing in her excitement. "That's good, isn't it?"

"As far as it goes. Big enough to keep us going for a while, but not good enough to help much."

"But it's a start." She refused to be disillusioned.

He didn't answer and she searched for a new topic of conversation.

"Your hair is pretty hanging loose like that."

She looked at him in surprise. "You think so?"

"Yeah. Bible says a woman's hair is her crowning glory. Not hard to understand when you see it hanging down like a waterfall. Been a long time since I've seen a woman dry her hair."

She'd heard rumors that the sheriff had once been married, so she figured he was talking about his wife. For a moment she was disappointed, but then she realized she wouldn't want him to forget the woman he had loved. A man like Jay Longer had room in his heart to love again. Her brush strokes became more sensuous as she relaxed in the warmth of the fire and the inner glow caused by the tender expression in his eyes.

"Do you ever miss Denver City?" he asked.

"No. I miss Mary and Harper and Lily, but I don't miss the city. I've learned to love the solitude of these mountains. I'd hate to have to move back to town."

"Me too." He leaned back, staring lazily at the fire. "I used to hate it here, too different from Phoenix. But now I've changed my mind. I'd like to build a cabin in this spot and sit and enjoy the scenery until I'm too old to see any more. It would be hard to live any place else, but few women would want that kind of life, I guess."

"Oh, I don't know," she said. "I guess it would depend on the woman.

He leaned forward, "What about you, Patience? Are you the kind of woman who'd prefer a cabin to a mansion? What about that gold we're looking for?"

"That gold isn't just for me. It's for the people I care about. I want to make life better for them. I'm not a mansion person, Jay. I've never had a real home, so this dugout is paradise to me." She could see in his eyes that he wanted to say something, but the door burst open, and he jerked back in his chair.

Wilson entered, carrying his rooster. "Supper ready? Say, P, how come you're just sitting there with your hair down? What are you doing?"

Patience sprang to her feet. "I'll fix supper."

Wilson sat down in the chair she had just vacated. "When did you get back, Jay? I wanted you to show me how to make a peashooter like Butch has. The next time he pops me, I'm going to pop him back."

Jay frowned. "Anyone ever mention your timing stinks?"

Wilson looked bewildered. "What? What did I do now?"

Chapter Sixteen

Bellyache. Bad." Moses stood in front of Jay early the next morning, looking sick as a dog.

"All of you?"

The Indian nodded. "Bad whiskey."

How had the women gotten liquor? he wondered. He had hoped to wind up the week on a promising note. So far, Mule Head was yielding only enough gold to get by.

"Loaded cart in mine."

"You left a cart in the mine?"

She nodded.

"Can't you bring it out?"

Paling, Moses grabbed her seat. "Go now." Turning, she trekked off, doing the green-apple quickstep.

Dropping the wild turkey he'd just shot, Jay glanced at the mine entrance. The women had left a loaded cart in there. If they were too sick to work, that meant he had to go in after it or cause even further delay. He broke out in a cold sweat just thinking about it.

"Turkey!" Patience rejoiced when he deposited the bird on her doorstep a few moments later.

"It's been hanging around the shaft. I thought it would look better on your table."

"I'd say!" Picking up the bird, she held it up for inspection. "Nice and plump! We'll have him for supper." She looked up, grinning. "I'll even make dumplings."

Jay smiled. "I'll be looking forward to that."

"Not half as much as I will," she teased, enjoying the way he immediately colored.

Settling his hat jauntily back on his head, he started off for the mine.

Patience called after him, "Where're the shady ladies today?"

"Sick."

"All of them?"

"All of them," he confirmed grimly.

Wilson came out of the dugout carrying his dinner pail. He frowned when he spotted the limp turkey dangling from Patience's right hand.

"Uh-uh," she *tsk*ed before he could set up a loud protest. "Turkeys are not put upon this earth as pets. They're meant . . . for other purposes."

Wilson's eyes flew to Selmore, who was still safely tied to a tree.

"With the exception of Selmore," she allowed. Leaning forward, she tapped her cheek. "Big kiss."

Grumbling, Wilson gave her the perfunctory peck. With a sympathetic look toward the deceased bird, he stepped toward the trail, whispering to Selmore, "I hope it wasn't anybody you knew."

Jay paused at the mine entrance, trying to see inside the dark hole. The narrow chamber stretched relentlessly down the tight corridor.

Undoubtedly, the cart was sitting at the point farthest from the entry.

Kneeling, he lit the lantern, trying to control the tremor in his hand. This was insane. All he had to do was go in, find the cart, and push it out. He wouldn't be in the mine for more than a few minutes. He was used to that from checking the ladies' work each day. How much harder could this be?

Straightening, he took off his hat, wiped the sweat from his forehead with his shirtsleeve, and put the hat on again. Why was he doing this? Retrieving abandoned carts wasn't his job. He could think of only one reason why he would go into that pit: Patience and the boy. They needed the day's diggings.

When he left Denver City, determined to rescue Patience from the kidnapper, he had no intention of becoming attracted to her. Just do the job he got paid to do. Now he looked forward to seeing her every day. He'd never thought anyone could take the place of Nelly and Brice, and no one ever could. They'd always have a special place in his heart. But Patience and Wilson were beginning to fill a void he'd thought could never be filled again.

Taking a deep breath, he picked up the lantern and entered the shaft. A damp, musty smell met his nose, and he hesitated at the entrance. The cart was nowhere in sight. Great. That meant he'd have to venture in farther.

Edging deeper into the tunnel, he raised the lantern wick, flooding the shaft with light. The temperature was cooler in here. Lantern glare played along the walls, exposing shored-up timbers and overhead leakage. Water stood in shallow puddles on the mud floor.

Rounding a corner, Jay lifted the beam higher. The familiar tightening in his lungs warned him that in a few minutes he would be struggling for breath. Light flickered off the

walls, and his leaden feet picked up the tempo. Where was
that cart?

Following a left fork, he moved through the tunnel, his
breathing strained now. Rounding a third bend, panic
nabbed him. This was much deeper than he wanted to go.
The walls closed in and his lungs battled for air. Rationality
fought with phobia, but as usual fear won out.

Whirling, he started to run. Had to get out—now!
Gasping for breath, his left foot tangled with his right and
the lantern went flying. Diving headfirst, he managed to
grab it just before it smashed to the ground.

Struggling unevenly back to his feet, Jay leaned against the
wall, sweating in earnest now.

"Heh, heh, heh."

Jay's head shot up. "What?"

"Some days it jest don't pay a man to git outta bed, does
it, buddy boy?"

Cocking an ear, Jay peered into the darkness, hearing
nothing but the sound of his ragged breathing.

"Tee, heh, heh, heh."

He crooked his head from side to side, trying to find the
source of the sound. "What?"

"Some days it jest don't pay a man to git outta bed, does
it, buddy boy? *Tee, heh, heh, heh."*

"Who's there?" Lifting the lantern, Jay's eyes searched the
darkness. Light played along the cracks and crevices, revealing nothing. Someone snickered—he heard it.

Snort, snort, snigger, chortle. "Tee, heh, heh!"

Jerking the lantern back, Jay ran the beam along the walls
more purposefully. "Who's there? You're trespassing on
private property!"

"I know. Mine."

Nailing the beam in the direction of the voice, Jay hit pay dirt. What he saw made his blood curdle.

Perched on a ledge, a man, small of stature and sporting a long white beard, lifted five fingers and waved at him.

Stunned, Jay's heart pumped faster. Lowering the lantern, he tried to think. It had to be his imagination. This was not the ghost of Gamey O'Keefe. Couldn't be . . .

Waiting a moment, he lifted the light again, moving it back to the perch.

Grinning, the figure on the ledge devilishly wiggled five fingers at him. He cocked his head. "Yo? Hello?"

Lowering the light, Jay wiped at sweat running down his sideburns. He'd lost his mind; claustrophobia had turned to delirium. He was deranged, loco. Gone nuts.

"Yes, you see what you see, buddy boy. It's me. Shine that light over here. I want to get down, and my eyes ain't the best."

While Jay searched for his voice, the man bellowed. "Hey! You deaf? I said shine that light over here!"

The light shot up and over. The man hopped down off the ledge. "Thank ya. That's better."

Aghast, Jay watched the little old miner walking toward him.

"Gamey O'Keefe here. How ya doin'?"

Mesmerized, Jay reached out to shake hands when Gamey quickly drew back. "Wouldn't do that if I was you." He looked sheepish. "The hand's still a mite hot from the blast."

Putting his palm at the small of his back, Gamey stretched. "Rheumatism kickin' up on me again." He glanced back to Jay. "What's th' matter, boy? Cat got your tongue?"

"Who *are* you?" Jay whispered. "And what are you doing in the mine without a light?"

The old man grinned again. Slapping his hands on his knees, he leaned forward. "Who do you think I am?" He bent closer. "I'll give ya a clue. *Boo.*"

Jay edged backward, speechless. The ghost. The ghost of Gamey O'Keefe. But it couldn't be Gamey—he was dead.

"Now, now, buddy boy—you ain't scairt of me, are you? Ain't you the one who's been blowin' off 'bout not believin' in ghosts? Eh? That was you, wasn't it, buddy boy?"

"Gamey O'Keefe," Jay murmured, unable to believe his eyes.

Gamey bowed modestly. "In the flesh—oops—guess that ain't exactly the truth." He suddenly straightened. "Say, where's them ugly women today? That one they call Moses? Whooeee! That woman's so ugly, when she was born the doctor slapped her mother!"

Dumbfounded, Jay stared back. "Does Moses know about you?"

"Well, now." Gamey doffed his hat and mindfully scratched his head. "I reckon she does—don't everybody?"

"Then she's seen you?" Relief flooded the sheriff; he wasn't the only one losing his mind.

"Who, Moses?"

"Yes."

"No, she ain't seen me. I ain't gonna show myself to nobody but you, buddy boy."

"The name is not buddy boy."

"Oh, I know that, *Jay.*" He put more emphasis on the name than Jay thought necessary. "But that's what I'm gonna call you."

Why me? Jay agonized. He didn't want this responsibility, and he sure didn't need more aggravation! Why hadn't he ridden off for Denver City and left Patience here to deal with her mine and her . . . ghosts. No. He didn't believe in ghosts. Whoever this was, he was a living, breathing human being. Question was: what was he doing in the Mule Head?

Gamey hefted himself back onto the ledge and got comfortable. "I haven't showed myself to nary a soul since the accident. Been real ornery—causing all sorts of trouble with cave-ins and whatnots, but haven't showed myself to nobody." He laughed. "Not until today." A devilish twinkle lit his rheumy eyes. "Now, why do you suppose that is?"

Jay was powerless to say, but he didn't believe a word this man was saying.

"Say, buddy boy, you're not breathin' so hard. Ya feelin' better?"

Jay realized his breathing had stabilized. When Gamey appeared, the phobia had receded.

"That classtrefabio stuff? What is that?" Gamey asked.

"How do you know about that?"

Gamey shrugged. "I know everything."

Jay inched backward farther, convinced he was imagining the encounter. It wasn't happening. The phobia was doing bizarre things to his mind. There was no ghost. Gamey O'Keefe had been dead for thirty-six years. Folks in these parts knew of him, and someone had put this man up to pretending to be the ghost.

"You leavin'?"

Jay refused to answer. If he responded, he acknowledged his insanity. If he kept quiet, there was still hope he could shake it off. He continued backing up, one foot, then the other, round the first corner, one boot behind the other, then another, then another.

The man's voice pursued him down the corridor. "What's yore hurry? It gets lonely in here."

Jay rounded the last corner, and he turned and broke into a sprint.

Patience was working in the kitchen, humming softly to herself. She'd cook a supper tonight like Jay Longer had never tasted before. The turkey was young and plump, just right for good eating. She wanted something special for a sweet. Maybe peach upside-down cake. He'd like that.

She'd make good dumplings too. Take flour, baking powder, and salt, add milk, and drop them in the boiling broth and keep the lid on tight until they were done. No soggy dumplings for Patience Smith. The cook at the orphanage had taught her to create a masterpiece that would rival thistledown and taste a whole lot better.

She paused in her work, thinking how much better her life had become since meeting Jay. He had seemed so aloof back in Denver City and when she first met him here, but now he was almost nice. Most of the time.

She gasped. What was wrong with her? She had gone to Fiddle Creek last week and had plumb forgot to see if the telegraph lines had been fixed. She still hadn't gotten word to Mary, Lily, and Harper that she was all right.

"There you are! I was worried about you."

Late that afternoon, Jay glanced up to find Patience coming toward him. Shoveling more dirt into the sluice box, he continued working.

Pausing beside the cart, she shaded her eyes against the sun.

Jay had discarded his coat, and now worked in shirt-sleeves.

For a moment Patience could only stare at him. Ridges of taut muscles glistened beneath his shirt, open at the neck. She had seen appealing men, but she was certain there could be none more remarkable than this one.

The thought shamelessly intrigued her.

When Jay looked at her, she quickly looked away.

"Did you need something?"

"I've lost Wilson."

Lowering the shovel, he repeated, "You've lost Wilson."

She smiled. "Not permanently, but I haven't seen him in a while."

His eyes skimmed the area. "I'm sure he's around some-where."

"Have you seen him lately?"

Plunging the shovel back into the dirt, he dumped another scoop into the box. "He was here for a few minutes after school."

Patience studied the sun, wrinkles creasing the folds of her eyes. "That was hours ago. The sun will set soon."

"He'll be along."

"Could you see if you can find him? The turkey's ready to come out of the oven."

"All right. I'll drop what I'm doing and look for Wilson."

Patience decided to ignore the note of acrimony in his tone. "Thank you. Supper'll be ready soon."

Once he got a taste of her turkey and dumplings his mood would improve considerably.

Chapter Seventeen

Jay plunged through the underbrush searching for Wilson. No telling where he might be. Ran around like a rabbit most of the time. The boy needed responsibilities, needed a father to help him grow into a man, but it wasn't his job and it wasn't going to be.

He'd already allowed Wilson to get closer than he ever intended. He and Patience both. He had to stop this invading relationship before it went any further. No point in starting something you didn't intend to finish.

"Wilson!"

Where was that boy? Never seen anything like him. Out of one thing and into another. Give the kid his due. Once Patience straightened him out, he never pulled the same trick twice, which wasn't much consolation, considering he apparently had an unending supply of new ideas he hadn't tried yet.

Jay approached the mine with a knot in his stomach. He'd looked everywhere else, everywhere he knew to look.

Wilson had been told a hundred times to stay away from

the shaft; he prayed this wasn't the time he'd decided to test his mettle.

"Wilson!" *Wilson, Wilson, Wilson . . .* Jay's voice echoed back from the mine.

"Wilson!" *Bless that boy's hide. Where is he?*

Stepping closer to the entrance, the sheriff admitted this had been the longest day of his life. This was the third time today he had been forced to go into the mine. He wasn't sure he could do it again. The last time had been bad enough. Going back into that mine to get the loaded cart had taken all the nerve he had. Particularly after seeing that old miner who claimed to be Gamey O'Keefe.

He'd had to bring out the cart for his own sake. He couldn't live with the knowledge that he was a coward. Worse, he would never be able to face Patience again. Afraid of a so-called ghost. Now that he'd recovered from his first reaction, he was a lot more skeptical of Mr. Gamey O'Keefe. There could very well be another opening to the Mule Head, which would allow someone to come and go at will.

He didn't like that thought.

"Wilson!"

Jay's voice echoed back on a cold wind.

He didn't know why, but he knew the boy was in there. Simple knowledge that it wasn't his day sealed it. If anything happened to Wilson, Patience would be heartbroken. That thought alone made up his mind, because he didn't want to think that he cared about the child. He couldn't afford to care. Everyone he'd ever cared about had been taken from him.

Lighting the lantern, he entered the shaft. "Wilson? You in here, son?"

Overhead, timbers creaked. He mechanically set one foot in front of the other. *Gamey could arrange for one of his cave-ins*, he thought. Having met the outlandish ghost, he couldn't deny that he was eccentric enough to wreak havoc—

What am I thinking? I didn't meet the ghost! The encounter was a figment of my imagination! But in here, alone with his own fears for company, it was a lot easier to believe.

His footsteps wavered, and his ears picked up the sound of dripping water. *Plink, plink, plink.*

"Wilson, can you hear me?"

Maybe the boy *wasn't* in here. Premonition had led Jay astray more than once. Relief flooded him. There was no telling where that boy was—

"In here, Jay."

Jay's heart sank when Wilson's muffled voice reached him. Turning, his gaze searched the jagged crevices. "Wilson?"

"In here, Jay."

Running the light over the uneven clefts, Jay tried to determine where the voice was coming from. The boy was close. He could hear him clearly.

"Where are you?"

"In here."

Swinging the light around, Jay checked the passageway jutting to the right. A bat darted up, disappearing between two ragged clefts. "Wilson, what are you doing in there?" Wherever *there* was.

"Just sittin' here."

Jay followed the sound, holding the lantern aloft. It was here he had encountered Gamey earlier. His eyes warily searched the blackness. "Come out, Wilson. Patience's waiting supper for us."

"I can't come out, Jay."

Jay muttered under his breath. He wasn't in the mood for games. Dampness seeped through his coat. His hands trembled and his breathing grew more labored. "Wilson, get out here! P's looking for you."

"I *can't,* Jay!"

Jay swung around and the light pinpointed a small chamber opening. "Wilson?"

Wilson's voice came from inside the chamber. "Jay, why do you keep saying 'Wilson'?"

"Why don't you stop asking questions and get out here?" He was losing patience with this kid.

Dropping to his knees, Jay crawled through water to get to the chamber. He realized why he wasn't overly fond of children lately. They were too much trouble. Women were interruptions, and children were too much trouble, and he had way too much of both in his life.

"Wilson, how did you get in there?"

"Crawled in. It was easy."

"Well, crawl out. That should be double easy."

"Uh-uh."

"Come on, Wilson." Poking his head through the chamber opening, Jay rammed his nose straight into something hairy.

Warm and hairy.

Springing backward, he swiped at his nose, jarred by the putrid smell.

"Jay?" Wilson called.

"Wilson, what do you have in there with you?"

"A bear."

A bear! There was a *bear* in there! "Wilson, get out!"

"I can't; the bear's sitting in front of the door."

Jay racked his brain. *Wilson is trapped in a chamber with a bear. What kind of bear? Big? Small?* Did it matter? It was a bear.

A bear, a boy, a tight chamber.

"Wilson, listen. Now, don't panic." He glanced around for something to distract the animal. How did a bear get in there? The opening was barely big enough for a child to squeeze through.

The kid was trapped in there with a bear, and it was up to him to do something about it. For an instant he remembered Brice, his own son. Would he have hesitated if that had been Brice trapped by a bear? No, he would have taken this place apart rock by rock. He couldn't do less for Wilson. He hadn't wanted to let Wilson become important to him—or Patience either, for that matter—but it seemed like the heart had a way of ignoring what the mind knew was best. That thought scared him more than the bear.

"Wilson?"

"Yeah?"

"Did you hear what I said?"

"Yeah. 'Don't panic.' "

"Stay calm."

"I have to go to the outhouse. I have to go bad, Jay."

"You'll have to hold on—do you know anything about bears?"

"No, sir. I come from England, and I don't think they have bears over there. Leastways, none I've ever seen. But they might, 'cause I probably didn't see much of England after I was born."

"What's the bear look like?"

"Like he's real aggravated."

Black, cinnamon? Mama bear, cub? Jay knew his luck wouldn't let it be a cub. "What color is he?"

"Mmm, well, kind of black . . . no, maybe reddish brown . . . no, well . . . I don't know. My glasses are fogged up."

"Hold on, Wilson. I'm going to have to find a way to get the bear out of there."

Wilson's voice came back, urgent now. "You'd better hurry, Jay, 'cause I have to go to the bathroom real bad!"

Jay ran out of the shaft, returning a few minutes later carrying a pickax. "Wilson?"

"Are you hurrying?"

"I'm hurrying. Now listen. Where's the bear now?"

"Same place. Sitting in front of the door."

"He's just sitting there?"

"Yeah. Staring at me."

Jay's gaze skimmed the cramped area, trying to think of a way to lure the bear out of the chamber. He needed bait. "Wilson?"

"Yeah?"

"I'm going back to the dugout. Don't move. I mean it— *don't move a muscle* until I get back! Don't do anything to antagonize the bear. Hear me?"

"I have to *go,* Jay, real *bad!*"

"I'll be back in five minutes, Wilson. Five minutes." Whirling, Jay sprang into action.

Racing back through the shaft, he dashed to the dugout. Patience glanced up, smiling when he blasted through the door.

"Hi. The turkey turned out beautifully—" She gasped as he jerked the bird off the platter and whirled and sprinted off with it.

"No time to explain!" he shouted and disappeared out the door again.

"Jay Longer! Have you lost your mind?" Stamping her foot, she marched to the door and slammed it behind him. "Beans for supper *again!*"

Dashing back to the mine, Jay tore down the narrow passageway, juggling the hot turkey with both hands. "Wilson!"

He could hear crying coming from the chamber now. "Wilson!" Jay shouted, panic-stricken. "What's wrong?"

The bear let out a death-defying roar that ricocheted off the walls.

"Wilson!"

"What?"

"Are you hurt?"

The sobbing increased, more intense now.

"Are you *hurt?*" Had the bear attacked him? Sweat beaded Jay's forehead and rolled down his face.

Wilson mumbled something Jay couldn't make out and cried harder.

Jay glanced around helplessly. Ghosts, bossy women, and bawling kids. He couldn't take much more.

Desperate now, he tore into the meat, laying a trail of turkey away from the chamber. If the bear took the bait, the meat would lead it out of the mine.

"Better spread it thick, buddy boy. That's a *big* bear in there. *Tee, hee, hee, hee.*"

Jay closed his eyes. *Not again.*

Looking up, he saw Gamey sitting on an overhead ledge, swinging his stubby legs in a carefree manner. Lifting his hand, the old miner wiggled five fingers, waving at him.

Ignoring the apparition, Jay tore off a drumstick and crawled through water to the chamber entrance.

"Okay, Wilson, I'm back. Everything's going to be all right. Where's the bear now?"

"Sittin'—" *sniff, sniff*—"in—" *sniff*—"front of the door."

"Okay. I'm going to try and lure him out."

"He won't come out," Gamey predicted in a whisper. "You'll have to have a bigger turkey than that."

"He'll come out."

"No, he won't."

"Yes, he will."

"Who you talkin' to, Jay?"

"Bet ya he won't."

"Just shut up! Okay?"

"Okay," Wilson called back, pained.

"I'm . . . not talking to you, Wilson. I'm talking to . . . someone else."

Wilson couldn't hear Gamey in the chamber. "I don't hear anybody else. Are you okay, Jay?"

Placing his index and middle finger in the center of his tongue, Jay whistled loudly and beat on the chamber, trying to get the bear's attention.

"Ain't no use. I put him in there, and he ain't comin' out," Gamey taunted. He got to his feet, dancing a light-hearted jig.

Jay thought his exhibition disgusting. "You'd do that to a child? That's pretty low, isn't it?"

"Shore! I'm bad!"

Jay turned away. "You're more than bad; you're rotten to the core."

"I'm sorry, Jay!" Wilson sobbed harder. "I don't know why you're talking mean to me—"

The ploy worked. Roaring, the bear dropped to all fours. Gamey jumped up and down, having a whale of a time at Jay's expense.

"Here you go, boy. Come and get it." Jay fanned the tantalizing drumstick aroma into the chamber.

Growling, the bear sniffed, slapping out with his paw.

"Right here, boy." Shoving the steaming meat into the hole, Jay fanned it around, scenting the air.

"Right here, boy," Gamey mimicked, clapping his hands with glee. "He's gonna tear yore head off, buddy boy! Yore gonna be blowin' yore nose out yore ear!"

The bear slapped out again, catching the back of Jay's hand with its claws. Blood spurted. Swiftly retracting the decoy, Jay held the meat on the ground within the bear's reach.

Roaring again, the bear sniffed around the chamber entrance to capture the scent.

"That's it, boy. Come and get it," Jay coaxed.

"That's it, boy," Gamey heckled. "Come and eat Jay up!"

"*Shut up!*" Jay blazed, sick of Gamey's interference.

"I didn't say anything, Jay, honest!" Wilson agonized from the chamber. "I'm being quiet as a church mouse except when you talk to me!"

"See what you're doing," Jay snapped. "The kid thinks I'm talking to him!"

"I don't care."

Jay heard the bear suddenly drop on his belly, trying to tunnel his way to the smell.

"He's coming out, Jay!"

"Better run, buddy boy. The bear's comin' after ya! *Heh, heh, heh.*"

Jay continued to wave the drumstick, keeping it within easy smelling distance.

The bear squirmed, maneuvering his thick body through the tight opening. Gradually a head emerged, then hairy shoulders. The animal's back legs slid free. Jay tossed the drumstick into the passageway and jumped into a crevice, nearly tripping over the old miner.

Gamey bristled. "Hey! Watch it thar, buddy boy! You caught my bunion!"

The bear quickly located the meat and devoured it. Lifting his head, he roared, his nose sniffing the air. Loping forward, he found another chunk of meat, gobbled it down, and loped on.

Jay watched, hoping the animal's appetite held.

The animal's fleshy backside waddled down the tunnel, and Jay quickly dropped to his knees and crawled into the small cavern.

Wilson was huddled in a far corner, crying.

"It's okay, Wilson. He's gone."

Lunging into Jay's arms, Wilson clung to his neck. His frail body trembled. Jay held him tightly. "It's all right, son. You're safe now." He was getting a soft spot for this kid—and he knew it.

When the boy's terror subsided, Jay removed Wilson's glasses and wiped the dirt off them. Hooking the wire earpieces around the child's ears, he positioned the glasses back on his nose. His heart wrenched at the boy's tearstained face. "It's all right. You're okay, and that's all that matters."

Wilson swiped his sleeve across his nose and sniffled again. "Jay."

"Yeah?"

"P's going to be real mad at me."

"That's okay. I'll explain it to her, and she'll be so glad to see you're safe that she won't say a word."

Wilson looked glum. "Yes, she will. P knows lots of words, and seems like I must have heard most of them."

Jay grinned. "I've heard a few of them myself."

Wilson sniffed the air. "What did you feed that bear?"

"P's turkey."

Wilson stared at him, wide-eyed. "You did?"

"Yeah. She's probably going to have something to say to both of us."

Wilson frowned. "You scared?"

"Sure. She's hard to handle when she really gets going."

Wilson bit his lip. "I'll tell her you saved my life. That might help."

Jay smoothed Wilson's hair back off his face. "Why did you crawl in here? I've told you repeatedly to stay out of the mine."

"I was looking for gold for P. Guess that was kinda stupid, huh?"

"No one made you come in here? No one put the bear in here with you?"

Wilson shook his head. "He was already in here when I crawled through the hole. Pretty stupid, huh, Jay?"

"Not stupid, but what you did was dangerous. I don't want you in here alone."

"I won't do it again if you don't want me to." Wilson blinked back tears. "Hey, look. Your hand's bleeding!"

"It's okay. The bear just grazed me a little."

Wilson gazed up at him imploringly. "P needs the gold real bad. That's the only reason I was looking," he explained.

"Next time you want to look for gold, you come and get me and we'll look together."

"Okay."

"It's dangerous in here. You could get hurt."

"Okay. I'll come and get you."

"It's for your own good, you know."

"Yeah, I know. I'll come and get you next time. I don't mind." Wilson's teeth chattered, and Jay took off his coat and wrapped it around the boy. "I wish P didn't have to know."

"Well, I grabbed that hot turkey off the table and ran out with it. How do you expect me to explain that if I don't tell the truth?"

Wilson giggled. "I'll bet she was surprised."

Jay grinned. "I think you could say that." He ruffled Wilson's hair. "If you're ready, I guess we'd better go face the music."

Wilson emerged from the chamber and paused to wait for Jay.

The sheriff crawled out behind him, keeping a close eye out for the bear. He got to his feet and winked at the boy. "Can you imagine what would have happened if one of the women had run into that bear?"

Wilson laughed. "They'd be upset, all right. Screaming and carrying on!"

"Well, everyone but Moses. If she'd run into that bear, we'd probably be having bear stew. That's one tough lady."

"I like her," Wilson said. "She talks to me."

"She does grow on you," Jay said. He knocked mud off his knees. "I'm hungry. How about you?"

"Yeah, starving!"

"Let's see if we can sweet-talk that pretty P out of some dumplings."

"Yeah, and turkey!"

Jay patted his head. "No, just dumplings."

Wilson grinned. "Oh yeah . . . I remember."

They walked in silence for a minute, and then Wilson said, "Jay?"

"Yes?"

"I know what I want to be when I grow up."

"What's that, Wilson?"

"I want to be a lawman, just like you."

Jay stopped in his tracks, staring down at the boy. "What did you say?"

"I want to be just like you when I grow up."

Jay swallowed. He wasn't any role model for a kid. "Wilson, I'm not all that good. You can do better than me."

Wilson's face turned solemn. "You are *too* good. And you're nice. Is it hard being a lawman?"

"It can be." He was at a loss to know what to say.

"You have to be brave?"

"The good ones are, but look at me. I'm scared of Patience."

Wilson squinted his eyes in thought, "Well, that's different. P can be very strong-willed."

Jay laughed. "I believe that's called stubborn."

Wilson slipped his hand into Jay's, and the two walked hand in hand away from the mine. "Say, Jay, I about forgot."

"What's that, Wilson?"

"P wants me to ask you something."

"Oh? What's that?"

"She wants to know if you'll marry her."

Chapter Eighteen

M arry me?" Patience flushed a deep scarlet. "Did he *say* that?"

Jay casually ladled beans into individual tin bowls. "I just wondered if you had a specific date in mind."

Patience might have been mortified at Wilson's audacity if she hadn't recognized the teasing note in the sheriff's voice. "I don't know what's gotten into that child!"

Carrying the bowls to the table, Jay smiled. "Naturally, I warned him I wasn't interested in matrimony." He looked up, his smile bordering on deviousness now. "Not until more gold was coming out of the mine."

Blushing to her roots now, Patience poured coffee, longing for a deep hole to crawl into. She couldn't believe Wilson had repeated their conversation when she had specifically warned him not to!

Taking their seats at the table, they bowed their heads, and Patience asked the blessing. "Dear Lord, thank you for this food, and especially for Jay's and Wilson's safety. Amen."

Reaching for the bowl of dumplings, Jay spooned a helping onto his plate. "Where was Wilson going in such a hurry?"

"When there wasn't any turkey, he ate three biscuits, gulped down a glass of milk, and ran out to assure Selmore his kinfolk did not die in vain. In fact, he told me he was going to tell Selmore that his kin was a hero."

Jay chuckled. "The boy earned my respect today. Most kids faced with that situation would have panicked."

Patience smiled. "He's a strong little boy. Look at all he's been through, losing his parents, losing the old prospector who befriended him. He was sick when I found him. After he recovered, he admitted he didn't know what would happen to him after the prospector died, but then I came along."

"I guess that was the best thing that could have happened to him."

She flushed with pleasure. "Oh, I expect someone in Fiddle Creek would have taken him in."

"I wouldn't bet on it. Folks out here are doing well to take care of their own without taking in every motherless child that comes along. I'm not saying someone wouldn't have fed him and given him a place to sleep, but he wouldn't have the love he has here."

She looked at him in surprise. Who would have thought he'd understand? "I do love him. He's rather special."

"He is that."

Leaning back in his chair, Jay watched Patience work. He had said she was the best thing to happen to Wilson. What he had no intention of saying was that she was the best thing to happen to him too. He'd miss her when he moved on. But he wasn't the man for a decent, God-fearing woman like Patience Smith.

He thought of what Wilson had said, about wanting to grow up to be just like him. Remembered the hero worship shining in his eyes. Sure, he had just saved the kid from a bear, but that didn't account for all of the boy's reaction. Jay knew love when he saw it. The kid loved him, a worn-out lawman with no dreams, no future, and a gambling debt hanging over his head. He needed to think about moving on. The thought depressed him.

He considered whether to tell Patience about the ghost— if there really was a ghost, which he didn't believe by a long shot. There was too much of the flesh and blood about this Gamey O'Keefe. He never got close enough to find out for sure, but for Jay's money, the man looked too sturdy to be a spirit. From all he'd heard, ghosts were supposed to be a mite frail, just a "ghost of themselves," so to speak.

He smiled at his own humor but sobered almost immediately. Was someone trying to run Patience away so they could claim the mine? Well, he was a sheriff, and investigating was part of the job. He'd do a little nosing around in Fiddle Creek. If there was something going on, he'd find out what, and he'd put a stop to it.

Resting her elbows on the table, Patience laced her fingers together and gazed at Jay. Each day brought a new awareness of him.

She knew the way he walked, the way the corners of his eyes crinkled when he laughed, the sound of his now-familiar voice. Just having him near, sitting across the table from her, seemed so right. She hadn't missed the way he looked at her either . . . and could it be possible that he liked what he saw? Shivers assailed her.

"Thank you."

"For distracting the bear?" He shrugged. "Anyone would have done the same."

"No, for being you."

Avoiding her gaze, he handed her the bowl of dumplings. "Can't say I've heard that recently."

Setting the bowl aside, she said, "Then I'll say it again. Thank you for being you, Jay. Why do you find it so hard to accept a compliment?" She could see he was uncomfortable with the subject.

He slathered butter on a steaming biscuit. "You have a lot to learn about men."

"Such as?"

"Such as, men don't want compliments."

Her brows lifted. "They don't?"

"This one doesn't."

"Nonsense. Everybody likes compliments." She didn't know one person who didn't.

"I don't." He took a bite of beans.

"Really down on yourself, huh?" Picking up the bowl of dumplings, she spooned a helping onto her plate.

"I'm not down on myself, and I wish you would quit implying that I am. From the moment we met, your eyes have accused me of being indifferent. What right do you have to accuse me of anything? I'm doing my job, minding my own business. That should be enough for anyone."

"You are indifferent to me."

"I am not."

"Yes, you are."

Lowering his spoon, he leveled his gaze at her.

Edging forward in her chair, she stared right back. "You *are*."

Jamming his spoon into the beans, he took another bite.

She wasn't going to let him avoid the subject this time. He was quite proficient at hiding his feelings. "Tell me why you don't like yourself."

"Eat your supper."

"I'm eating." She slid a spoonful of beans into her mouth, studying him. She was in a feisty mood tonight. "I know," she ventured. "You hate yourself because of your red hair."

Glancing up, he caught her grinning.

"That's it, isn't it? Rather be dead than red on the head."

Shaking his head, he reached for a second biscuit.

"Yes, you hate your red hair. That's clearly the reason you're so down on yourself." She picked up her cup and took a sip of coffee. "You're downright embarrassed because of it. No one in your family other than old, fat Aunt Fanny has red hair, and you had to take after her." She smothered a giggle, loving the way she could frustrate him so easily.

The man patiently spread butter on a biscuit, appearing not the least frustrated. "I don't have an old, fat Aunt Fanny. My mother had red hair. My sister Jenny has red hair. And the color of *my* hair has nothing to do with my character. It so happens that I like red hair."

"Mmmm, me too," she mused. She hadn't been all that fond of it before meeting Jay Longer, but now it was a favorite with her.

His features sobered. "Wilson told me about your mother and father."

Patience nodded. "I'm told they were killed by a band of renegade Indians. Someone found me and took me to the orphanage." She met his eyes across the table. "What about your parents?"

She knew so little about the man she loved. And she did love Jay Longer. Each day brought a clearer—if not understanding, then complete acceptance, of that love. He didn't love her. Goodness, he was terrified of her. But he would love her someday. He would someday.

"Mother's dead. Pop's alive."

"Any brothers and sisters other than Jenny with the red hair?"

"No, only Jenny. She's married, with children of her own."

"Living where?"

"Phoenix."

"Phoenix?" She racked her brain trying to recall American geography. "Where is Phoenix?"

"Arizona Territory."

"You lived in Arizona? Isn't that the place with all the cactus?"

He nodded. "I lived in Phoenix most of my life."

"Why did you leave?"

He shrugged. "I was young, wanted something different."

"So you came to Colorado? Then what?"

He stared at his plate, and she thought he wasn't going to answer. She waited, her eyes daring him to remain silent. Finally he spoke, slowly at first, then picking up speed.

"I got married. We had a boy, and then both Nelly and the child got sick. You wonder why I don't have any faith in God—I'll tell you why. Nelly had strong ideas because of her religion. Wouldn't have a doctor. She died. Brice too. I lost them both. God took them. He could have let them get well; Nelly believed he would. She prayed about it, but he let them die. I lost my faith in God the day I lost my wife and son. It changed me. After Nelly, I knew I'd never love another woman, and I knew I'd never trust God again."

He took a drink of coffee, lost in memory now. "After I lost Nelly and Brice, I wandered around for a while, settled in Denver City, and took the sheriff's job. Got involved in gambling. Right now, Mooney Backus is hunting me to collect a debt I can't pay. That's the only reason I've stayed to help run the mine. I need the money."

Patience felt like he'd thrown cold water in her face. She'd been feeling sorry, wanting to take him in her arms and comfort him for his loss, only to learn he hadn't stayed because of her. He didn't care a thing about her. Why keep hoping for romance when obviously the man didn't have a romantic bone in his body?

Once a personal note was injected, he changed the subject. "There's a square dance in Fiddle Creek tomorrow night."

"Really?" After what he'd told her she wasn't in the mood for a party. To him she was nothing more than a way to pay off a gambling debt. The thought hurt—not that he'd ever given her any indication he was romantically interested in her.

"You should go," he observed. "A young lady like you needs a social life."

Toying with her food, she wondered how he could tell her that he would never love another woman then callously ask her to attend a square dance with him. She shook her head, then casually observed, "It's too cold to make the long walk."

"Would you pass the salt?"

She absently handed him the shaker. "So the square dances are respectable?"

"Far as I know they are."

Patience wondered. She had seen men dancing with each other in Silver Plume. She had also heard stories about

Fiddle Creek men and how they made such a spectacle dancing with one another, half drunk and shamelessly disorderly during their Saturday night forays. She didn't want to go to a square dance with anyone other than Jay.

Have you no pride? He just said he wasn't interested in other women. Still, if he asked, what would it hurt to go? Enjoy his company for the evening?

He handed the saltshaker back. "I'll watch Wilson if you like."

She glanced up. "What?"

"I'm not doing anything. I'll watch Wilson for you." When she glared at him, he clarified the offer. "While you go to the square dance."

Shoving back from the table, she stood up, her hackles rising. "You're not going?"

"Me?" He laughed. "I hate to square-dance."

"Then why did you ask me to go?"

"I didn't *ask* you to go; I merely said you should go."

"Oh, really?"

He looked back mulishly. "Really."

Picking up the bowl of dumplings, she heaved its contents at him. Dough and gravy hit him, sending him reeling backward on the stool. He wiped his eyes, nearly blinded, but he could see well enough to catch the gleam in her eyes. He cringed instinctively, halfway expecting to have the beans hurled at him too. She glared at him for a moment, then turned on her heel. Marching to the door, she jerked it open and slammed it shut on her way out.

A minute or two passed before the door opened again, and Patience stuck her head around the corner. "You're not coming after me?"

He brushed dumplings off the front of his shirt. "Not on your life." What kind of fool did she think he was?

She slammed the door again.

⁓

When a knock came at the door the following evening, Patience laid her sewing aside.

"Want me to let Jay in?" Wilson asked.

"Yes, and if he wants to talk to me, tell him I'm busy."

Wilson's eyes appraised the cramped quarters. "Won't he know I'm lying?"

Crawling into her cot, Patience jerked the blanket over her head.

Setting Jellybean aside, Wilson went to open the door. "Patience's busy," he relayed.

Looking inside the dugout, Jay's eyes traveled to the conspicuous hump in the middle of the cot. "I want to talk to her."

"She's busy," Wilson repeated.

"Doing what?"

His eyes gestured toward the cot. "She's real busy, Jay. She can't talk right now."

Stepping around the boy, Jay closed the door, holding his index finger to his lips. Tiptoeing to the cot, he lifted the corner of the blanket to reveal Patience's head.

She stared up at him.

"You look busy."

"I'm asleep," she murmured.

"I can see that, and I hate to bother you, but the square dance starts at eight. It's seven-thirty now, and it's a forty-five-minute walk to Fiddle Creek."

"So?" She jerked the cover back over her head.

He lifted the corner again, and his gaze ran lazily over her. Goose bumps raced down her spine. "I had that coming, but let's not argue. Let's go to the square dance."

"No."

"Are you going to wear what you have on, or would you like to change?"

"Please go, P." Wilson held Jellybean in his arms, his face a mask of concern. "It'd be fun."

Nodding, Jay dropped the cover back into place. "Wilson, tell P I'll wait outside."

"What about me?"

"Guess you'd better get your dancing shoes on. We're going dancing."

"Oh, boy!" Wilson dropped Jellybean and ran to grab his coat.

⁓

Jay and Patience lagged behind Wilson. The boy carried the lantern despite a full moon overhead lighting the trail.

"You look mighty fetching tonight," Jay admitted, helping Patience descend a slippery slope.

She knew he was only being nice. If only she had a pretty dress and shoes to wear—anything other than the prospector's clothes. "I feel very foolish about throwing those dumplings at you."

"Why? I like dumplings."

Grinning shyly, she refused to look at him. "To eat—not to wear."

"Well, I was being insensitive. Forgive me?"

Her smile widened. "You're forgiven."

Without thinking, she slipped her hand into his. His warmth was reassuring. He might vow to never love another woman, but that didn't mean *she* couldn't love *him*. Secretly, down deep in her heart, where no one would ever know.

The square dance had already begun when they arrived. The chandeliers above the dance hall burned brightly.

Wilson spotted a few of his classmates sitting together on the sidelines and reluctantly went to join them.

Offering Patience his arm, Jay led her to the floor, where the musicians were just beginning a new set of square dancing.

The caller went to work.

> *"Allemande left with the old left hand*
> *Honey by the right, then the right and left grand!"*

Bowing to one another, Patience took Jay's hand, and he twirled her gracefully around. They moved across the room, passing each other twice before joining the other couples in a square.

> *"Side couple turn their ladies;*
> *Ladies turn side couples.*
> *Gentlemen turn side couples,*
> *All hands round, back again.*
> *Pass on through and a do-si-do*
> *Like a chicken in the bread pan a-pickin' out dough!"*

Laughing breathlessly, Patience collapsed into Jay's arms at the end of the third square.

Several men approached Patience, asking her if she would do them the honor of dancing the last dance with them. She refused graciously, waiting for Jay to ask her.

He gripped her hand. "Let's sit this one out. All right?"

She nodded, relieved.

He led her to a remote corner and then brought her a cup

of punch. "Hello, belle of the ball," he teased, fondly smiling down at her. The fabric of his shirt made his eyes look as blue as a field of cornflowers.

"Thank you for bringing me tonight." She gazed up at him, cheeks flushed, eyes sparkling. "I'm having a wonderful time."

"Wilson seems to be enjoying himself. He and his school friends have emptied the punch bowl twice."

She laughed, thinking about the expert way he had guided her through the complicated square-dance formations. "Sheriff Longer, you're good! Do you dance often?"

He smiled. "Only when I have to."

She feigned amazement. "Other women have thrown dumplings in your face?"

"I'm afraid they've thrown more than dumplings," he confessed, "but none have had your charming persuasion. Besides, you make very good dumplings."

Wrinkling her nose, she made a face.

The music slowed, the fiddle sang sweetly. She hummed along, remembering the words. "I love this song," she confessed. "Do you know it?"

"I've heard it."

Softly, she began to sing, "I dream of Jeanie with the light brown hair," only she substituted *Jay* for *Jeanie,* and *red* for *light brown* hair. Her gaze locked with his, willing him not to look away.

In soft, whispery tones, she sang the words for his ears only, in a voice pure and sweet as a nightingale's. Others around them faded away, and they were in a world of their own.

That moment something changed between them. Patience could never be sure exactly what, but something changed. They both were aware of it.

After the dance, Jay walked Patience and Wilson home. Wilson, yawning, promptly said good night and slipped inside. Jay said good night, then turned to walk back to his shack. Suddenly he spun around. "Patience?"

She looked up expectantly. "Yes?"

"I was wondering . . ." He hesitated.

"Yes?"

"If it wouldn't offend you, I'd like to kiss you good night."

"It wouldn't offend me," she returned softly. "Actually, I've been hoping you would."

"You were?"

She nodded, smiling.

They stood for a moment, neither one certain of what to do next.

"Should I come to you?" she asked hesitantly.

"Oh . . . no, of course not. I'll come to you." Approaching her, he tried to position himself properly.

With darting, chickenlike neck gestures, they hemmed and hawed around a few moments, struggling to come to a meeting of the lips.

When it finally happened, Patience felt a stab of disappointment. She'd not seen stars—or skyrockets. Nothing at all like that romantic novel she'd read.

"See you in the morning," Jay murmured.

"Yes." She smiled, trying to hide her frustration. Was it her? Surely he could do better than that. "See you in the morning."

Chapter Nineteen

Moderation now seemed to be a thing of the past. Jay drove the shady ladies with a passion, working them long after the sun went down over the mountaintop. He suddenly had a will to live—and if he was to survive the gambling debt, he had to make the mine pay off.

Only a minimal amount of gold was coming out, but Jay knew there was more, much more, buried deep within that black, abysmal creation called the Mule Head. Otherwise, whoever was trying to scare Patience away wouldn't be setting up residence in the mine.

Once or twice, he thought of telling her about his encounters with the "ghost," but he never did. She didn't need to know; the old man hadn't shown himself to anyone but Jay—and wasn't likely to. Jay figured the less Patience knew about the strange goings-on, the better.

Unexpected floods, unexplainable fires, collapsing timbers, strange noises, and obnoxious belching sounds occurred in the mine on a routine basis now, but the shady ladies didn't seem to mind.

Jay was determined to get to the bottom of this mystery

without alarming Patience and Wilson. If the mother lode was in the Mule Head, he was going to unearth it. He had taken the job to save his own neck; now he'd made up his mind to save Patience's also.

Moses approached him as he worked outside the mine one afternoon. "Man at assay office say no weigh gold for two weeks."

"Tell him we have to have it sooner."

"Told him." She shook her head no.

Jay paused, resting on the handle of his shovel. There wasn't another assay office around for thirty miles. Consequently, the one in Fiddle Creek was running behind.

Lifting his hat, he wiped the sweat off his forehead. If he had a choice, he'd do business elsewhere. Sage Whitaker was an ill-tempered old coot. Area miners were having to wait weeks to get their ore assessed, but Jay couldn't wait weeks. Already the ladies were starting to complain about low wages.

Smiling, Jay winked at the sober-faced woman, knowing she could arm wrestle a man out of his hide if she was pushed. "Why don't you see if you can get Sage to cut us some slack?"

Moses returned his look stoically. "Diplomacy?"

He hadn't realized she knew the word. Her English was broken at best. "You know what *diplomacy* means?"

She nodded. "Boy teach me: Be nice until I find big rock."

He chuckled. Wilson. "Unless we can find another assayer, we're going to have to get along with Sage."

Moses trekked off, apparently to see what she could do about the situation.

Tossing a shovelful of dirt into the sluice box, Jay

wondered what sort of man would take Moses on. Most miners were so hungry for female companionship they'd marry anything in a skirt. "That Moses would be a handful." He spoke the thought out loud.

"Not for me, buddy boy. I'd take her on in a minute."

Gamey reclined on a nearby rock, arms scissored behind his head, lazily soaking up the sunshine.

Jay hadn't heard him approach. "That might be a mistake," Jay pointed out. "She could whip you without breaking a sweat."

"You got your own problems, buddy boy. Especially in view of what you've been thinking about that Patience woman lately. Better leave now, afore you suddenly find yourself tied down to a woman and an eight-year-old boy."

Jay shot him a cross look. "How do you know what I'm thinking?"

"Been watching you. Ain't hard to tell when a man's got a woman on his mind."

Jay was getting used to the old man's observations and sudden visits. They were daily now—and annoying. He switched the topic back to Moses. "Thought you said Moses was ugly."

"Oh, she is. Ugleeeeee. But she's got possibilities," Gamey allowed. "Winters get mighty nippy up here. That woman's bulk could provide some powerful warmth to a man."

"Winters shouldn't bother you," Jay goaded. "You're dead."

The old man sat up. "Don't believe that I'm dead?"

Jay threw another shovelful of ore into the sluice box. "You're about as dead as I am. What do you want? The mine? Or are you working for someone—someone who thinks I'm stupid enough to believe in ghosts?"

The intruder shifted positions. "You ever been in love, buddy boy?"

"Might have."

"Don't try to tell me you haven't, 'cause I know you have. Her name was Nelly, and she had your boy, Brice."

Jay froze, anger overflowing him. Whoever was trying to claim-jump the Mule Head had done his homework. Considering he and Nelly had lived in these parts while he was mining, it wouldn't be any trouble to learn about his past, but he didn't like anyone digging around in things he'd rather not have to talk about.

Guarding his tongue, Jay said quietly, "Well, guess that saves me the trouble of telling you." Taking his shovel, he moved on downstream. "Someone's coached you real well, haven't they? But everything you're saying could have been learned in Fiddle Creek. So who's paying you to go to all this trouble?"

Gamey tagged along behind him, ignoring the question. "Some other little gal got yore heart now, eh?"

"Not that I'm aware of."

"Liar."

"I said, *not that I'm aware of.*"

"And I said, *liar.*"

"Okay, so you tell me who has my heart now." Jay felt like a fool discussing the subject.

"Patience. You're sweet on her—but not sweet enough. If you was, you'd take her back to Denver City where she could be with them other orphans. I ain't ever gonna let her alone, ya know. She won't bring any gold outta this mine." Smiling, he winked. "You can bet on it." Trailing behind,

Gamey aggravated Jay. "Cute little bugger. Shame she got mixed up in this mine."

"She deserves better," Jay agreed.

"Who?" Gamey baited. "Go ahead, say her name. You ain't got no secrets from me."

Jay refused to be drawn back into the conversation.

"Sweet on her, are ya?"

"No," Jay denied.

"Are too."

"I'm not."

"Big liar."

"I *admire* her," Jay conceded. "That doesn't make me sweet on her." Patience wasn't like most women. She accepted people for what they were, and with the exception of the time she flung a bowl of dumplings in his face, she was usually even-tempered.

And if he felt different than he was saying, well, it was no one's business but his.

"Even had a good time at the square dance, huh, buddy boy?"

"Good enough to suit me."

"But?"

"The last thing Patience needs is a man like me in her life."

"Cain't agree. You ain't no blue-ribbon prize, I'll grant ya, but she could do worse."

"Look, do you mind if we just drop the subject?"

The old man shrugged. "What else we got to do?"

"*I* have work to do."

But pretty soon Gamey was heckling again. "Like to hitch up with her, wouldn't ya?"

Jay didn't bother to answer. He'd learned the less he said

the quicker Gamey would tire of badgering him and leave—go wherever he was camped out for the charade.

"Oh, you'd like to all right, but you've got this idea yore not good enough for her."

"You talk too much. Go away. You're wasting your time here. Go tell whoever you're working for that it isn't going to work. This mine belongs to Patience and the boy."

"You ain't so bad," Gamey said. "You ain't necessarily anyone I'd choose for *my* daughter, if I had kids, but you've been behavin' yoreself lately. Quit gambling, haven't ya?"

"You tell me."

"You have—mighty hard habit to shake, but you did it. Guess you got real ashamed of yoreself and realized yore ma would be real disappointed to see how you'd turned out. It's hard for a man to get away from the way he was raised. Now ya need to get Backus off yore back."

Jay whirled, temper flaring. "How do you know about Backus?"

"His thugs, Red and Luther, been lookin' everywhere for you—bound to find ya real soon, if I was to tell 'em what I know."

Plunging the shovel back into a cart, Jay wondered exactly how much the old coot did know about him. So Red and Luther were nosing around town. He hadn't seen them since he'd left the hotel and moved into the miner's shack. He'd hoped they had given up and gone back to Denver City, but no such luck.

"You don't like me knowing yore business, do ya? Ghosts can go anywhere they want to without being seen. I can find out anything I want."

"Way I heard it, you were supposed to be locked in the

mine forever. Gamey O'Keefe couldn't go wandering around like you are now."

Gamey looked startled. "Eh! Where did ya hear that?"

"Around. If you know so much about me, then you should know that I don't like you or anyone else butting into my business."

"I know *that!* I'm jest tryin' to tell you, you ain't as hopeless as ya think."

Jay's laugh rang with irony. "I'm the epitome of success."

"Shoot, no, you ain't that neither, but you've had a run of bad luck. So what? You want to talk bad luck?"

The old miner raised his hat and scratched his head. "I was sixty-two years old when I blowed myself up. *Sixty-two,* and not a penny to my name, but I ain't never considered myself worthless. Why, I'd worked one hopeless claim after the other—seen the elephant a hundred times, but always had the gumption to keep going. Gamey O'Keefe give up? Not on yore life. Drank too much, yes; 'ssociated with women too much, yes; got discouraged, yes; complained a lot, yes. But give up? Never entered my mind. I've lived through winters so cold I've seen horses froze solid standin' up, and the horns on cattle freeze and burst off from the pith. I suffered through summers so hot you'd swear you was in hades. I've witnessed fires sweep entire towns and lay 'em out in ashes. I've seen grown men cry when everything they'd worked for went up in a sheet of flames or their claim didn't pan out.

"Shoot, buddy boy, gettin' what you want out of life takes a powerful lot of effort. Nothin' worth havin' ever comes easy. Jest 'cause you lost yore wife and boy, couldn't make a mine pay off—because you found out you couldn't work 'cause of that phobia thing—why, that's sissy stuff.

Stop beatin' yoreself up. If that's all life's got to throw yore way, consider yoreself lucky."

At his age, probably most of what he'd said had a grain of truth, except for that part about blowing himself up, Jay figured. "For a man who claims to have blown himself to pieces, you seem to be well preserved. I'm guessing your job is to scare me off; if that's the case, you're doing the opposite. Why boost my morale?"

"I don't know." Gamey scratched his beard. "Shore as shootin' I don't know—maybe I'm startin' to like ya, buddy boy."

"Then why are you trying to scare me and Patience out of the Mule Head?"

The old man stiffened. "Didn't say that, did I?"

"You didn't have to. Now clear out of here and don't come back."

Gamey scoffed. "Too hard on yoreself. Ain't dead yet, are ya? Never met a man who didn't have somethin' to learn and wasn't the better for learnin' it."

Jay considered his prospects. Come spring, he would turn thirty. Thirty, flat broke, with the future of a salmon spawning upstream. He had nothing to offer a woman. Patience was intelligent and pretty. Though she didn't know it, she could have her pick of eligible suitors. What did she need with a broken-spirited man like him?

"Look at it this way: you were decent enough to help her," Gamey reminded him. "You cain't be all bad."

Jay laughed caustically. "She didn't have a whole lot of choices now, did she? There wasn't anywhere else for her to turn."

Gamey dipped his hands in the stream, letting water trickle through his fingers. "There ya go again, selling yourself short, buddy boy. Now take my gold—which you won't—but for right now, we'll pretend you will. You're convinced that with enough time you're going to find that gold, ain't ya?"

"I'll sure be doing my best."

"Won't find it."

"I'll keep looking."

"Ya lookin' for Patience's sake, or do ya want it to save yore hide from Mooney?"

"You tell me."

"Well, at first it was the latter, but now yore tiltin' more to the former."

"That just goes to prove you *don't* know everything."

Smiling, Gamey gradually began to fall behind. "Ya still got a powerful lot to learn about women, buddy boy."

"Yeah," Jay conceded. "But not from you." When he looked again, the miner was gone, disappeared over a ridge.

Jay leaned on his shovel, thinking about the little man who seemed to know so much about him. Someone had coached him well. Question was, who? He'd never talked much about Nelly and the boy. Some things lay too close to the bone for general conversation, but he guessed it was no secret. People in these mountains were interested in each other. With no newspapers and the hit-or-miss mail service, they didn't have anything else to do. So they talked. Not hard to find out anything about someone if you wanted to bad enough.

Mooney Backus, now, he'd probably been rampaging around, blowing off steam. Him or those goons he employed. Bragging about what they'd do to him. But this so-called ghost, he wasn't working for Mooney. Whoever had hired him to pull this scam had brains, something notably lacking in Backus.

Brides of the West

Why didn't this Gamey, or whoever he was, show himself
to anyone else? to Patience? Seems like a woman would be
easy prey. He must have a reason to appear to Jay only
when no one else was around. It didn't matter, except that
it looked like whoever was behind this wanted to run him
off more than he did Patience.

Jay paused in the act of lifting a shovelful of dirt. Maybe
he was on to something. Whoever wanted the Mule Head
knew Patience couldn't work the mine by herself. Get rid
of Jay, and she would have to leave. The unknown claim
jumper could move in and take over.

He whistled through his teeth. Shrewd. Except it wasn't
going to work. What kind of no-account varmint would he
be to walk out on Patience and Wilson?

Jay Longer didn't run.

Two nights later Jay knocked on Patience's door. She
unhooked the latch and opened it, surprised to see him up
so late. She supposed he'd been asleep for hours.

"Did I wake you?" he whispered.

"No, I can't sleep." Opening the door wider, she allowed
him entrance.

"Is it too late?"

"No," she whispered. "I'm grateful for the company."

He stepped inside the dugout, closing the door quietly
behind him. Wilson was asleep on his pallet before the fire,
his arm gently curved around a kitten.

Moving to the fireplace, Patience slid the coffeepot over
the flame. Her hair was loose tonight, a dark auburn cloud
swinging below her waist. "What are you doing up so late?"
she whispered.

222

"Had something on my mind; I couldn't sleep either."

Seating herself at the table with Jay, she gazed at him.
"Is something bothering you?"

"Patience, there's something you ought to know. At first
I thought I'd keep it from you, but you should know.
There's someone in the mine who's pretending to be
Gamey O'Keefe."

He couldn't keep the information from her any longer.
The old miner was getting reckless. Today he'd initiated
two minor cave-ins, one trapping the shady ladies for over
two hours before Jay could dig them out. Moses was furious. She and the other women were getting tired of the
hassles.

Patience's jaw dropped. "You've seen the ghost?"

"There is no ghost," he confirmed. "My guess is that
someone is trying to steal the mine, and they've hired an
old miner to be the ghost of Gamey O'Keefe. In the process
they've learned a lot about me." Jay gave her a level look.
"The man is human flesh and blood. He roams wherever he
wants and shows up unexpectedly to throw me off."

Patience stood up, returning to the fire. Pouring two cups
of coffee, she inquired softly, "Someone is trying to steal the
mine?"

"You shouldn't be surprised. Man is greedy, and the Mule
Head is rumored to have the mother lode, whether it does
or not."

Carrying the tin cups to the table, she set them down.
Ladling two heaping teaspoons of sugar into hers, she
cautiously reached out and laid her hand over his. "Jay,
we've been working hard lately. Why don't we take the
afternoon off tomorrow? I'll fix a picnic, and we'll find a
nice place to eat in the sunshine." She smiled encourag-

ingly. "Doesn't that sound nice? The shady ladies can surely do without us for one afternoon."

Shoving back from the table, he stood up. "Sorry I bothered you."

"Jay—" Springing up, she hurried around the table, realizing she had hurt his feelings. "I'm sorry. . . . It's just, well . . . an odd story. Moses hasn't said a word about seeing anyone. Are you sure it's a man?"

Jay's eyes turned grave. "I see him every day, Patience. I talk to him. He wants to scare you off."

Her features softened. "Jay . . . if you say you see him, then I believe you. It just seems strange . . ."

He'd been working too hard. His claustrophobia must be bothering him. Did the condition have side effects that might cause him to see things?

"You don't believe me, do you?" His expression was as blank as a tinhorn gambler's running a bluff.

No, she didn't believe him, but she couldn't let him see that. "I believe you think you see him—," she began.

He interrupted her, his eyes bright with anger. "Don't try to con me, Patience. I know what I saw."

"I'm not trying to con you," she stammered. "I didn't mean—"

He changed the subject. "I'm going into Fiddle Creek tomorrow morning."

She blinked. "Why? What about the women?"

"They won't work the mine tomorrow; we need fuses and a few other supplies."

"But Jay—"

Before she could answer, he left, slamming the door behind him.

She sank down in a chair, her thoughts troubled. She shouldn't have let him see that she doubted him, but what else could he expect? Her shoulders slumped in despair. She'd depended on Jay, and now he was seeing little men in the mine. . . . She had to help him.

But how? This was something she had no experience with. What if Jay turned violent? What would the shady ladies do? She visualized her crew. Well, led by Moses Malone, they'd probably beat him to a pulp. No man would be a match for that bunch.

She'd heard a sound in the mine today, but after thinking it over, she knew what it was. These mountain winds could blow fiercely sometimes. She'd heard it moaning through the trees. But hearing the wind was different from seeing and talking to someone who wasn't there.

Patience took a deep breath and straightened her shoulders. Tomorrow she would insist that Jay rest, and she'd cook him a good lunch. Suddenly the gold didn't seem so important compared to Jay.

He'd be all right. He had to be.

Chapter Twenty

The next afternoon Jay sent the shady ladies into the mine before taking a gold pan and wandering upstream. He needed some time alone. Might do a little panning for nuggets.

Patience had stood in the door of the dugout watching, but he ignored her. She didn't believe him. Well, that was fine with him.

Thought he was crazy, huh? He'd show her. He'd show them all. Mooney Backus and his thugs, that little runt who called himself a ghost, and Patience. Particularly Patience. Somehow, even though Jay admitted he wasn't good enough for her, he'd expected her to trust him.

He swirled the pan, letting loose gravel wash out while the heavier flakes of gold settled on the bottom. Picking out the scattering of flakes and a couple of nuggets, he dropped them into a drawstring tobacco pouch he'd gotten from an old-timer in Fiddle Creek.

He felt lower than a snake's belly today. For two cents, he'd pack up and leave. Or he would if it weren't for Mooney Backus. He sighed. He was honest enough to admit that Mooney wasn't the only reason he stayed. There were Patience and Wilson. He'd never intended to let it go this far. Although he wouldn't admit it to Gamey, the day seemed a little brighter when he could see Patience and hear her voice. But he'd never let her know how he felt. Couldn't. She was a fine woman, and she deserved better than he could give her.

And some low-down varmint was trying to steal her mine.

In a sudden burst of temper, he picked up a rock and slung it at a pine tree.

He heard snickering and glanced up to see Gamey perched on a limb of a neighboring cottonwood tree, watching him pan for gold.

"You don't seem to be in a good mood this afternoon. I'd guess you let it slip out, didn't ya? Jest couldn't stand it. Bet you had to tell her about me."

"You can relax; she didn't believe me."

"Well, now—" Gamey squinted and scratched his mangy beard— "that's a real shame. For you—not for me."

"Get out of here, Gamey."

"No, not until I help ya."

"You can't help me."

The little man eased carefully down from an overhead branch, dropping to his feet in front of Jay. "Yep, buddy boy, you've got me pegged dead center. I've done told you: no one but you is gonna see me, and no one—not even Moses, though goodness knows I've got an itchy feelin' for that woman—is gonna get their hands on my gold."

Slamming his gold pan to the ground, Jay lit on it with both feet. Trouncing on it, he jumped up and down, venting his pent-up frustrations. Up and down, up and down,

he stomped the pan, mangling the tin and fouling the air
with a string of epithets that made Butch Miller sound like
a choirboy.

He'd had it! Cave-ins, floods, egotistical ghosts, Mooney
Backus threatening to kill him, Patience thinking he was
seeing things, Patience and the gold, Patience and the boy,
Patience, Patience, Patience!

"Leave me alone! You hear me? I don't want to ever see
your face around here again! Torment someone else! *You
hear me? I've had it with you and your nutty ways!*"

Hammering the pan with the heel of his boot, Jay
viciously ground it into the gravel bank. Rage burned out
of control. He pounded the tin with the heel of his boot,
cursing the day he was born.

When a shadow crossed the ground, he glanced up.
Standing beside the stream, Patience had witnessed his fit
of temper. Her baffled gaze shifted from his boots to the
throbbing vein in his neck to his anger-splotched face.

Regaining his composure, he paused, his hiked foot in
midair. "Yes?"

She murmured, "Supper's ready."

Giving the tin one last brutal stomp, he refused to look
at her. "Okay."

She continued to stare at him as if there were something
more that needed to be said. But he wouldn't meet her
stupefied gaze.

"I'll be along in a minute."

"Are you all right?"

"Fine. Never better. First-rate."

She walked away, turning back to look over her shoulder,
frowning.

Muttering under his breath, Jay gave the mangled gold

pan a swift kick, sending it skittering into the stream, and followed her up the hill.

Supper was a tense affair with Jay eating in silence. He still looked angry, but there was something about him that broke her heart. He seemed shamefaced, as if her seeing him pitch that violent tantrum bothered him. Well, it bothered her too.

What had come over him? Jumping up and down and cursing that way. If Wilson had been anywhere within hearing distance—and he probably was—he'd no doubt learned several new words. She'd have to stock up on soap.

What really bothered her was the way Jay had been shouting at someone but there was no one there.

She cut a wedge of dried-apple pie and set it in front of him. "More coffee?"

"Yes, thanks."

She sat down across from him, watching him eat. "Is there anything you want to talk about?"

He raised his eyes and looked at her briefly before shifting his attention back to his pie. "We already talked."

"I see. Anything you want to add?"

"Nope. Subject closed."

He finished his pie and left, and she conquered the desire to throw his plate at the door he had slammed behind him. A reluctant smile curved her lips. Well, she knew what it was to be provoked. Hadn't she flung a pot of dumplings at his head just a few nights ago? So something had provoked Jay. Who and what? She'd made a mistake last night when he'd confided in her about Gamey. Now she had to regain his confidence.

Patience left Wilson trying to braid the cat's tail while she stole a few minutes alone with Jay the following night.

The scene yesterday at the stream still bothered her. Jay was behaving so strangely lately. Even so, he continued to stand by her when it seemed they were fighting a losing battle. Any day now, she expected Moses and the shady ladies to walk out. There was barely enough gold coming out of the mine to pay them a paltry sum at the end of a long week. And the constant interruptions were more than annoying—they were dangerous. Patience was beginning to think they were an indication of something more sinister than just plain bad luck. And now Jay thought he was seeing the ghost.

She made her way across the mountain, shivering in the night wind. If she went to him, he couldn't walk away; he had no place to go. She should never have let him see she didn't believe him. Tonight she would try to regain lost ground. If he didn't trust her, she couldn't help him. Jay needed her, and she had to be there for him.

Pausing in front of Jay's shack, she called softly, "Are you awake?"

A moment later the door opened and he appeared in the doorway. In the background she saw a rosy fire in the fireplace. He frowned when he saw her huddled against the biting wind. "Something wrong?"

"Can I come in?"

Standing aside, he allowed her to enter.

Hurrying to the fire, she undid her scarf, permitting her hair to fall unrestricted around her shoulders.

She'd seen the way he had looked at her the other night

231

when her hair was down. The decision to wear it loose tonight had seemed good at the time, but now she had her doubts, considering the way he stared at her, like a thirsty man seeing a stream of fresh water.

Something inside her stirred, responding to the look in his eyes. He was older than she was, and she had an idea what he was thinking: that he was too old for her with nothing to offer a woman. Somehow, she had to change his mind.

Jay broke the silence. "Where's Wilson?"

"Braiding Jellybean's tail."

"How can he do that?"

She shrugged. "Not easily, but it keeps him occupied. How was your trip to Fiddle Creek?"

He busied himself stacking dishes. "Routine."

She wondered what the unexpected trip was really about; she found a box of fuses in the cellar when she'd gone for another jar of pickles, so obviously he hadn't been completely honest about his reason for going. Had he been in Fiddle Creek asking questions? trying to gain solid evidence that someone was trying to jump her claim?

Lifting her hands to the fire, she warmed her fingers. "It's so cold. Jay. I worry about you here, alone in this drafty shack."

He stooped and put another stick of wood on the fire. "I'm thinking it's time I went back to Denver City."

"Why? We need you here."

He shrugged. "I should have left sooner, but I thought you'd give up and see reason. I don't know, P; seems like I have to get away, regain my perspective."

"Are you leaving because of me?" She almost whispered the words.

"That's part of it. Seems like everything I do these days is because of you."

Patience caught her breath. She'd never been alone with a man like this. What would Lily and Mary and Harper and Ruth say? She could just imagine. He stepped closer to the fire, and she turned to face him, aware of the isolation of the cabin. She shouldn't have come. What had she been thinking?

Suddenly—she didn't know how—she was in his arms and he was holding her close. She knew she should pull away, but somehow she couldn't make the effort to move.

"This is crazy," he murmured, but he didn't try to break the embrace. Stroking her hair gently, he said softly, "I was thinking about the look on your face today when you found me at the stream."

She held him tightly, feeling a spurt of alarm. "Jay, what was that all about? Everyone loses their temper at times, but the incident today was more than a simple fit of anger."

"Gamey O'Keefe."

"Jay," she complained, "we're not going to start that again!"

"All right, don't believe me," he said, apparently willing to let it go for now. "What brings you out this time of night?"

Sighing, she rested her head on his shoulder, absently fingering the woolen fabric of his shirt. She felt surreal, as if being in his arms was a dream—one she didn't want to awaken from. "If it's true, why can't I see him? After all, I own the mine. If he wants to frighten someone, why not frighten me?"

She didn't want to talk about the ghost, but Jay seemed determined to have his say. He lowered his face in her hair, whispering. "Maybe he doesn't like to provoke beautiful women."

Her eyes drifted closed, relishing his nearness. It felt so right to be in his arms—*he* was so right for her. Why couldn't he see that? "Does he say why he appears only to you?"

"Of course not; he wants me to believe that he's a ghost, but I don't. What I believe is that he's been sent here to convince me that someone will never let us work the mine. Once you leave, they'll move in and stake a claim."

She held him tightly, wanting desperately to believe him, even though the thought of someone trying to trick her out of the mine was distressing. If this . . . *man* truly did exist, her future looked dim indeed.

She'd had enough talk of the mine and ghosts for tonight. The gold was important, but she had something else on her mind. Tilting her head back, she looked deeply into his eyes. "Do you ever think of me?"

He shifted. "What kind of question is that? We were talking about ghosts."

"But we're not now. We're talking about you . . . and me. . . ." She smiled up at him. "Do you ever think of me?" Some days she thought of nothing but him.

"I'm thinking of you right now."

"Then you feel the attraction too?" She was both relieved and frightened by the revelation. If he felt the same magnetic pull that continually drew her, there might be hope. . . .

"Yes, I feel it," he admitted. His voice dropped to a low, husky timbre. "I don't want this to happen, Patience. I'm wrong for you."

"Why are you so afraid of your feelings?" she asked. She wasn't afraid of hers. She raced to embrace them.

"I don't want to fall in love again, Patience. I have nothing to offer a woman."

She gazed up at him, aware of how hard he was fighting the way he felt. "Don't you think that's for the woman to decide?"

"No, it's what I've decided, and I don't want to complicate matters between me and you. You're young, beautiful, alive. You need a man who will match your spirit, not an ex-gambler who can't pay off his debt."

"I've found that man."

"You're young and impressionable, Patience. You know nothing about me."

"Then tell me about you, Jay Longer. What are these thoughts you find so frightening?"

"They're foolish thoughts, and I'm a fool for thinking them."

"There's nothing foolish about you," she assured him.

He hesitated, and then said softly, "At night, before I drift off, I find myself wondering why you like sweet potatoes so much—or questioning your love affair with pickle sandwiches."

Laughing, she contentedly nestled deeper against the solid wall of his chest. He smelled of woodsmoke and mountain air. "I was expecting to hear something a little more romantic."

"That wasn't romantic enough?"

"No. Try again."

"I'm not very good with romance." He held her closer. "What do you want me to say?"

"Tell me what's in your heart."

"I can't . . . not now, Patience. Maybe never—"

She laid her finger across his lips. "Then tell me the sort

of things a man might say to a woman when he loves her
so much he can think of nothing else."

His mouth moved to the nape of her neck, lingering hesitantly. "If I were to say such things, let alone think them,
I would be twice a fool," he confessed.

Eyes drifting shut, Patience held him close. The fire
crackled, swathing them in a warm cocoon. "Then tell me
what is in your heart."

"I wonder how you make your hair smell so good, or
why your eyes turn the color of warm honey when you
smile," he whispered. His breath fell softly upon her ear.

"Hey! There you are!"

Wilson's voice jerked them back to sanity. Patience had
not heard the door open.

The boy stood in the doorway, holding his cat. "What're
you doing?"

Springing apart, Patience tidied her hair, disappointed, but
knowing the interruption was for the best. What must Jay
Longer think of her, throwing herself at him like this? Her
cheeks flamed. "It's late." She hurriedly tied the scarf
around her hair. "I have to go."

Brushing past Jay, Patience pointed Wilson back out the
doorway. "What are you doing out at this hour of the
night?"

On the way back to the dugout Patience walked so fast
Wilson struggled to keep up.

"P?"

"What?"

"Are you mad at me?"

"No, of course not. What makes you think so?"

"The way you're walking, like Moses when she's working
on a temper fit."

Patience stopped so abruptly, Wilson bumped into her. "I do not walk like Moses."

"Well, when she's upset about something, she steps out fast, like that. You upset about something, P?"

"No, Wilson. I am not upset about anything."

She had behaved in a way she would have trouble explaining to her friends back in Denver City. Going to a man's cabin this time of night with her hair down and throwing herself at him like a common hussy. She could only pray the others would never learn of her bold behavior. And then to have Wilson walk in on them . . .

She walked slower now, letting Wilson keep up with her.

"P?"

"Yes?"

"Did Jay decide to marry us?"

"He didn't say anything about it."

Wilson sighed. "Well, I wish he'd hurry up. Then he could move in with us instead of staying in that cabin."

Patience's face burned. "I'm not sure he wants us."

Wilson stopped dead still. "Not want us? Of course he does. I'll talk to him."

Patience stopped, goaded beyond endurance. "You listen to me, Wilson. If you ever talk to Jay Longer again about marrying me, I'll . . . I'll . . ."

"You'll what?" he asked, interested.

"I don't know, but I'll think of something."

They walked on in silence, with Patience remembering the natural feel of Jay's arms around her. Whether he admitted it or not, they belonged together. Somehow *she* had to convince him of that. Not Wilson.

Chapter Twenty-One

Early the next morning, on his way to fetch Moses and the shady ladies, Jay decided to drop by Fiddle Creek and see if the old whittler Chappy was around.

The air was fragrant with the scent of pines, the sky a pearl gray, the scattering of fluffy clouds touched with peach glow from the searching rays of the as-yet-unseen sun. Jay paused to enjoy the scene. Seemed like he had learned to appreciate the mountains. The cold didn't bother him the way it used to.

He thought of Patience, the way she had felt in his arms last night, the scent of her hair. The man who won her would be lucky. He turned his face resolutely toward Fiddle Creek. He'd give all he owned if he could be the one. Realizing the turn of his thoughts, he laughed bitterly.

All he owned? A horse and saddle? Not much to offer a woman. A rich man he wasn't, and unlikely to become one. One thing he could do for her: find out who was behind the problems at the mine.

He rounded a stand of scrub pine and jerked to a halt. Down the trail a ways stood the "ghost" of the Mule Head in earnest conversation with a tall, burly man with a bushy black beard and clothes as disreputable as Jay's had been when he was in disguise.

Jay was too far away to hear what they were saying, but the big man was doing most of the talking. Gamey's ghost didn't seem all that happy, and Jay got the impression they might be disagreeing about something.

The two men separated and Jay felt torn, but he decided to follow the bigger man. The old miner was probably going back to the mine, using a different entrance than the main one by the dugout. But Jay lost the man he was following because he didn't want to get close enough to be seen.

In Fiddle Creek he bought two cups of coffee and carried them outside to where Chappy had already taken his post outside the mercantile.

"Thankee." Chappy took the hot coffee. "What brings you to town so early?"

"Wanted to talk to you."

Chappy's expression didn't change. "About what?"

"About a man—tall, broad shoulders, black beard, wears an old battered hat and a shirt that used to be blue and gray, far as I can tell."

Chappy took a drink of coffee. "Silas Tucker."

"What do you know about him?"

"Worst claim jumper in these parts. Supposed to have a nose for gold. Thinks there's a mother lode in the Mule Head."

"Mother lode?"

"Yep. Don't know if it's so or not, but Tucker thinks it is."

Jay nodded. "Tell me about a little old miner who is pretending to be the ghost of Gamey O'Keefe."

Chapped grinned reluctantly. "Frank Innis. Tucker's

240

paying him to be the ghost. Promised him a cut of the gold if he can run the woman off. Frank ain't up to working much anymore. Was a good one in his day, but got stove-up in a cave-in a few years back. You've seen him?"

"Yeah, but no one else has."

Chappy turned serious. "Frank's all right. He may work for Tucker, but he's solid."

"Trying to take a mine away from a woman doesn't seem too solid to me."

Chappy shook his head. "A man will do funny things when he's hungry enough, but give Frank a chance. He'll do what he thinks is right."

Jay didn't argue, but he had his doubts. At least he'd gotten what he came for. "Thanks, Chappy." He held out his hand. "Appreciate it." He took a couple of steps away and turned back. "How come you didn't tell me all this before?"

Chappy smiled. "You never asked."

On his way out of town Jay saw Silas Tucker talking to a bunch of men. Working his way around behind the livery stable so he could get closer, he listened in growing anger as Tucker outlined the plan to scare Patience into leaving.

He looked up at the sun. Getting late. He still had to collect Moses and her crew, but now he knew what he was up against. He'd put a spoke in their plans if it was possible. Silas Tucker and Frank Innis weren't going to cheat Patience. He wouldn't let them.

He knew the truth now. This so-called ghost was Frank Innis. Just like he suspected, Gamey O'Keefe was dead and gone or never even existed. The problems with the mine were human problems.

But the man pretending to be Gamey's ghost hadn't

caught on yet. He showed up the next day right on sched-
ule, as if he had been waiting for Jay to come. "I know
where that gold is. Know exactly—could take ya there in
a minute, but I won't."

Jay grunted, ignoring the man as he set a charge.

"Has anyone ever told you that you're bullheaded?"

Jay shot him a penetrating glance. "Give it up."

"Never." He rolled his eyes and studied the roof of the
shaft. "It's my mine, ya know."

"I believe you've mentioned that, Frank."

Disbelief crossed the man's face. He sat up halfway, eyeing
Jay. "Frank?"

Turning, Jay smiled. "Frank Innis, isn't it?"

The miner's eyes narrowed. "Don't know what yore
talkin' about. Name's Gamey O'Keefe."

Leaning on the shovel handle, Jay surveyed the imposter
coldly. "That's not what some say. Some say you and Silas
Tucker are in cahoots. You're working for Silas to scare
Patience—and me—out of this mine. Rumor is, Tucker's
promised you a hefty cut if you stick around long enough
to get the job done."

The old man paled. "You're talkin' crazy. I never heard
of Tucker—I've been dead over thirty years."

"You're about as dead as I am." Jay picked up a pick and
rammed it into the shale wall. "How much gold do you
suppose is in the Mule Head?"

"In the Mule Head?"

"How much gold is in here?"

The miner squinted up at him. "Is this here a trick question?"

"Just curious. How much gold is actually in the mine?"

"A lot. The mother lode. Pay dirt. Tons."

"And you know where it is."

"Exactly."

"How would you know that, Frank?"

"I've always known where the gold is—know just where
to find it, but someone else always owned the claim. You
know any reason why I should tell someone else how to
find my gold?"

Jay eyed him in speculation. At least he had stopped
claiming to be a ghost for the present. Probably because
finding out that Jay knew his real name had shocked him
into admitting the truth.

"I'm betting you and Tucker would own the claim right
now if you'd known the old prospector had died."

"She got a bill of sale? Ya know if it's held under purchase
it has to be under a bill of sale and 'certified by two distin-
guished persons, honorable folks, as to the genuineness of
the signature and the consideration given.' "

"She's got all she needs. Are you saying you and Tucker
could find 'two honorable folks' to sign anything for you?
Doesn't seem likely to me."

Frank looked offended. "This mine can't be more'n a
hunnert square feet, and a 'jury of five persons shall decide
any question arisin' under the previous article.' "

"You memorized it all, didn't you? Why—since you
don't have a mine? Or did you think the information might
come in handy in claim jumping?"

"And last but not least, 'soon as there is enough water for
workin' a claim, *five days' absence* from said claim, except in
case of sickness, accident, or reasonable excuse shall forfeit
the property.' "

"So if you can scare Patience into leaving for more than
five days, you and Tucker are home free. That your game?

What if Patience offered to cut you in on the profits? Give you more than Tucker ever dreamed of giving you?"

The old man didn't flinch. "Cain't negotiate if I don't know who or what yore talkin' about."

Jay shook his head. The old coot was loyal—he'd give him that. "What good is the gold if nobody can have it?"

"Ain't worth a ball of spit," Frank conceded.

"It could make some people's lives a lot easier," Jay said, thinking of Patience, Wilson, and the girls in Denver City. They desperately needed the money. Patience couldn't last much more than a week at the rate they were going—Moses and the women were getting antsy about missed pay.

"Nobody ever made my life easy." The little man started backing up, stepping deeper into the shaft.

"Give it some thought," Jay called. "Do something nice for once—*Frank.*"

"Honest, Patience! I *heard* him! He was talking to somebody, but when I asked him who he was talking to, he said, 'Nobody, and stop asking so many questions, Wilson!' Then he walked off real mad-like."

Patience ladled stew onto Wilson's plate, finding it increasingly difficult to defend Jay's odd behavior. She had caught him on several occasions mumbling, talking out loud, arguing with thin air. And his ongoing obsession about Gamey O'Keefe was getting serious. Perhaps she should insist he see a doctor next time one passed through Fiddle Creek.

"Maybe he was talking to himself—people do sometimes," she offered.

"They talk *bad* to themselves?"

"Sometimes," she acknowledged. "Has Jay been talking bad in front of you?"

Wilson nodded. "Real bad—but he didn't know I heard him."

Patience frowned. "Where were you?"

"I wasn't hiding or anything," Wilson upheld. "I was just sitting on a ledge eating a biscuit when I heard him start yelling and cussing, waving his shovel in the air and saying, 'Get away, you—' "

Patience whirled on him sternly.

"I didn't say it!"

"You'd better not!"

"Well, *he* said it, anyway." Wilson halfheartedly drew a trail through his stew. "He couldn't have meant for *me* to get away because he didn't know I was even there, and he's never called me that, no matter how mad he gets."

"Where were you when you heard this?"

"Sitting on a ledge—" Wilson stopped.

Patience's hand shot to her hip. "In the *mine?*"

Developing an unusual preoccupation with his meal, Wilson started spooning stew, cramming his mouth so full an answer would be rude.

"Wilson, you are to stay *out* of the mine."

He stared back at her, cheeks round as a chipmunk's.

"The women are blasting in there now, and it's extremely dangerous!"

Nodding, he chewed emphatically.

Unfolding her napkin, she sighed. "In regard to Jay's odd behavior, I wouldn't worry. He has a lot on his mind lately—and we have not said grace yet. Will you bless the food, please?"

Swallowing, Wilson bowed his head and scrunched his eyes tightly shut. "Please help us, God. We're in big trouble."

Patience slid him a sideways glance.

"And thank you for this good, nutritious stew. Even though we don't have any meat, carrots and onions are better than beans any day. Amen."

"Amen," Patience echoed.

Wilson reached for his spoon. "We're not doing so well, huh, Patience? Moses is shouting a lot lately because of all the accidents."

The third cave-in in a week happened early this morning, and the women had lost another day's work clearing the shaft. Patience thought she must have the worst luck in the world. Unless . . .

She shook Jay's strange wanderings away. "No, I'm afraid we're not, Wilson."

The boy's features turned solemn. "Do we have to go to Denver City?"

"It's possible. We have no money, and we're not mining enough gold to pay wages. I'm going to be honest; we're down to needing a miracle, Wilson."

"But I don't want to go to Denver City. I like it here."

"I know. I don't want to go either, but we have to do what's best for your welfare." She leaned closer. "I can't take care of you here, Wilson. Not unless the mine starts producing."

"If we go to Denver City, can I take my animals?"

She shook her head, swallowing around the knot suddenly forming at the back of her throat. "I'm sorry—your animals wouldn't be happy there, Wilson. This is their home."

Tears formed in the young boy's eyes. "What'll happen to

Jay? He's ours now. He doesn't have anybody, and we love him."

Sighing, Patience pushed her plate aside. "I don't know about Jay." She wished she did. Oh, he'd go back to Denver City—that's where his job was—but she wasn't sure she'd see much of him after that. He'd retreat into an impenetrable shell and—

"Why is he acting so *nutty?*"

"Wilson, can I tell you something?" He suddenly seemed like the old, wise-beyond-his-years Wilson in whom she'd always been able to confide, and right now she badly needed a confidant.

"Certainly. May I have more stew, please?"

"Yes, you may, and I'm very proud of you. Your language has improved considerably."

"I'm working on my behavior," he divulged. "And I'm trying to teach Butch the proper way to express himself without making Teacher blush." He took a swallow of milk. "I'm embarrassed for him sometimes, but he just won't learn."

"Where are that boy's parents?" Patience mused, more rhetorically than not.

"Miss Perkins says she thinks he's being raised by wolves." He looked up from his plate. "Could that happen?"

"No. Miss Perkins was only teasing."

"Oh." He took another sip of milk, carefully wiping the white mustache rimming his upper lip. "What did you want to tell me?"

"You have to promise not to say anything to anyone about this."

"Who would I tell? Hardly anybody ever tells me anything."

"I sure don't want you telling Jay."

Wilson quickly took another drink of milk.

"Jay says he's seen Gamey O'Keefe." She absently ladled carrots and onions onto Wilson's plate, watching his reaction.

He peered back at her questioningly.

"The ghost—Jay says he's seen the ghost," Patience repeated, hoping he would think the notion ridiculous.

"Did he like him?"

"Wilson! That's insane. There's no such thing as a ghost!"

"Who said?"

"Everybody *says.*"

"Not everyone. I heard Moses and the other women talking, and they believe there's a ghost—though they've never seen him. But Moses said they're getting tired of him causing all these cave-ins and stuff."

"When did they say that?"

"Today." His eyes lowered back to his plate. "When I . . . *wasn't* in the mine."

Her heart sank. If Moses walked out, she was doomed. She'd have no other choice but to return empty-handed to Denver City. Then what? She couldn't impose on Pastor Siddons and his wife much longer, and neither could the other single women.

"I'm so confused. I don't know what to believe. The number of accidents and cave-ins is unusual. How much bad luck can one person have?"

"Jay said he saw the ghost, didn't he?" Wilson spoke as though the matter were settled.

"He says he has, and on more than one occasion."

Wilson nodded gravely. "Maybe Jay just needs someone to love him, huh, P? Then he won't be seeing ghosts."

She smiled. "Maybe so." She could love him. Very easily, if he would permit it. She had walked away from him that night in his cabin, but she couldn't stop thinking about him.

"We love him, don't we?"

Patience looked away. "Your stew's getting cold."

"But we do love him, huh? I won't tell him if you don't want me to. Honest."

"Yes, we love him," she conceded.

"A lot."

She nodded, fighting back tears, and started to clear the table. "A whole lot."

"Wilson and I are worried about you."

Jay glanced up when Patience kneeled beside him the next morning. Icy water bubbled in the stream.

"He overheard you yesterday—you have to be more careful. Granted, everyone talks to themselves on occasion but—"

"He overheard me what?"

"Talking to yourself."

He turned to face her, carefully placing the gold pan on the bank. "I wasn't talking to myself."

"He heard you."

"He heard me talking to Frank Innis, the so-called ghost of the gold mine." He got to his feet, pulling her up off the cold ground.

She shivered. Seemed like it was colder here close to the creek.

He motioned toward a ledge of rock, waiting to speak until she was seated. "Listen, Patience. I went into town yesterday and asked some questions. What I found out was more or less what I had expected."

She watched him, wanting to believe. He seemed so

earnest. . . . He sat down beside her, and she fought an urge to reach out and smooth back his hair, the way she did Wilson's sometimes. Her heart ached for him. He'd worked so hard. Too hard. Maybe there *was* a curse on the mine and it was making Jay sick.

"Hear me out—I'm not losing my mind. I know what's going on. The ghost isn't a ghost at all, just like we've always known. His name is Frank Innis, and he works for a man by the name of Silas Tucker."

"Frank Innis, Silas Tucker," she murmured, trying to speak calmly. "That's interesting. . . ."

"Chappy says they're trying to convince you and everyone else the mine is haunted so you'll give it up."

"But, Jay, everyone in Fiddle Creek *already* thinks the mine is haunted. That's why they won't work here. If they know it's a scam, then they'll change their minds and come work for us after all."

"No. No, they won't, Patience. That's the problem. I'm the only one who has seen the ghost of Gamey O'Keefe. He doesn't show up in town. I just happened to see 'Gamey' and Tucker meeting down the mountain a ways, and since I'd seen Frank pretending to be Gamey, I went on into town and dug into Tucker's background."

"And what did you find out?" Humor him. That's all she could do.

"I learned he has a sidekick named Frank Innis, who fits the description of the man I'd seen in the mine, and the sidekick hasn't been around for a while. I overheard Tucker bragging that after you give up, he knows how to rid the mine of the ghost. That's what he's planning. Something to fool people into believing he's gotten rid of Gamey O'Keefe. It will work too. Can't you see that?"

Patience watched him, sure he believed what he was saying but unable to accept the strange tale herself. "Why does he just appear to you, Jay? I'm the one he's trying to scare off. Why doesn't he show himself to me?"

"They've got that all figured out. Get rid of me, and you won't have a crew. Without a crew, you'll have to give up. And if no one else sees him, then, when I try to tell the truth, I won't be able to get anyone to believe me. They'll think I'm seeing things; Gamey's ghost has got to me."

That was so close to what she was thinking, it startled her into letting him see her doubt. She tried to recover, but he'd caught her expression.

He drew back, the excitement dying from his eyes. "See? Even you don't believe me. You think I'm losing my mind."

"I didn't say that."

"You didn't have to. It's there in your face for me to see. You don't believe I've seen him, do you?"

"Of course, if you say so." She knew he wouldn't be convinced by the weakness of her response and tried desperately to think of something to restore his pride, but he moved away from her.

"All right, that does it. I want you to go back to Denver City until I can get the mine producing. Take the boy with you. I'll expose those two thieves and hire a crew, but I want you out of the way in case things get rough."

She shook her head. "I'll not leave you alone. If you're right on this, why would you expect me to run? It's my mine too, and my future that's at stake. I'm not leaving."

"Patience—"

"I'm *not leaving.*"

He sprang to his feet. "Of all the stubborn, hardheaded women . . ."

She stood up also, facing him. "Calling me names won't help. Are you going to *make* me go back?"

He stared at her, his expression frustrated. "I can't *make* you do anything you don't want to do, but you owe it to the boy to put his welfare first."

"I *am* putting his welfare first. That's exactly what I'm doing, and you know it. How dare you talk to me like that!"

That was why she clung to the mine in the first place—for Wilson and the others. She hadn't been this stubborn and endured so much for self-interest. The Mule Head was their only hope for a bright future—for all of them.

"I know that look on your face," Jay fumed. "You're digging your heels in, as stubborn as a mule. Too contrary to admit you're wrong."

"I'm not wrong." Patience's temper flared, hotter than a pine-knot torch. "The gold is there. I can't just walk away from it."

"Maybe you can't, but I can." Jay's face flushed with sudden rage. "I've had enough. Why should I stay here, working my fingers to the bone, when you have the faith of . . . of . . ."

"I'm *trying* to believe you," Patience said, making an effort to curb her temper. "But be fair. No one but you has seen that man."

He threw up his hands. "Have it your way. There is no Frank Innis or Silas Tucker. I'm a raving lunatic, and you can run the mine by yourself. Well, be my guest, honey. I've had enough."

He stalked off, leaving her to stare after him. She should have hung on to her temper. Should never have crossed him. What if he had been telling the truth, and she had refused to believe him? What would she do if he didn't come back?

Patience opened the dugout door and looked out. Jay hadn't come to supper tonight, although she had cooked his favorite: panfried catfish that Wilson had caught in the cool sparkling waters of the little creek.

Closing the door, she cleared away the remains of the meal and washed the dishes. After Wilson lay sleeping in front of the fire, she sat in the old rocking chair, staring into the flames, reliving their argument. What would she do for a crew? If Jay wasn't here to guard the women, they wouldn't be allowed to work.

Why had she let him walk away? It felt like he had ripped her heart out and taken it with him. What would she do if he never came back? She had grown so used to having him around, had looked forward to seeing him every day.

She sat before the fire until the flames burned low and the creeping cold drove her to her bed. Wrapped in a blanket, she lay staring into the smoldering coals, seeing Jay Longer in the flickering shadows, until she cried herself to sleep.

Chapter Twenty-Two

Patience waited at the mine entrance before sunup with a lump of lead for a heart. Would he come? Wilson was outside, feeding his animals, completely oblivious to the storm raging inside her.

She watched the trail, ears straining to hear the approach of the shady ladies. When she first heard them coming, she couldn't believe her ears. They plodded up the trail, Moses in the lead, Jay trailing along behind. Patience sank down on a nearby boulder, her knees too weak to support her.

He glanced at her and then looked away. Moses and the other women walked past her into the mine.

Patience waited until Jay stopped in front of her, not smiling. She wet her lips. "You came back."

"Yeah."

"I was afraid you wouldn't."

"If I had any sense, I'd be halfway to Denver City by now."

"I'm glad you stayed. I'm sorry. I shouldn't have doubted you."

He looked away. "I have to get to work."

She watched him walk away, but the sun shone in her world again. She'd fix him a good dinner. If the way to a man's heart was through his stomach, Jay Longer wouldn't know what hit him.

"Please, God," she breathed, "don't let anything else go wrong."

Later that morning, a fracas broke out in front of the mine, bringing Patience running. Wilson left his beloved animals to join the uproar. The shady ladies milled around, making more noise than a flock of hens. One convict, looking more groggy than usual, staggered around in circles, muttering something about wanting to take a pickax handle to that ghost.

Moses stood, arms akimbo, dark brows drawn together, lips set in a bitter line. As Patience joined them, she glared in her direction. "We quit!"

"Quit? You can't quit, Moses!"

"*Quit.*" Moses sported an angry bruise between her eyes.

This morning's incident was the last straw. Someone had rigged the women's picks so that when they swung them the heads flew off and hit them squarely between the eyes. One of the ladies had been knocked cold and hadn't come around for a full ten minutes.

"I know it's hard to work with all these accidents, but if you'll be patient just a little longer—" Patience looked to Jay for support.

He looked the other way, stubbornness etched on his stoic features.

The shady ladies picked up their shovels and walked off with Moses, mumbling something about there not being enough gold in Colorado to put up with this.

Patience watched them leave, realizing what it meant. There wasn't a man, woman, or child left willing to work the Mule Head.

Trying not to cry, she turned to Jay. "Shouldn't you walk them to the prison camp?"

"I'll follow them back. Are you all right?"

Dropping her face to her hands, Patience whirled and ran to the dugout. She sank down at the kitchen table, letting the tears flow. How could he ask her if she was all right? He had stood there and said nothing as the women walked away. Didn't he *care* they had no other help to work the mine?

Where are you, God? He'd promised to be there in time of need. Why didn't he do something about all of these accidents? She raised her head, wiping away tears. They couldn't all be accidents. Not *all* of the pick heads coming loose at once. One, maybe, but not all of them at the same time. Jay was so sure someone was trying to drive them away. Had he been right all along?

Her heart hardened with resolve. No one was going to drive her away from what was rightfully hers. She would fight as long as she had breath.

Forgetting the convicts, Jay pitched the shovel aside and angrily strode toward the mine, with no thought of his phobia. For the first time in a long time, rage blinded him. He didn't care about the gold. Mooney Backus could do whatever he wanted to him, but without the gold Patience was sunk. She wasn't chasing luxury; she was fighting for survival. And he was going to fight Frank Innis to the death, if that's what it took.

Snatching up the lantern, he entered the mine, shouting, "Frank! Show yourself!"

A bat darted up and away, vanishing into the darkness. "Frank!"

Frank . . . Frank . . . Frank echoed back.

Moving deeper into the shaft, Jay's eyes searched the darkness. "Enough's enough!"

Overhead, timbers snapped and splintered down. Jumping aside, Jay avoided the flying debris.

"Cut it out, Frank! For once in your life fight like a man!"

Water rushed through the mine. Grasping the wall, Jay struggled to keep his balance. A whirlpool swirled around his thighs. The shaft plunged into darkness as the lantern fell from his hand and the current swiftly carried it away.

He could feel his lungs closing. Struggling for breath, he held tight to the sides of the ledge. "If you want to fight someone, fight me. Let Patience have the gold. You've lived your life—she's young, got most of her life ahead of her. She needs the means to take care of the boy and three other women who don't have a chance in this world without that gold. This plan of yours and Tucker's won't work. I'll personally dog you for the rest of my life, Frank. That's a promise!"

An explosion rocked the mine, splintering rock and pitching timbers through the air.

The thought hit him: He was going to die. This was how his life would end, alone in a black hole. He should have enough sense to be afraid, but he wasn't. Blackness closed around him, filling his senses, squeezing the life from his lungs.

Walls collapsed and buckled.

Racked by coughing spasms, Jay clung to the wall. Dust

fouled the air, and a thick grit filled his mouth and stung his eyes. The air supply in the narrow chamber dwindled. "You're evil, Frank," he choked out. "You can kill me, but you won't kill her spirit. She'll stay and fight . . ."

A sheet of fire burst overhead. Angry flames licked across the ceiling, searing the timbers.

Strangling, Jay struggled for breath. And for life. Plowing through the rising water, he blindly felt his way back through the shaft. He didn't want to die. The realization hit him hard. If he died, Patience would have no one.

She needed him.

And he needed her.

He didn't want to die. The revelation was exhilarating and sobering. The meaning of life, which he had forgotten, suddenly came back. Wallowing in self-pity was for cowards. It took guts to stand up and fight back.

The ground vibrated beneath his feet. He inched along the shaft wall and edged toward the entrance.

Timbers shattered; dirt and shale hurled through the air. The tunnel became a living, roaring nightmare.

Stumbling out of the shaft, he fell to the ground, gasping for breath, only seconds before the mine entrance violently collapsed shut.

Patience raced for the mine, heart in her throat, when she heard the roar of an explosion. A big explosion. Much bigger than Jay or the shady ladies ever set off. Dust and rocks blasted through the mouth of the mine. The crash of falling debris boomed like cannon fire.

Wilson, white-faced, came running. "Jay! Where's Jay?"

Patience saw him lying facedown a few feet from the shaft. She and Wilson caught him by the arms, pulling him away from the mine as another explosion rocked the earth.

"Wilson, bring water. Hurry."

She knelt beside Jay, her fingers groping for a pulse. *Dear God, let him be all right.*

 ⌒

Jay felt a cool cloth on his face. P was softly calling his name. She tenderly dabbed the wet cloth back and forth over his battered face.

"Jay . . . please . . . wake up. Please . . . Jay."

Cracking one eye open, he scowled. "What for?"

With a sob of relief, Patience dropped her head to his chest, hugging him tightly around the waist. "I thought you were dead."

He struggled to sit up, massaging the knot on the back of his head. "I thought I was too."

She lifted the hem of her apron and wiped fresh tears, then glared at him. "You scared the life out of me!"

Getting to his feet slowly, he knocked the dust off his denims, grimly surveying the blocked entrance to the mine. "I can assure you, this wasn't my idea."

"Oh, Jay!" She turned to survey the damage. "Not *again!*"

Reaching for his hat, he dusted it off before settling it back on his head. "Are you convinced now that we're fighting a losing battle?"

Whirling, she grasped the front of his shirt, catching him off balance. "We *can't* let those evil, claim-jumping thugs beat us!"

Gently loosening her hands, he said quietly, "They already have, Patience. Face it."

Her face crumbled. "But what will I do? I have no money—nothing for Wilson . . . "

His eyes softened. "Patience, it's over. Moses just quit and took her crew with her. We've dug that shaft out too many times to do it again. We don't have enough funds to buy fuses and dynamite, and we couldn't hire another crew if our lives depended on it."

She gazed back at him, defeat shadowing her eyes. "Wilson's and my life do depend on it."

"No, they don't." Taking her by the shoulders, he made her look at him. "I'm not a quitter, but I know when I'm beat. You and I sure can't dig that shaft out again. We're beat. Men like Frank Innis and Silas Tucker are never going to let anyone get that gold."

"But—"

"No *but*s. You're not going to talk me out of this. I'm taking you back to Denver City. You don't belong here. You deserve to sleep in a warm bed, take decent baths, and go to sleep with a full belly every night. You need pretty clothes and proper suitors." His eyes gentled. "You need a husband, Patience—one who can give you all you deserve."

"But the gold would pay off your gambling debts."

A muscle flexed in his shadowed jaw. "We don't have the gold; we never will."

Meeting his eyes, she bit back tears. "What about us?" He tried to look away but she wouldn't let him. "What about *us?* You can't deny there's something between us—something incredibly special, Jay. You can't just walk away from me and Wilson—"

Pain shot through him. Five years dropped away, and he was losing the one he loved again. "There is no *us,* Patience. I thought you understood that."

"No," she whispered. "I didn't understand that."

He gently broke the embrace. "I worked your mine. That's all I promised."

"Yes," she said brokenly, "that is all you promised."

The hurt he saw in her eyes cut him deeper than any knife could, but he wasn't the man for her. She deserved more than a loser unable to pay his gambling debts, a man who would be hounded or shot, depending on how much he could come up with.

Tears rolled down her cheeks.

"Don't start that," he warned. "We gave it our best shot, and we lost. I have to see if Moses and the other women made it back to the prison. It's my obligation. If they decided to run, that's also my obligation."

"And I'm *not* your obligation." Before he could answer she whirled and walked off.

He watched her climb the hill to the dugout, her small frame buffeted by the cold wind, and he wanted to stop her, hold her, kiss her until the hurt left her. But he knew he couldn't. Right now she felt wounded and betrayed, but someday she would understand what he'd just done. She would realize that he loved her enough to set her free.

Hot tears formed in his eyes, and he self-consciously wiped at the moisture, mentally castigating his weakness.

Someday, she'd thank him.

The thought didn't cheer him the way it should. He didn't want her thanks. He wanted her beside him, in his arms. He could close his eyes and smell the sweet wildflower fragrance of her hair, see the way her eyes sparked with laughter.

He stumbled over a loose rock, almost falling. She only thought she loved him. Sheltered by life in the orphanage, she had no experience with the relationship between a man and a woman. She'd find someone her own age. Someone who could give her the kind of life she deserved.

The thought almost choked him. He couldn't bear thinking about Patience in another man's arms. How could he walk away? But for her sake, he had no choice.

She would go back to Denver City and make a life. He'd see her from a distance—but he'd keep that distance. That was the problem now; he'd let down his guard.

But never again. *Never* again.

Chapter Twenty-Three

W hat time is it?"

"Ten minutes later than the last time you asked." Chappy held the miniature hummingbird he was carving up to the light. Thick clouds formed a low-hanging, pewter-colored ridge in the west. "You got it bad, haven't you, son?"

Perched on the hitching rail, Jay watched loaded wagons moving up and down the street. Oh, he had it bad, all right. Once his anger cooled, he realized that he couldn't walk away; Patience and Wilson were his life now. He'd given himself quite a talking-to back at the mine, but the walk down the mountain had done a lot to clear his thinking.

Yes, he was too old for her, and no, he wasn't good enough—probably never would be—but he loved her, and he wasn't going to let any other man have her. He'd let down his guard, but God had turned that into a blessing. All his doubts and insecurities had hardened into resolve. Patience belonged to him, and he wasn't planning to give her up.

Trouble was, he didn't know how to tell her. *How do you tell a woman that you've fallen in love with her against every deter-*

*mination not to, and that you're not a prize catch for any woman,
but that you'll gladly spend the rest of your life taking care of her
and the boy—if she'll have you?*

He'd work night and day to pay off his gambling debt and
get his life back in order—if she would forgive him for the
way he had acted. And if God would forgive him for the
last five years of bitterness and blaming his ills on everybody
but the man responsible for his misery: Jay Longer. All he
had to do was ask.

His blood raced with expectancy when he thought of
Patience. He missed her: the touch of her hand, her smile,
the sound of her voice. A foreign feeling, to be sure, but
one he couldn't deny.

"Gonna marry her?"

"If she'll have me."

"Unless I miss my bet, she will." Wood chips from
Chappy's knife flew to a scattered pile at his feet. "You
never talked much about yourself. Where'd you say you
come from?"

"Phoenix."

"Phoenix, huh?" Chappy paused, brushing the shavings
off his lap. "Suppose you got family there?"

"Some. Sister, father."

"Mother?"

"She died in '59."

"Sorry to hear it. Your pa in good health?"

"I haven't seen my father in a while, but I suspect that
he's in good health for a man his age."

Jay thought about the long hours Gordon Longer worked,
delivering babies, treating dyspepsia with doses of bismuth,
rheumatism with bicarbonate of soda laced with lemon
juice. He had apprenticed four years by his father's side

before marrying Nelly. His life had turned out different from what anyone expected.

"Suppose you'll be going back someday?"

"No—don't ever plan to." Jay's eyes skimmed the ragged, snow-covered Rockies, and he knew he would never go back. He loved this land; loved the way the sun kissed the mountain slopes, the wildflowers that bloomed in the high meadows, the clear streams, and the abundant wildlife. The rugged pioneers who had settled here were good people for the most part. He was proud to be one of them. Together, he and P could make a good life for Wilson. He wasn't sure about kids of his own—the thought of Brice still hurt—but Wilson needed a father. "Colorado is home now."

Smiling, Chappy turned the carving over in his hands, critically examining his work. "What d'you think the woman will do now? Heard the Mule Head sealed tighter than a tick this morning. Crew walked off—left the woman empty-handed."

"I'll open it again." Jay had been doing a lot of thinking the past few hours. Odds were against them, but if Patience wanted to reopen the mine, he was going to hire another crew, even if he had to go to Denver City to do it. Right now, he had to work up the nerve to face her. She couldn't be too happy with him at the moment.

Chappy's voice broke into his thoughts. "You talked to Frank yet?"

"Yeah. I've talked to Frank, but I've got a few more things to say to him. He almost killed me."

Chappy glanced up. "Doubt if he knew you were in the mine. He'd have thought you were taking the women home."

"Patience or the boy could have been inside. He should

have thought of that. Don't try to make me change my mind about Frank Innis. If it weren't for Innis and Tucker, Patience would own the mother lode right now. You know that—don't you?"

"You hear all kinds of rumors about mother lodes in these parts. Ninety percent of the time it's just speculation."

"Frank admitted it's there. He and Tucker wouldn't be trying to steal the Mule Head if it was a dry hole."

Chappy glanced up a second time. "You gonna let them get away with it?"

Jay eyed him. "What do you think?"

The old miner laughed, flashing a gold tooth in the cold air. "Didn't think you would be a man to set by and watch a woman being swindled."

The two men sat in comfortable silence.

"It's close to three, isn't it?"

Chappy consulted his watch. "Yep, a few minutes afore three."

Eventually, Jay got up, pulled his collar closer in the rising wind, and ambled off.

Rubbing the carving between his hands, Chappy watched him go.

Jay set out for the Mule Head an hour before dark. He'd concocted a speech—not necessarily a persuasive one, but one he hoped Patience would accept:

"Patience, I'm sorry. We'll reopen the shaft. I'll go as far as I need to go to hire a new crew. I'll throw Innis out of the mine—and oh, by the way, I love you, and I want to marry you if you'll have me. We can raise Wilson together, here in the foothills. . . ."

The discourse ran over and over in his mind. What if she

refused him? What if she insisted on going back to Denver
City and marrying the likes of Conner Justice? The man
was town mayor, well established, and well thought of in
the community. Lost his wife and child a few years back.
P deserved a man like Justice. But Jay wasn't in a giving
mood. He would work hard to be a husband she deserved;
he would make her proud. And he would take care of Mary
and Lily and Harper—he'd never let them be in want of
anything, if only Patience would have him.

The brief afternoon's separation had been a revelation for
him. For someone who thought he didn't need anyone,
he'd discovered he needed her.

Content for the first time in a long while, he whistled.
Brisk, pine-scented air filled his nostrils. The sky, overcast
and dreary, failed to make a dent in his mood. Pewter-
colored clouds promised snow by nightfall, but he knew
by that time he'd be with Patience and Wilson, hopefully
sitting before the fire, eating popcorn, being a family.

Family.

That sounded so good. He closed his eyes, walking on.
*Forgive me, God. I've put you out of my life the last five years,
and I'm asking for forgiveness. I've been blind to how good you've
been to me. For a long time I couldn't think about anything but
Nelly and Brice. I couldn't get past that black hole that kept me
imprisoned, but today you've given me back a reason to live.*

Near the mining camp's outskirts, the sun momentarily
streaked through the clouds, touching the frozen earth
with pale, icy fingers. Savoring the knowledge that
Patience and Wilson waited a mile or so up the mountain,
he trekked on.

Up ahead, he spotted Edgar Miller's outhouse. The small
building with a half-moon notched in the door was active

this afternoon. Edgar himself emerged, fastening his suspenders on his way back to his shack.

Jay drew closer and frowned, spotting one of Mooney Backus's thugs walking up ahead. The ruffian had caught up with him again.

Slackening his pace, Jay let the man get well ahead, figuring he'd just as soon not inflame an already volatile situation.

Suddenly veering off the road, the thug made a beeline for the outhouse, loosening his suspenders on the run. He wouldn't miss three hundred pounds by much, so he'd be a tight fit for the small quarters, but when nature called, she sometimes shouted.

The door swung shut behind him with a slam.

Ordinarily, Jay would have left well enough alone. But this wasn't an ordinary day or an ordinary opportunity. This particular thug—along with another—had beaten him to a bloody pulp, and Jay wanted retribution.

Glancing around the deserted area, he noted he was the only one on the road. Pausing in front of the door, Jay grinned. Revenge was sweet. Bracing his shoulder against the door, he mustered all his strength and shoved. The outhouse toppled backward amid a flurry of the man's startled oaths.

Whirling, Jay broke into a sprint. Jay didn't plan to be within a country mile when the thug crawled out.

He'd covered half of that country mile before his pace started to moderate. Trotting along, he threw his head back, laughing out loud. He imagined the look on Red's face when the structure went down. Confident the man would never know who or what hit him, Jay relished the brief victory.

All at once three hundred pounds—give or take a few ounces—slammed into him from the back, felling him like gunshot. Jay's eyes stung from the putrid smell. The thug's clothes reeked.

Anger flushed the man's fleshy cheeks. His nostrils engaged, retracted, fury boiling over in his eyes. He pinned the sheriff to the ground. "I'm gonna break your neck, Longer!"

Jay struggled to break the headlock, but wasn't having much luck. The guy had one hundred pounds on him.

Then he saw it coming. Planting his knee in the middle of Jay's chest, the thug drew back, murder in his eyes. A belated thought crossed Jay's mind: *You should have toppled the outhouse on its* door, *lunatic!* It was his last coherent thought before Red knocked him cold.

Snow began falling shortly before dusk. Pacing the banks of the stream, Patience tried to blow feeling back into her hands. Her eyes anxiously searched the trail. Where was Jay? He'd been gone for hours now. Was he not coming back? The thought both frightened and angered her. How could he just walk off and leave her and Wilson to fight for the mine alone? Was he completely heartless?

Her mind sought to justify his absence: Maybe Moses and the other women had run off—failed to return to the prison. Of course they would run if they smelled freedom. Jay had to go after them—the women were his responsibility.

While she assumed he was still in the vicinity of Fiddle Creek, that didn't necessarily mean that he was.

Wilson, huddled on a fallen log, was losing heart. They had been waiting since early afternoon. Now his hands and feet were trembling with cold. Teeth chattering, he voiced Patience's worse misgiving. "Maybe he isn't coming."

Her tone was more caustic than she intended. "Don't say that. He's coming." She'd thought he wasn't coming this morning, but he had showed up. He'd come tonight.

Her eyes stubbornly returned to the trail. He wouldn't walk away and never come back. He might have shortcomings, but he wasn't cruel. Nothing would convince her of that. There was a reason he hadn't come back—she had to believe that. If only she waited long enough, he would come.

Another hour passed. Snow blanketed bare tree branches. Wind whistled through pines that were taking on spring finery.

Periodically, Patience's gaze returned to the trail. Wilson's followed. Yet no matter how long and hard they looked, Jay's comfortable, familiar figure failed to appear.

"Are we gonna stay here forever?" Wilson finally asked.

Patience continued to pace. Her feet had lost feeling fifteen minutes ago. Where could he be? In her heart she believed he would never betray her welfare, yet what could possibly delay him this long?

A new thought hit her. Had he fallen off the mountainside—broken a leg or hip?

Another hour passed, then another. Wilson's lips were starting to turn blue. Sinking down beside him, Patience stared blindly at the falling snow. It was so late. They couldn't wait much longer.

"We better go now, huh, P? It's dark, and we still have to walk back to the dugout."

Patience's eyes yielded to the trail, as she desperately prayed that Jay would appear, but she had to conclude he wasn't coming. Getting up from the log, she ignored the pain in her icy limbs.

"Are we going now?"

She stared at the trail. Empty. "We can go now."

Wilson's eyes darted to the deserted road, his voice strained with emotion. "He really isn't coming, is he?"

"No." Patience stiffened her resolve. She needed to be strong for Wilson, but she was crying inconsolably on the inside. "He isn't coming."

"Well, maybe a bear got him or something. There're a lot of them around, you know."

They started walking.

"Maybe he's at the dugout instead. That's it, P! I bet he's at the dugout right now, waiting for us! I bet he's waited all afternoon, wondering where we are."

When Patience looked at him she saw that the child's glasses were frosted over.

He peered back at her. "Don't you think?"

"Perhaps, Wilson . . . perhaps."

Their footsteps left deep tracks in the snow. They labored to walk. Bitterly cold wind howled about, snow blinding them now.

Wilson suddenly started crying. Softly at first, then deep sobs. Patience knew he'd tried to be brave for her sake, but his love for Jay overwhelmed him.

But Jay didn't love them. He didn't care that they had sat in the cold, waiting all afternoon for him.

"Shush," Patience said quietly, blinded by her own tears. She was suddenly tired, so awfully tired.

Jay slowly came around, aware of sounds. Logs whispering and popping in the fireplace, a ticking clock, the metallic chink of a spoon scraping across the bottom of a kettle, a cat lapping cream from a saucer, the faint brush of slippered feet against a wooden floor.

Smells permeated his thick fog: woodsmoke, a subtle detection of lye soap coming from the woolen blanket, meat sizzling in a skillet.

Ensnared in a murky haze, he struggled to orient his thoughts, but his mind refused to serve him. A fire raged in his gut. The smallest motion caused excruciating pain.

Breaking into a cold sweat, he started shaking, his feverish body burning up beneath the heavy blanket. He threw the cover aside and struggled to sit up. His head swam, and blackness momentarily encased him.

Hands penetrated the darkness, bearing a cool cloth. He moaned and allowed himself to be lowered back to bed. Even the small act of kindness brought a cry of anguish from his swollen lips.

He stilled the faceless hands, trying to speak. "Patience . . . ," he murmured.

A dipper of water touched his parched lips and he drank thirstily. Water spilled over, splashing onto his bare chest. Each point the droplets touched brought more torment.

"Patience," he whispered hoarsely. "Patience . . . need to get to the Mule Head."

When he'd drunk his fill, his head was gently lowered back to the pillow. A pungent smell filled his nostrils, and he cried out again. Hands that had once been benevolent became instruments of anguish.

Jay prayed for death, but the pain continued.

"Patience . . . Patience . . . " Hands restrained him; he struggled to sit up. He had to get to her; she would be waiting for him. "Have to go . . . Patience . . ."

He fought consciousness; the hands ministered to his body. The pain was unspeakable.

When the ordeal finally ended, he was lying in a pool of sweat. Once again he was gently turned, the damp cloth cooling his heated body. The sheet beneath him was whisked away and replaced with a soft, dry one.

"Have to get word to Patience," he mumbled, praying that the angel of mercy would understand. Patience was waiting for him; if he didn't come, would she leave?

The angel didn't understand. A woman's voice penetrated his fog. "You have been severely injured. Don't move." Unrelenting hands pressed him back into the mattress.

Groaning, he lapsed back into unconsciousness.

Chapter Twenty-Four

The covered wagon pulled into Denver City and stopped in front of the parsonage. The hefty driver jumped down and hurried to help Patience down. Wilson tumbled from his perch on the back of the wagon and stood beside her, staring at the hustle and bustle of town.

He reached out to take her hand. "I don't like it here, P."

"You will, Wilson. Give it a chance." She took the satchel the driver lifted down and handed the second one to Wilson. "How much do I owe you?"

"Nothing at all, ma'am. It was a pleasure to have you along. You take care now, hear?"

He climbed back into the wagon seat and slapped reins on the horses' rumps, driving away.

Patience sighed. Well, here she was, but it wasn't the homecoming she had dreamed about. She looked down at the old prospector's trousers, wondering what the others would think of the way she was dressed.

The front door opened and Mary ran down the walk, followed by Lily and Harper.

"Patience! Oh, Patience!"

She was hugged, laughed and cried over, and pushed and pulled up the walk. At the porch steps she remembered Wilson and turned back to find him standing at the gate, looking lost.

Patience hurried back to take his hand. "Come, Wilson. We're home."

"Home?" He peered up at her through his bottle-thick glasses. "It doesn't feel like home, P."

"It will." She tugged at his hand. "Come on. Trust me; it will get better."

He followed, pulling back slightly.

Mary stooped down to his level. "I'm Mary. Who are you?"

"Wilson."

"Well, Wilson, this is Lily and Harper. We're glad to meet you."

Harper reached for the satchel he carried. "I made sugar cookies today. Got a batch cooling. You like cookies, Wilson?"

Wilson nodded. "I suppose . . . if I have to."

Patience followed the women into the parsonage, gazing around at her old home, which looked familiar but strange in some way, as if she didn't belong here anymore. She felt hemmed in, missing the space and majesty of the mountains. Even the air smelled different.

Pastor Siddons and his wife welcomed her back and gladly accepted Wilson. She had never doubted their generosity, but just the same, she didn't want to be here.

That night she lay awake in the room she shared with Mary, staring at the wall as her tears soaked the pillow. Where was Jay? He hadn't come back to Denver City. That was the first thing she'd asked. Was he all right? How could he just walk away and leave her and Wilson?

God? Are you there? Be with him, and, O God, help me. How can I give him up? Let me see him one more time.

A week later Patience pulled an apple pie out of the oven and placed it on the table to cool. The Siddonses were so good, but she and Wilson were an added burden. She knew the good pastor and his wife would never complain about two more mouths to feed, any more than feeding Mary, Harper, and Lily, but there had to be a limit to the number of people who could live in this small house.

Patience turned away to look out the kitchen window. She'd had such dreams, planning to bring them bags of gold, showing them how she could take care of them. Maybe that had been her problem. She had been so wrapped up in *her* plans, *her* wants—*her*—so sure that was where God was leading her, but had she ever bothered to ask *him* to show her what *he* wanted? Maybe the problems at the mine were a judgment on her.

If she had left with Jay when he had wanted her to, they would both be back in Denver City. Now she was here alone with no idea where he was or how to find him. Instead of being rich and successful the way she had planned, she was a failure.

A failure at money, and a worse failure at love.

Lenore Hawthorn's wedding had taken place on the thirty-first of December as planned. She'd worn a simple gown instead of the lovely creation Patience was wearing when she had been kidnapped. The bride's and groom's families were still feuding.

Patience sighed. She missed Jay. Last night Mary had heard her crying and slipped over into her bed to comfort her. The two had held each other; Mary had cried too, confiding that she was so sickly and her asthma was such a burden she was sure no man would want to marry her, which made Patience feel even worse that the mine hadn't worked out. She'd had such plans.

Wilson entered the kitchen, interrupting her thoughts. "I'm worried about my animals. Are you sure they're all right?"

"Chappy promised to take care of them until we come back."

"Are we ever going back?"

"Maybe someday." Probably not, but she couldn't tell Wilson that. Without Jay she couldn't fight Silas Tucker and Frank Innis. She couldn't hire a crew. With Jay's help she might have been able to hang on, but alone she didn't have a chance. And by now someone else had probably jumped the claim. They had no place to go back to.

"P?"

"Yes, Wilson?"

"I miss Jay."

"So do I."

"I thought he'd come after us. Doesn't he love us anymore?"

The boy was getting upset. Since they'd left the mine he'd been confused and unhappy.

Patience untied her apron. "Tell you what. How would you like to visit Jay's office? He won't be there, but you might like to see it anyway."

"I'd like it better if he was there."

"Oh, Wilson. He'll come back someday. We just have to

wait." She took his hand. "Come on; let's go see that office."

The trip to the office was a partial success. Wilson had liked seeing where a real sheriff worked, and she could see him imagining Jay sitting behind the desk, but walking back to the parsonage, he seemed downcast.

When they entered the kitchen, he noticed the empty pie dish before she did.

"Somebody ate all the apple pie!" he exclaimed. "Every last crumb!"

"I'll make another one, Wilson."

"When? You're busy all the time. Since we've come back you're always busy cooking and cleaning." Patience could see that he was getting worked up again. "I *hate* it here! I hate not having Jellybean and Selmore. I hate Jay. I hate Denver City. I want to go back to the Mule Head."

"I'll make another pie shortly," Patience said calmly, aware that Wilson's outbursts were due to grief. He missed Jay. He was not adjusting well to his new surroundings.

Nor was she. Tossing for hours at night, she found sleep impossible. She yearned for Jay. Mornings she was drained of emotion.

Harper called her a thousand fools for falling in love with a lawman, but deep down she didn't regret one moment. Her biggest concern was for Jay. Was he ill? Did he need her? Were his nights as unbearable as hers?

Picking up a handful of dirty dishes, Patience pushed through the swinging door, Wilson's voice following her.

"I hate school! I hate towns! I hate my teacher! I hate this kitchen, I hate this house, I hate this table, I hate these dishes, I hate this butter dish, I hate . . ."

Mary wasn't feeling well, so she changed rooms with Lily for the night. Patience helped her get settled into the small room at the rear of the house, while Lily moved her things into the room Mary had shared with Patience.

The household quieted down for the night. Wilson had been upset, angry, wanting to go back to the Mule Head and his animals. She couldn't blame him because she felt the same way.

Now, with Lily sleeping, Patience sat on the side of her bed, holding Jay's shirt. She had laundered it for him, but he never returned and she couldn't bear to leave it behind. Her fingers caressed the worn material, remembering his face, the way he smiled, the light in his eyes when he looked at her.

She began to speak hesitantly at first, but gaining in confidence, as if the shirt could hear her. She held it against her, pretending she held Jay. "I know you had a reason for not coming back. I don't understand it yet, but someday I will."

He wouldn't have left without a word unless there was an explanation. She had fought this battle in her mind, finally conquering her doubts. Something had prevented him from coming back.

"I love you so much, and I still have faith in you and faith in God. I truly believe he intends for us to be together someday."

She believed that with all her heart, and she had enough faith and trust in the Lord that no matter how bleak it seemed, he was there and he had the situation under control. At his own time and in his own way he would bring them together.

She held the shirt to her face, wetting it with her tears, talking to the shirt, not as if it were Jay, now, but a personal confidant. "I know how hard it is for him to trust. Losing Nelly and Brice hurt him so much. He loved them so deeply, and when a man really loves a woman, he doesn't forget her that easily. I admire that in him, and I pray that he'll soon feel that same love for me. And for Wilson. We won't take Nelly's and Brice's places, and we won't try to. We'll make our own place in his heart."

Lily spoke from the darkness. "Patience? I'm awake."

"Oh! Oh, Lily, I'd forgotten you were here. I'm sorry. I didn't intend to bother you." Patience wiped her eyes.

"You didn't. I just wanted to let you know I could hear you."

"I guess I sounded silly, talking that way to a shirt."

"No, it wasn't silly." Lily sounded sad. "You love Jay very much, don't you?"

"Very, very much, Lily. I can't find words to describe how much I love him. It's like he's a part of me, like I'm not complete without him. And the really crazy thing about our relationship is—it's sort of romance between Jay and Wilson and me. It's like we've all three fallen deeply in love with each other, and not a one of us knows how to make the love permanent." Her breath caught in a sob. "I'm so afraid that Wilson and I have lost Jay."

Lily sighed. "I've wondered what it would be like to love that way, but I've never been attracted to a man, never seen anyone I wanted to spend my life with. I'm afraid sometimes that my life will never change. I'll just go on helping the Siddons and getting older and lonelier."

Patience reached out in the darkness and took her hand. "Don't feel like that, Lily. Your time will come."

"I'm not so sure." Lily's voice brimmed with tears. "I've watched you and Ruth find love, but it seems like there is no one for me. I'm afraid God intends for me to live and die and never know the love of a man."

Slipping out of bed, Patience crawled into bed with Lily and held her tightly. The young girl's shoulders shook with sobs. As children they had comforted each other; tonight Patience was swept back to a lonely childhood full of dreams. Lily had the same dreams.

Why, God? Why can't our dreams come true? I know you love each of your children and plan only the best for them, but sometimes the waiting gets terrible hard, Father. Please give us either more patience or less hurting—we can't stand the pain anymore.

Long after Lily had fallen asleep, Patience stared into the dark, thinking of Jay and about what Lily had said. In her longing for Jay, had she blinded herself to the truth? For all her brave words in defense of Jay, and her talk of faith and trust, she couldn't forget the hammer blows of his words back at the mine: *"There is no us, Patience. Thought you understood that."*

Maybe, Lily, you're the lucky one, not me. Loving and not having that love returned . . . well, maybe that hurts more than never loving at all.

Chapter Twenty-Five

Late one afternoon Jay found himself walking up to the mine shaft. The gray, overcast day with miniature flakes of blowing snow peppering the air only deepened the growing ache in his heart.

He walked slowly, not completely recovered from his injuries. After being beaten half to death by Mooney's goon, someone had found him and delivered him to the town midwife and self-styled nurse. She'd taken care of him, bringing him back to life by her sheer bullheaded refusal to give up. He owed her a lot.

But sometimes he wished she hadn't bothered. Patience was gone, believing he had abandoned her. How could he go back to Denver City and face her, broke and with a tale of not being able to come to her because of his injuries? Why would she believe him?

He walked the familiar path, fighting memories at every turn. Pausing at the top of the hill, he stared down on the mine. Snow drifted deep around the dugout, obstructing the doorway. The irrational thought that he should clear it away crossed his mind.

He squinted, trying to remember, and the scene began to take shape in his mind: Smoke curled from the dugout's old smokestack; Selmore was staked outside the door, and Jelly-bean pawed the air at a passing bug.

He watched, transfixed, when Patience stepped out the door, her laughter carrying on the icy air. Pausing at the clothesline, she waved up at him, her eyes bright with mischief. The gentle breeze caught her hair and tossed it like a kite on a windy day.

She waved again, calling his name.

Hesitantly lifting his hand, he smiled, waving back.

Blowing him a kiss, she started to hang wash. The musical strains of "Jeanie with the Light Brown Hair" floated across the barren countryside. He could hear the soft refrain she had half sung, half whispered to him at the square dance . . . how long ago was it? It could have been a million years. Or maybe it all had been a dream.

He stood on the hilltop for over an hour, oblivious to the wind and the cold.

On his third outing, he took along a shovel. This time, when he reached the top of the hill, he continued down the steep incline.

It was over a mile to the mine. Today he wore snow-shoes, so walking came easier. But by the time he reached the dugout, his strength was sapped.

Resting for a spell, he sat on the log, trying to invoke Patience's image again. This time his imagination refused to cooperate. How long had it been since he'd last seen her? Three, four weeks. He couldn't remember.

After he'd rested, he got up and started to slowly shovel snow away from the dugout door.

"Better save yore strength, buddy boy."

Closing his eyes, Jay wondered why Frank was sticking around. Hadn't Patience deserted the mine? If so, Tucker had moved in, to be sure.

"Surprised ta see me? It's not like I have places to go, things to do."

Frank was up to his same old rhetoric, but with a different tone. He didn't sound as ornery or as pleased with himself. He emerged from nowhere and paused in front of the dugout. "Missed you, buddy boy."

Jay ignored him. Frank had what he wanted; Jay wasn't going to congratulate him on his good fortune.

The old man leaned against the dugout. "Pert near got yoreself killed. Gonna have to be more careful."

"I'll concede that I'm just plain stupid. Since you didn't finish me off that day in the mine, I thought I'd let one of Mooney's thugs have a shot at it."

"Now, buddy boy, I didn't *hurt* ya, did I? I was jest makin' a point."

Jay shoveled snow aside, ignoring him.

"Mad at me, ain't ya?"

"Actually, I don't give a hoot about you, Frank."

"Yeah, yore mad all right." Frank scratched his beard sheepishly. "Guess I was a might hard on that girl and the boy."

Jay refused to look up.

"Got my own woman troubles, ya know." Frank moved to sit on a log, hands folded, watching Jay work. "Come on, son . . . so I *am* a heartless, angry, old man . . . I *did* save yore life."

Jay glanced up.

"I was the one who found you and brought you to Elga's cabin."

"That was you?"

Frank nodded. "That was me. Fool thing you done, shoving that outhouse over with Red sittin' in it."

"Well—" Jay lifted another shovelful of snow—"face it; I do a lot of foolish things."

"There ya go, bein' hard on yoreself agin. You was on yore way back to the Mule Head when it happened, wasn't ya?"

"Before I was . . . detained."

"Then what's the problem? You didn't run her off. You was comin' back—or least ya would have if ya hadn't let yore orneriness get the better of yore common sense. Son, you don't fool around with a man Red's size. Ain't anyone ever told ya that?"

Pausing for a moment, Jay's gaze traveled to the mine. "She thinks I deserted her—stalked off and never came back. She didn't have a chance against you and Tucker after that. She gave up her dreams and went back to Denver City."

"Yeah—shore hated to hear that."

Jay met the old prospector's eyes, aware that his injuries were still apparent. "Why would you hate to hear it? That was your plan, wasn't it? Run her off, scare her witless so she'd give up the mine? She'd still be here, Innis, if it wasn't for me. She wasn't scared of any *ghost.*"

Frank hung his head. "Yeah, she's purty spunky."

Jay kept shoveling. It was a while before he spoke. "Have you heard anything about Patience?" he asked softly. "Did she make it back to Denver City all right? Is she well?"

"Hear tell she's well. Got a friend over in Denver City—I've been keepin' up since I knew you couldn't. Her and the boy are stayin' with the pastor and his wife, along with the other girls. She's being taken care of, buddy boy, better'n when she was livin' up here, fightin' that mine."

"Wilson?"

"Wilson? Mick Johnson, a fellow miner, passed through Denver City last week. He says rumor is the boy hates everything—suppose it's his age."

Jay's voice dropped to a ragged whisper. "I love her, Frank."

"Yeah, I know, buddy boy." The old man scratched his head. "I was in love once—didn't turn out much better than you and the girl, but I can shore remember how I felt about her."

Jay rammed the shovel into another drift, angry now. "I fell in love with her. I told myself a thousand times I wouldn't, but I did. Fell in love with both of them. The time we spent here . . ." Jay's eyes traveled the mine area. "We were a family, Frank. God gave me a second family, and I didn't realize or appreciate it."

"Yeah, well, now there's still time to do somethin' about it. Not all's lost. She might be in Denver City, but that ain't the jumpin'-off place. You got a swift horse—go after her."

Jay noticed that Innis crossed his arms when he kept shoveling. "Why are you shovelin' that snow?"

"I have to do something to pass the time."

"Shovelin' snow's only gonna sap yore strength. Better save it, son, for better things."

"Are you ever ashamed of what you did to her?"

When Frank didn't answer, Jay looked up, expecting the old miner to be gone. Instead, he sat there, his arms folded across his bony chest, staring out across the mountains.

"Frank?"

The old man glanced at him, eyes misted over. "Ashamed, you ask. Yeah, I'm ashamed. She's a good woman. Reminded me of someone I used to know. Never deserved what I did to her, and I liked the boy too. Never had a son or grandson. Seemed like you and Wilson sort of filled that need."

Jay stared at Frank in disbelief. "So you blew up the mine with me in it? Thanks a lot, *Dad.*"

Frank shook his head. "You ain't takin' me as serious as you ought to."

"I'll take you serious when you talk serious. You set out to drive us away from the mine."

"Yeah. I did that. Gonna go after her, aren't you, boy?"

Jay knew he'd eventually have to return to Denver City and face Patience. It also meant that he had to explain the thug, the beating, and the gambling debt to the town council. He paused and leaned on the shovel handle. "I haven't a thing to offer her—no gold, no solidarity. Nothing."

"Aw, shucks. Gold ain't no problem. You are gonna go after her, ain't ya? Shame to let a purty little thing like that git away."

"She's better off without me."

Frank shook his head. "Feelin' sorry for yoreself agin."

Maybe he was. Jay had faced the grim reaper and lost the woman he loved. Law didn't pay anything. If anyone had a right to feel sorry for himself, he did. His mind returned to the days of his youth when his family lived on Pop's fees: fresh eggs, vegetables from a grateful patient's garden, a butchered hog come fall, fryers and stewing hens throughout the summer.

There were times when an outbreak of cholera gripped the community and Doc Longer wouldn't see his family for days. When he did come home he'd be so tired he could do little more than eat leftovers and fall into bed for a few hours' sleep. People came and went at all hours of the night. He could never be counted on to be around at important times like Christmas and birthdays.

Delivering babies, tending the terminally ill, hovering

over the desperately sick—never enough time for his own
family. Law was the same way. Once Jay returned to
Denver City his time would belong to the citizens. Patience
and Wilson would be better off without him. He wanted
wholesome meals on his table, new shoes for his children
every winter, a house, and a team of horses to take his
family for a Sunday afternoon ride.

Slinging his shovel over his shoulder, Jay walked away
from Innis and the dugout.

"Hey . . ." Frank sat up on the log. "You leavin' for good?"

Jay never looked back. He slowly made his way through
the deep snow and eventually disappeared over the hilltop.

Seven more days passed before Jay ventured back to the
mine. He had vowed he was never going back. Patience
was gone, and he sure didn't value Frank's company.

Yet shortly after dawn Sunday morning, he set off in
search of her memory. Climbing the steep hill, he made his
way slowly down the other side of the incline.

A cold sun glinted off the deep snow. His heavy boots broke
through the crusty surface. He plodded toward the mine.

The little dugout looked bleak in the early morning light.
What a difference her presence had made.

Sitting down on the log, he stared at the dugout, wondering what Patience and Wilson were doing on this Sunday
morning. They'd be in church, worshiping God.

Suddenly he missed the comfort of a worship service.
Nelly had been big on going to church, and she'd seen they
never missed a meeting. He'd had something to believe in
back then, before he'd lost his wife and son and his faith in
a loving God.

A hawk soared overhead, riding the air currents. Jay breathed in the cold, clean air, drinking in the beauty of this remote corner of the world. God's world. He started to push the thought away, then paused, unaccustomed to his new feelings. Yes, God's world. The silence was so deep it was like being in a holy place. Like a cathedral.

He watched the hawk, letting his thoughts soar . . . up . . . up . . . into the dazzling blue of the sky. "Are you listening? Was I wrong? Do you really care?"

A sweet, subtle warmth began somewhere in the frozen wasteland inside him, where he kept his memories of Nelly and Brice, spreading outward like the rays of summer sun, thawing, healing.

The truth hit him again with the clarity of church bells. He'd stumbled out of faith, blinded by the pain of losing the two people he'd loved the most. He'd given up on God, but God had never given up on him. It was good to finally trust again.

He sat in silence, letting the peace of this lonely mountaintop seep into his soul. Faith. He'd never lost it; he'd just put it aside for a while. The belief in a loving God who truly cared for his own, that faith was the only thing that could see him through this life. It had taken a young woman and a little boy to make him see the difference.

Cold saturated his bones, aggravating his injuries. Oblivious to the pain, he sat lost in thought.

He'd vowed never to take a risk that involved love again. Never would he take someone into his heart; it wasn't worth the pain. He'd always get hurt. Love would fail him. Erect those barriers. But he was powerless. P had come along and—

"Hey! You! Buddy boy!"

Jay glanced up when he heard Frank's voice. His eyes searched the area for the miner. When was he going to give up and leave him alone?

"In here!"

Jay looked, but Frank, for once, didn't show himself. "What do you want, Frank?"

"I'm trapped."

"You're what?"

"Trapped. Over here."

Now what game was he playing? "Where?"

"In the mine."

Getting up, Jay walked in the direction of the mine. Frank was more trouble than a kid. And more aggravating, he might add. "Where are you?"

"In here."

"Where?"

"Toward the front of the shaft."

"What are you doing in there?"

"Quit talkin' so much and get in here, will ya?"

Turning away, Jay went back to the log. Frank got himself in there—he could get himself out. Jay didn't care what happened to the old fellow.

"Hold on a minute, buddy boy. I got myself a problem this morning. A bad one."

Jay sat back down. "Join the crowd."

"I'm serious. Git back over here."

"No."

"Just git over here!"

Getting up again, Jay walked to the entrance of the sealed shaft. "You are getting on my nerves, Innis."

"I hate to tell you this, but I'm stuck."

"Stuck?"

"Stuck."

"How could you be stuck? You come and go as you want."

"I don't know how it happened. One minute I was moseying through the mine, and the next I was trapped. Cain't move a muscle, buddy boy. You're gonna have to help me."

"What do you expect me to do about it?" Jay wasn't a miracle worker, and he'd had his fill of Frank Innis. In spite of what Frank had said the last time they'd talked, he wasn't convinced the old miner had a change of heart. Innis and Tucker had accomplished what they'd set after. Patience was gone. They should be happy.

"Help me figure out a way to get unstuck."

"The shaft's sealed. I can't get in there. Is there another entrance?"

"Yeah, about three feet from where yore standin'."

He *knew* it.

Jay laughed. "When did you ever think about *my* needs when you were causing all the cave-ins and rigging up the women's picks to knock them senseless, trying to run Patience off? Remind me again, Frank, why I should lift one hand to help you?"

"I'm serious, buddy boy. You gotta do something. I'm a mite uncomfortable."

Jay shifted on one foot. Guilt nagged him. Not five minutes ago he was asking the Lord for forgiveness and mercy. He had to help the old man, even though everything in him wanted to walk away.

"Are you in pain?"

"In a lot of pain. Now get to thinkin'. What are we gonna do about this?"

Kneeling, Jay ran his hands around the entrance, now

crumbling. "The dirt's packed pretty tight. I can't get to you."

"Yes, you can. Think."

Jay knelt, his eyes assessing the situation. He could hear Frank clearly—that meant there was an open hole some-where. "Where are you?"

" 'Bout fifty or so feet inside the shaft. Ya know that outcrop of shale just to the left as you come into the mine?"

"Yes." Jay knew it well. Went by it every time he entered the mine shaft.

"That's where I am. Wedged in between two big rocks."

Rising, Jay looked around for something to dig with, but his shovel seemed to have disappeared.

"You can't *dig* me out," Frank called. "You're gonna have to *blast* me out."

"Blast you out? Why, that would—"

"Kill me?" Frank mocked. "I'm tough as cowhide. I'll survive the blast, but if you leave me here I'll die a slow, agonizing death. Air's runnin' out, buddy boy. Ya have to do something—there's a couple of sticks of dynamite in the dugout. Go get 'em."

Jay glanced toward the dugout, puzzled. "Patience didn't keep explosives in the dugout."

"Just go look," Frank said crossly.

When Jay returned, he was carrying the two sticks of dynamite he'd found in the dugout. They had been lying in the middle of the kitchen table, a placement he found bizarre.

"You find 'em?"

"I found them."

"Good. Tell me when you're gonna light the fuses. I'll plug my ears."

"You better plug more than your ears—" This was insane. He couldn't kill the old man, no matter how tempting the thought. When he lit the dynamite that shaft was going sky-high.

"Jest do what I say! You ain't gonna hurt me!"

"You just said you were in pain!"

"Don't worry 'bout me! Just light the fuses!"

Jay searched his pockets. "I don't have any matches." How was he going to get out of this? Did Innis have a death wish?

"Good grief, boy! Have I picked an idiot to free me? There was matches layin' right next to the dynamite. Didn't ya see 'em?"

Jay stiffened. Name-calling now. Anger surged and he wished he had a match. A box of them. "I didn't see any matches."

"Well, go look."

"Hold on."

"Yeah, like I'm goin' somewhere," Frank muttered.

Jay was back in a minute.

"Got 'em?"

"I have them."

"Get to blastin'."

Jay began to set the charge, praying. *Lord, stop me. Revenge is the devil's tool, and you've been too good to me to let me fall again. I don't know how I'll get him out, but I refuse to light the fuse.*

"Now, you are going to Patience, ain't ya, buddy boy?"

Jay glanced up. "What?"

Suddenly Innis stepped into the open. His eyes twinkled with devilment. Outside the mine; he'd been *outside* the shaft all along. Jay's jaw dropped.

"I said, you *are* gonna marry the little Smith gal, ain't ya?"

"Innis—what kind of game are you playing now?" This was getting downright aggravating! Jay straightened, about to walk away, when Frank walked closer, holding a match.

"What's your answer?"

"It's none of your business what I do about Patience and the boy."

"You *are* gonna marry her, ain't ya? You ain't gonna let that pride of yours stand in the way of love, are ya?"

"Okay—yes. Soon as I'm well enough I'm going back to Denver City. If Patience will have me . . ." He paused. That was a big *if*. Would she have him?

"Gonna take good care of the boy, see that he gits a good education?" Innis asked.

"What's the sudden interest in Patience's and Wilson's futures? You never cared before."

"I told ya. I took a likin' to the boy." The old man's features softened. "I'm old—don't have much time left here on earth, and I shore don't need the gold, so I've been thinkin' that before my days are through I might ought to do something worthwhile."

Jay frowned. "What are you talking about? Because of you and Tucker—"

"Aw—I was jest fillin' time with Silas. Had me a little fun 'hauntin' ' the mine, owner after owner. That ole coot prospector wouldn't scare off. Then the woman came along, and I thought to myself, *Frank, you ought not to scare women and children,* so I decided to go to work on you." He scratched his beard. "That didn't work out either—but then I kinda liked the boy—never had any kids myself, and the little tyke's kinda cute with all his animals and his grown-up talk."

Leaning forward, Frank struck a match and touched the end

of the fuse. "So, if you're watching, Lord, I'm doin' somethin' nice for a change. Shore hope you make note of it."

Jay backed up, his eyes on the sizzling fuses.

"Innis—you're *nuts*. That shaft's going to blow sky-high—"

"I'm ready, buddy boy! Let 'er blow!"

Jay dived for the old prospector, trying to pull him to safety at the same time a thunderous explosion rocked the Mule Head, showering dirt and catapulting debris straight up.

Dust settled and Jay slowly got up, his eyes searching for Frank. *"Frank!"* The name echoed over the mountainside. There wasn't a sign of the old prospector. Dropping to his knees, Jay frantically dug into the shale, trying to locate the old man.

A ray of sun suddenly caught a shining speck on the ground. A moment later a second ray caught another, then another. The brilliancy that suddenly surrounded Jay was blinding.

Scraping up a handful of nuggets, Jay studied the findings. Slowly lifting his head, he looked around, realizing that he was sitting in a pile of more gold than he'd ever seen in his life.

Huge, unbelievable stones covered the ground as far as the eye could see.

Bursting into laughter, he scooped up handfuls of the enormous nuggets, tossing them into the air, delirious with joy. The mother lode! He had hit the *mother lode!*

His laughter died away as his eyes searched for Frank. Had he done this? Had he finally relinquished the gold?

"Frank," he called hesitantly. "Are you still there?"

In the distance he heard distinct footfalls and an unmistakable *heh, heh, heh.*

Jay grinned. Why, that old fool!

Chapter Twenty-Six

J ay's here."

Patience glanced at Wilson from the open oven door,
wiping a stray hair out of her eyes. "Who?"

"*Jay.*"

Lugging the heavy roaster to the cooling board, Patience
set it down with a thump. "That isn't funny, Wilson."

"I'm not being funny. He's really here."

Patience turned, her heart hammering against her rib cage,
halfway believing him. "Where?"

"At the front door. He doesn't look like riffraff anymore,
Patience. He looks *rich.*"

"Rich?"

Wilson nodded. *"Really* rich. I've never seen Jay looking
so good."

Dropping the hot pads, Patience touched her hair, wishing for a comb. "Dear God, please let it truly be him," she
whispered. It had been nearly two months since she'd
returned to Denver City, and she hadn't heard a word
from him.

Shrugging, Wilson sneaked a bite of the roasted hen. *"Filthy* rich, actually," he murmured.

Racing down the hallway, Patience wondered what he really looked like and immediately decided that it didn't matter! He could be wearing sackcloth and ashes for all she cared. *Please God, let it be him.*

Rounding the corner, Patience came to a sudden halt. Standing before her *was* the most handsome man she had ever seen in her life.

Lily stood in the doorway, her gaze fastened on the handsome sheriff and a goofy grin on her face.

Jay's eyes met hers over Lily's head. Gazing at one another, there was no need for words. His expression told her everything Patience needed to know.

Giving a squeal of joy, she flew into his arms, nearly bowling Lily over in her exuberance.

Clasping her tightly to him, Jay kissed her. Rockets exploded, colored lights flared, and the roar in Patience's ears sounded like a dynamite blast.

"Patience Smith!" Lily gasped.

The taste of him, the feel of him—Patience couldn't get enough! The shameless, passionate embrace was embarrassingly prolonged.

When they finally parted, Patience took both his hands, smiling up at him. "You're a little late."

"I have a good excuse." Leaning forward, he kissed the tip of her nose. "By the way, I love you."

"Mmm," she whispered, returning the embrace. "I love you too."

Quickly and without taking a breath, he told her about his injuries and why he hadn't followed her to Denver City immediately.

Shutting her eyes, she willed back tears. *Thank you, God. I knew there had to be a reason.*

Lily cleared her throat, closing the front door. Realizing her lack of propriety, Patience quickly apologized. "I'm sorry, Lily—it's just . . . I'm so *glad* to see him!"

"Can't blame you," Lily murmured.

Still holding tightly to the sheriff, Patience pulled him inside the parlor, where the pastor, his wife, Mary, and Harper sat. He looked so . . . different today. Dressed in a suit of pearl gray worsted, under a brass-buttoned greatcoat, his snowy white cravat studded with what must surely be a diamond set in pure gold, he bore little resemblance to the scruffy miner or the town sheriff. From the crown of his beaver hat to the toes of his polished boots, he was bandbox fresh and a joy to behold.

"Look, everyone! Sheriff Longer is back."

The minister rose immediately, reaching for Jay's hand. "Good to see you, son! We've been worried about you."

"Thank you, Pastor." Removing his coat, hat, and gloves, Jay handed them to Lily, who had followed them into the parlor. He grinned and winked at the flushed young woman. Once everyone was comfortably seated, Patience reached for Jay's hand, unable to leave him alone.

"Pastor, Mrs. Siddons—I've come to ask for Patience's hand in marriage," Jay began quietly. "I know you're not her parents, but she thinks of you fondly. It would be well and good if you were to grant that permission, but I must warn you, I love this woman with all my heart and soul, and I will marry her no matter what you say." He turned to look at Patience. "Me and God had a misunderstanding for a while, but we've worked it out." He smiled. "Like you say, P, God is good."

"Oh, Jay." Patience was so proud of him she could burst. "You said that so well!"

He nodded, courtly indeed. "Thank you, Miss Smith. I thought I did a rather good job myself."

"Marry her!" The pastor's grin widened. "Why, that's wonderful, son." He glanced at Patience fondly. "You have my and Mother's deepest blessing."

A grin spread across the sheriff's face. "I think you should know that Patience is an extremely wealthy woman, sir. She and Wilson and Lily, Harper, and Mary will want for nothing." His gaze met Patience's. "Absolutely nothing."

Patience covered her mouth with both hands. Rich? Her?

"You hit the mother lode, sweetheart."

"Oh, Jay!" Springing to her feet, she flew back into his arms. There would be time later for him to explain everything. Right now it was enough to know that he loved her enough to marry her—rich or not!

Pastor Siddons smiled. "Wealth is subjective, Jay. Good health, love—"

"Two million isn't, Pastor."

Patience's soft intake of breath filled the stunned silence.

"Two . . . million," Mary repeated lamely. *"Dollars?"*

Jay grinned. "Give or take a few hundred thousand."

"Well, goodness," Harper fanned herself. "Ain't nothin' sub—subject—whatever you said, about *two million dollars!"*

Later, Patience drew Jay into the parsonage kitchen, where they could be alone. The door closed behind them and she turned into his arms.

"Oh, I've missed you so," she whispered. His mouth lowered to take hers. Between patchy kisses, he managed to tell her in greater detail why he had failed to come back that day. He explained how he would have died if Frank Innis hadn't found him and taken him to Elga's house.

"But the money," she whispered. "Were you making that up?"

Chuckling, he held her tightly. "The money is real. Innis gave us the mother lode, darling."

Frowning, Patience looked up at him. "Innis?"

"The man I told you about—the one posing as Gamey O'Keefe's ghost. He admitted he'd been trying to scare us into leaving, so he and Silas Tucker could jump the claim, but seems like Innis felt guilty for what he'd done. He convinced Tucker he'd lied about the mine having the mother lode. He's the one who helped us find the gold."

"Oh," she said lamely. "There really was a man?"

Resting his lips on her hairline, he whispered, "It doesn't matter if you believe there was or wasn't. He believes in us."

Laughing, he kissed her bewilderment away. "There is so much we have to catch up on and to learn about each other. On the way over here I looked up Red and Luther and paid off the gambling debt. I knew you wouldn't mind." He held her closely. "I'll make you and God a solemn promise: I will never wager money again."

"Oh, darling, I love you *so,*" she whispered. "Then, we truly are rich?"

"Honey, we can burn money for firewood." He grasped her shoulders, slightly moving her back so he could meet her eyes. "Chappy Hellerman told me you hadn't deserted the mine, that he was holding the deed. Strange, I never saw him around, but apparently he made it known you were away on business."

She smiled. "I never gave up the dream, and I trusted

Chappy to guard my secret. When you didn't come back I knew I had to really think about Wilson's future—but deep in my heart I knew you would come for us. If for no other reason you would return to Denver City and your job. I knew when you did, I would chase you shamelessly until you were mine." She kissed him briefly. "What d' you think of them apples?"

"I love them—and I love you more."

Closing her eyes, Patience thought about what the money would mean to Mary, Harper, and Lily. "Thank you, God," she whispered.

"This is all well and good, but what about me?"

Springing back, Patience saw Wilson sitting at the table, calmly stuffing cookies into his mouth.

"What about you?" Jay reached over and rumpled the boy's hair. "You can have your own zoo now, kid, complete with elephants and giraffes, if you want."

"I'd like an elephant, perhaps one giraffe, but that isn't the point." The child wasn't to be deterred. "I *know* you'll take care of me because Patience will make you."

Jay's tone gentled. "Wilson, I would take care of you regardless, but knowing you, you're about to make a point. What is it?"

"The point is you *hurt my feelings.*"

When Jay glanced at Patience, she shook her head warningly. Wilson had been angry with him from the moment they left the Mule Head. It would take a while for the child to forgive and trust again.

Kneeling beside the table, Jay said softly, "I'm sorry I hurt your feelings. Do you want to tell me what I did so you won't resent me anymore?"

Wilson's countenance turned grave. "Patience and I

waited all day for you to meet us, but you didn't come. It was cold, and we waited all day. You didn't come."

"I didn't come because I couldn't. Because Red beat me up. I did a stupid thing, and I paid for it by temporarily losing the two people I love most."

Tears brimmed to Wilson's eyes. "You love *me*, Jay? Honest?"

"Honest." Leaning closer, he said. "Next to P, I love you more than anything in the world. We're going to be a family, Wilson. You, me, and P."

"And now you love God again?"

Jay nodded. "I never stopped loving him—he hurt my feelings, Wilson, like I hurt yours. But now I know he never stopped loving me."

Throwing his arms around Jay's neck, Wilson hugged him. "That day, when you didn't come, I thought it was because you didn't like me."

"Never," Jay assured him. He reached out and took Patience's hand, drawing her into the circle. She smiled back, her love overflowing for this man. "And from now on I won't be pushing over any more outhouses. But that's another story entirely." His eyes met hers. "When you need me, I'll be there for you."

"Always?" P and Wilson parroted.

Drawing the two of them to him, the sheriff whispered, "Always."

Epilogue

Someone knocked on the front door, and Lily hurried to open it, feeling anyone else would be anticlimactic after Jay's arrival. What a day this had been! She swung the door open and stopped with her heart in her throat. There facing her was the best-looking man she'd ever seen. Even more handsome than Jay Longer, to her notion.

"Afternoon, ma'am. The name's Claxton. Cole Claxton."

Lily stared up from her five feet two inches, thinking she hadn't known God made men that tall. For a minute, she longed to be blonde and beautiful, instead of having plain brown eyes and hair the color of maple syrup, to say nothing of the smattering of freckles across her nose. Freckles weren't beautiful.

"M-Mr. Claxton," she stammered.

"I was told I could find my old friend Jay Longer here."

"Oh, yes." Lily opened the door wider. "Come in. I'll get him."

She hurried to the kitchen, surprising Jay and Patience by bursting in on them. "Oh, Sheriff. There's someone here to see you."

Jay turned slowly. "To see me? Who?"

"He said his name was Cole Claxton."

Jay took Patience's hand and hurried through the kitchen and down the hallway to the front door. "Cole! Come in, man. How are you?"

The two shook hands, and Cole's eyes slid past Jay to linger on Lily and her heart fluttered. "Just passing through. Thought I'd stop and say hello."

"I'm glad you did." Jay glanced toward the crowded living room and stepped out on the porch, motioning for the women to follow. They sat down in the rocking chairs Pastor Siddons kept there. A pale sun rose high in the winter sky. Lily pulled her woolen shawl closer, too excited to stay in the house.

Patience and Lily listened as the two men reminisced about past experiences. Lily caught her breath in wonder at the bravery of the lawmen and what they considered harmless escapes. To Lily, they seemed suicidal. Wilson crept out to join them, listening with shining eyes to the tales of adventure. Lily remembered her manners and brought cups of warm cider.

Finally Cole stood up. "Well, it's been nice, but I've got to be on my way." He shook Jay's hand and nodded to Patience and Lily. "Maybe I'll ride through this way again before too many years." He caught Lily's eyes and she felt light-headed. He put on his hat, and said, "Ma'am," and left. She watched him walk down the path, mount his horse, and ride away.

Jay grinned, drawing Patience into his arms. "Lily, don't get any ideas about Cole Claxton. He's married."

She turned to face him, frowning. "Why are all the good men taken?"

Jay threw back his head and laughed. "But he's got
a passel of friends who've yet to take the marital plunge—
good-looking, ornery men." He reached over and tugged
a lock of her hair. "You've got good taste, lady. I've known
Cole Claxton for a long time. He's from Missouri. Got two
brothers, Cass and Beau—both happily married. The
Claxton men are lawmen—best in the country. Only a
special woman can lasso men like the Claxtons."

Lily gave him back look for look. "You were a man of
the saddle once."

Jay chuckled. "And I was lassoed."

Mary and Harper joined them on the porch. Patience
slipped her arms around the two newcomers, and her smile
included Lily. "It's so good to be back together again. All of
my plans for us have come true. We'll never have to worry
again. A lot has happened since we left the orphanage, but
our journey is over. We've finally found a home."

She released the women and stepped into Jay's waiting
arms. "A real home with real love."

Smiling, Lily's eyes followed Cole Claxton—man of the
saddle. He rode out of town, straight and tall. So . . . Mr.
Claxton had a passel of unmarried friends . . .

Ornery lawmen.

"Patience, I wouldn't hurt your feelings for the world,"
she murmured, though nobody noticed. "But don't count
this girl out on finding her own true love. Miracles still
happen—and I can lasso with the best of them."

A Note from the Author

Dear Friends,

Words cannot express my gratitude for the loyal readers who have followed the Brides of the West. The series started with three books and grew to six. Now we come to the end of the brides' journeys, and though I'm sad to part with this family, I'm satisfied that each woman has found true contentment, whether by marriage to that special man, or—like Mary, Harper, and Lily—through God and the knowledge that life is unique and not everyone finds happiness in the same way.

Now I look ahead to a new HeartQuest series titled Men of the Saddle. Much like the brides, these young men are rugged pioneers who paved the way for freedom, democracy, and yes, love in the Old West. And who knows? Lily might even bump into one of these handsome strangers. . . .

Meanwhile, I'm busy with another fun series for Tyndale House: Morning Shade Mysteries. The stories involve my usual quirky characters, a small (fictional) town in Arkansas, people who love the Lord, and the oddest mysteries. Of course, eighty-seven-year-old Stella Diamond can't let a good mystery lie, so she and the self-appointed, bumbling town constable Hargus Conley bump heads when an occasional strange happening pops up—like the recent bizarre case of the furniture mover. Someone is breaking into homes, rearranging and redecorating! *A Case of Bad Taste* was released in July 2003, and *A Case of Crooked Letters,* the second book in that series, will be available in spring 2004.

God continues to pour out blessings on the Copeland family. My husband and I have purchased a small motor home, and we now camp with good friends as often as our busy schedules allow. We spend a good deal of time shamelessly spoiling our five grandchildren (and kissing their faces off), having picnics and Bible studies with our church family, and each day thanking God for the wonderful life he has given us. Not without its problems, but most assuredly under his watchful care.

Until we meet again—

Lori Copeland

About the Author

Lori Copeland has published more than seventy romance novels and has won numerous awards for her books, most recently the Career Achievement Award from *Romantic Times* magazine. Her recent novel *Stranded in Paradise* marked her debut as a Women of Faith fiction author. Publishing with HeartQuest allows her the freedom to write stories that express her love of God and her personal convictions.

Lori lives with her wonderful husband, Lance, in Springfield, Missouri. She has three incredibly handsome grown sons, three absolutely gorgeous daughters-in-law, and five exceptionally bright grandchildren—but then, she freely admits to being partial when it comes to her family. Lori enjoys reading biographies, attending book discussion groups, participating in morning water-aerobic exercises at the local YMCA, and she is presently trying very hard to learn to play bridge. She loves to travel and is always thrilled to meet her readers.

When asked what one thing Lori would like others to

know about her, she readily says, "I'm not perfect—just forgiven by the grace of God." Christianity to Lori means peace, joy, and the knowledge that she has a friend, a Savior, who never leaves her side. Through her books, she hopes to share this wondrous assurance with others.

Lori welcomes letters written to her in care of Tyndale House Author Relations, P.O. Box 80, Wheaton, IL 60189-0080.

Turn the page for an exciting preview from

A Case of Bad Taste

Book 1 in Lori Copeland's new
Morning Shade Mystery series.

→

ISBN 0-8423-7115-X

Available now at a bookstore near you.

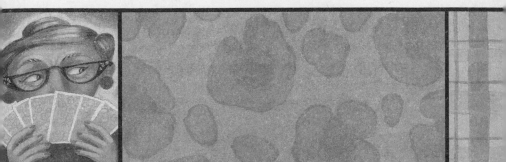

The paper's thin this morning," Stella complained as she shuffled into the kitchen. The paper was always like that on Saturday.

I poured a bowl of Honey Nut Cheerios and waited for the coffee to drip through. I needed the caffeine before I could confront the morning.

"Look at this!" Stella exclaimed. "There's been a break-in!" She rattled the paper to fold it over. "At Lucille Stover's place. Why, we were just talking about her at our bridge game. Remember? I told you about that."

I remembered. The subject of Lucille's awful couch and chair with the monkey fabric had dominated the bridge game. "Was anything taken?"

"Don't think so, but Hargus Conley is investigating."

"I'm sure he'll take care of the situation." I poured my coffee and added cream.

"*Humph*. He's not worth the paper it takes to print his name," Stella said, her eyes glued to the article about the break-in. "It says here that the back door was left open and the culprit came in that way. *Tsk, tsk.* Lucille was playing bingo and Harold was with her. They got home about eleven o'clock and found . . . well, my goodness!"

"What?" I was interested in spite of myself.

"Nothing was taken!"

"Nothing?"

"Nothing."

I sat across from Stella, waiting for the rest of the story. "Well, then, why did someone break in? Were they frightened away before they could take anything?"

Stella read on. "Nothing was taken, but . . . but the living-room furniture was moved around. Hmm. Odd."

"The furniture was moved around?" That was bizarre, even for Morning Shade.

"That's all."

"Why would anyone do that?"

"I don't know. Why, Frances and Pansy were talking about how Lucille lines her furniture around the wall. 'No creativity at all,' Pansy said." Stella shook her head and turned the page.

"Lucille must have been very shaken."

"I'd imagine. I think I'll just go down to the Citgo and see if anyone knows anything more."

Coming Soon!

HEART QUEST®

OVER A MILLION BOOKS SOLD!

WILD HEATHER

Olivia Hewes and Randolph Sherbourne are drawn toward a forbidden love that will mean betraying both their families.

DANGEROUS SANCTUARY

Kent Anderson is committed to making Camp Hope a sanctuary for his campers. But when Georgia MacGregor joins his staff, her troubled past threatens to endanger them all.

Visit **www.heartquest.com** today!

BOOKS BY BEST-SELLING
AUTHOR LORI COPELAND

Visit **www.tyndalefiction.com**